THE ROSE AND THE GHOST

LOCKE & STEEL BOOK TWO

L. E. MEDLOCK

STONE SOUL PUBLISHING

For my sister Becky.
May the wind carry you wherever you desire,
and may you always find a path back home.

CHAPTER ONE

The knife is slick in my palm. Rayne lies stretched across the bed, his limbs twisted in pain. He can't speak; the wound in his throat took care of that.

"Very good." The professor's hand is warm and solid on my shoulder, his voice soft in the darkness. "Next, the heart."

Even wet with blood, my hands are steady. I place one on the man's ruined torso, the other poised with the blade against his chest. The blood drips over my fingers, runs down my wrist, drops on the once-white sheet. I lower my hand, make the cut. Rayne's eyes fly open.

I jerk awake. My teeth are clenched so hard that my jaw aches and the scream caught behind them stays trapped. Shaking, I sit upright. Light pours through the porthole, casting Steel's sleeping figure in a dull glow. Our cabin is a narrow slot in the wall, split on the left by a single bunk dressed in partisan white sheets. The other side holds a shallow basin and a broken mirror.

We're on the ship on the way to Boulogne. Nowhere near the professor, or Rayne. It was just a dream.

The sheets are twisted around my body, tight rivulets of cotton cutting into my skin. Last night—this morning—I'd collapsed on the bunk in exhaustion, too tired to do more than grunt. I rip them off, stumble out of bed and over Steel's legs to the basin. Some benevolent sailor has stocked it with water, and I plunge my hands into it, rub them together until my bones ache as badly as my teeth. The water is clear, not cloudy.

Dreams aren't real. Dreams can't hurt.

Exhaling, I wipe my hands dry on my skirt, avoiding the dark stain soaked into the wool. The light streaming through the porthole is amber; early afternoon. We must be nearly there.

I pick my way back across the narrow cabin and sit on the bunk. This close to Boulogne, we'll be in French waters. England is far behind us. England and the Agency.

My body feels heavy, and I struggle not to bend, not to crack. Everything I left behind—Eve, Jacob, Maia—I'll never see them again. I might never step foot in England again.

If I'd been more thorough, questioned my orders sooner, maybe I could have stopped Rayne. Maybe I could have saved him.

Enough of that. My bun is loose, half undone from where I'd slept on it. I pull my hair free, scrub my hands over my scalp. We're in French waters. We're safe. Nothing else is worth thinking about.

I glance at Steel, who lies on his side, his long legs stretched across the length of the cabin. Blue smudges cup his eyes and a thin wrinkle keeps his brows from merging. Asleep, he looks nothing like the powerful demon he is. Somehow, that unnerves me more than if he'd been breathing smoke and brimstone.

A faint cry drifts down from somewhere on deck; we're about to dock. I stand to shake Steel awake, then draw back my hand.

The binding spell no longer lies between us and without it, we're no longer agent and demon, no longer partners. I don't know what we are.

"Steel," I call. His brows creep closer together, and I say his name again, louder. Silver gleams under his eyelashes. "We've almost reached Boulogne," I tell him and he shifts, pulls himself into a sitting position.

"What time is it?" he asks, his voice hoarse the way it is when I wake him at dawn.

"Gone noon, I think." The dream lingers, staining the walls of my mind scarlet. I think of speaking it aloud, making it real—but no, it's better not to look.

"We should go up on deck," he says, standing. "It'll be easier to get away when we dock." He slips through the door into the corridor, leaving me alone.

The waves crash against the hull of the ship, rocking me. He couldn't wait to put distance between us. Perhaps he doesn't trust me as much as I thought. For the first time in months, I wonder if I should let myself trust *him*.

I crush the thought. Steel came back for me, stayed with me when no one else did. If he doesn't trust me, then it's because I haven't earned it. I twist my hair back into its bun, square my shoulders, and follow him.

***

Boulogne-sur-Mer has none of the warmth that I expected: I'm hit with the cold first, almost as cold as London itself, and the stench of brine and fish sweeps past on a stinging wind that flings saltwater at my face. There's some comfort in the way the other passengers gape at the town, in as much awe as I am. Boulogne may be nothing special, but to those of us on the ship—to me—it's the gate to a new world.

White buildings stippled with square windows line the quay. Trees sprout among them, green and brown leaves interwoven with cheery red roofs. The quay itself is dotted with people and small carriages. Bystanders rush to greet the newcomers, full of cheek-kisses and delighted *bonjours*; families and friends reuniting.

"Now, what?" I whisper, but Steel isn't at my side.

Alarm flares and my heart kicks into a gallop. I peer through the crowd, remind myself not to call his name. There—he's in the middle of it, squeezing around an embracing couple. He ducks past a man in a bulky coat and reaches my side.

"What are you doing?" I ask, my voice sharp with an irritation I didn't intend to reveal. "We can't split up."

He opens his jacket, shows me the outline of a wallet tucked into his inner pocket. "We need money."

"Oh." I thought he'd left me here. Rayne's face flashes before my eyes, the gloating expression after I'd slapped him, after I'd walked right into his trap.

"I can't smell any demons," Steel says and I tear my mind back to the quay. "We should find out when the train leaves; I doubt there's more than one a day."

I rally myself. "The station will be in the centre of town, I expect."

"Good. I'll meet you there." It takes me a minute of listening to his voice fade before I understand what that means.

"Steel," I call, then wince at myself. It's too late, anyway; Steel has vanished among the passengers and the townspeople.

I stand in the middle of the street as people stride past. It's been nearly three months since I've been more than twenty feet from the man and now he's gone.

Nearby, a busker strangles music out of an ancient fiddle, his hat upturned on the street and filled with half a dozen francs. People gaze at my grimy clothes, wide-eyed. Damn that demon.

An elderly woman looks at me with pity. She stops, rummages through her bag, pulls out a coin and presses it into my hand. Then she pats my shoulder and walks away.

Blinking, I clutch the single coin. In the windows across the street, I see my reflection; my face worn and my hair blown half-wild in the wind, my skirt stained and my jacket rumpled. Seven years at Turner's side and I'm back on the street, with no future in front of me but what I can carve out for myself.

The old fear looms, clawing up so quickly that it must have been there all along: how will I survive? Steel's case—finding his family's murderer—won't last forever, and then I'll be alone, with no job and no family to help me.

I swallow, hard. I can't afford to deal with emotion, not yet. I seal away the fear. My stomach growls its first complaint, long overdue. I pocket the coin, and my hand brushes my warrant card, the identification Monaghan gave me when I took over from Turner as an agent months ago.

What was it that she used to say? There's always work to be done. Time to focus on the work.

I eye the townspeople and pick a woman in a bonnet and apron with a friendly face. At my halting enquiry, she directs me to the train station, full of sympathy and shrewd glances at my stomach, no doubt assuming I was cast off by some rake. That would be an easier story than the truth.

The station isn't far, across a broad river and nestled beside a park. Steel was right, though; the train for Paris doesn't leave until the next day. I hover at the station's entrance, wincing as the wind cuts through my jacket. The light is already fading, the November sun skimming towards the horizon like it can't bear to stay in this bleak part of the world for a minute longer. We need food and somewhere to stay for the night, and Steel's not even nearby.

I blink at the thought. He's nowhere within a one-mile radius of my location, and somehow I'm certain of it. Odd.

Standing here is going to give me pneumonia. I tug at my jacket, smooth my frazzled hair, and head for the nearest inn.

The first one I find that's warm inside and doesn't contain the kind of men who look like they might give me trouble is a run down little family place, occupied by fishermen tucking into their dinner and a few older couples drinking wine by the bottle. The wooden tables are shiny from use, and the rough brick walls and beamed ceiling seem to swallow the late November chill. A piano and a violin sit growing dusty in the corner.

The innkeeper's skin is as coarse as old leather and his face doesn't soften when I offer a smile and a *bonjour*. "I'm looking for work." The language sits awkwardly on my tongue, hampered by my cropped London accent. Turner always thought it was useful to know the language of our nearest neighbour—thank God someone at the Agency had pragmatism.

"I don't need any help."

I persist. "I'll do anything. Clean the rooms, wash dishes, whatever you need. I'm not a crook," I add, at the suspicion in his eyes. "I just need to earn some money for food."

He shakes his head and repeats, "I don't need any help."

I deflate. After a moment, the man pushes a small glass over to me.

"Here," he says. "This should warm you up. No charge," he adds, when I offer the single franc the old woman gave me.

"Thank you." The wine does warm me, sinking down my throat with a tangy heat, leaving me with the presence of mind to consider my next step.

A draft of cool air brushes my nape and I turn to see Steel on the threshold, scanning the tavern. His gaze finds me and he strides over with a curt, "Where have you been? I've been looking all over town for you."

"At the station, where you told me to go," I retort. "What was so urgent you had to rush off without me?"

"I was trying to keep us fed and safe."

"So was I." Silence fills the space between us as the rest of the tavern's patrons speak quietly to each other.

Steel sighs and takes a seat next to me. In apology, I push over my half-drunk glass of wine. He takes it with a rueful grimace and downs the dregs. "The train?" he asks.

I shake my head. "Not until tomorrow. Did you make any progress?"

He shrugs. "Some. No one here is that wealthy. You?" I lay my single franc on the counter between us and he grimaces again. "Now what? It's too cold to wander around town at night."

"I'm not sure." I scan the room until my gaze lands on the abandoned piano and on the violin perched on its lid. Once, Steel had talked about magic as if it was music, the rise and fall of its energy like arpeggios. I point at the instruments. "Do you play?"

He glances at them and then at me. "A little. Why?"

"Give me your hat." He hesitates, then takes off the Homburg and hands it to me. I stand, leaning over the counter. "Do you mind if we use one of your instruments?" I ask the innkeeper. "Play for a little coin?"

The man looks as bemused as Steel, but he shrugs his indifference.

"Play for money?" Steel asks, following me as I make my way over to the corner. "That's your idea?"

"If a street performer can do it, so can you." I raise my brows at him, half a challenge, and he snorts.

"It's been a while," he warns. "I'm quite rusty." Contrary to my expectations, he picks up the violin. He notices my surprise. "We couldn't afford a piano at home. A fiddle, though—Even my father knew a few songs on the fiddle." He drags the bow over the violin's strings, wincing when the notes ring sour.

I leave him to tune it, turning to the tavern. The other customers have grown quiet, watching us with curiosity. Swallowing, I step forward, holding Steel's hat in both hands. It's just a few fishermen and farmers. They hardly compare to a group of policemen at a crime scene.

"Hello," I begin. My voice wavers and I clear my throat. Keep it short. If Steel's any good, he'll win over the crowd. If not—I didn't even consider that he might not be. A bit late for that now. "We'd like to play a song or two for you this afternoon. Any appreciation you can show would be welcome." I give the hat a little shake for emphasis.

Steel has finished tuning the violin. He ignores his audience, staring at a fixed point in the near distance. He picks out a few notes, a low melody that draws lingering conversations to a close and attention to him. Then, as he warms up, the melody quickens, painting a picture of spring woodlands and country dances. The music lifts the tavern's mood, a bright contrast to the whistling wind outside. When the song draws to a close, he flows without pause into another. If he's rusty, I can't tell. He could be playing at the Royal Albert Hall for an audience of thousands, rather than twenty-odd French fishermen in a rundown old tavern.

This song leads to a third, and then to a fourth, as if, now that he's started, he doesn't want to stop. When he finally lowers the violin, it's with such a look of grief that my heart twists for him. He banks the expression as a smattering of applause rolls through the tavern. I collect francs with a smile, hovering when someone feels inclined to be a miser until they relent and toss in a coin. Steel plays again a few hours later, when the crowd changes and the late night patrons settle in.

When we finish, the innkeeper brings us each a plate of braised lamb with under-cooked vegetables and crusty bread. He deposits them with a gruff, "For your trouble," and leaves.

Steel counts out our earnings. "Not bad," he comments. "Perhaps I should think about taking this up as a career. Lucifer knows I have few other options."

I spear a carrot and bite into it with a crunch. "You play well. Not that I know very much about music," I admit.

"Thank you," Steel replies, tearing into the lamb.

"Where did you learn?"

"My father taught me."

He hasn't said much about his father. I find myself thinking of my own, but all that comes to mind is the man's dour voice telling me to earn more money. What we had was never enough for him. "Was he with your mother?"

"No, he was killed by Revenants, burned to death by their fire." Somehow, Steel keeps eating. "That's why we were there."

I frown. "What do you mean?"

He shakes his head.

I fall silent, puzzling out our next steps as I watch night creep into the edges of the room. The London murders will have the police on edge, worried that the Ripper will try to escape through France. Not that they have to worry about that; right now, the Ripper will be putting together a plan to replace me. He's lost three agents in the last four months: he'll be recruiting as fast as possible to get the Agency back on its feet and rebuild his power base.

And then... I can't guess what his move will be after that. Monaghan might as well be a stranger to me now. Yet it's hard to think about him as anything other than the man who plucked me from Whitechapel and gave me a job, gave me a purpose. It's hard to think of him as a murderer.

I try to bury the thought. I can't think about the professor now—only what our next move should be. We're here for Steel.

"Are you all right?" the demon asks.

"I'm fine."

He doesn't look convinced. "You're thinking about the professor."

This man can read me too easily. "He wasn't real," I reply. "The man I thought I knew was just a facade designed to get him what he wanted—power." I want to believe that I won't see Monaghan again, but some part of me suspects that he won't just disappear, that he'll be there until I face him again.

"He still has the power to publish our likeness in the papers," I say, steering the conversation back on track, "at which point nowhere in Europe will be safe."

"Don't tell me I need to start wearing spectacles again," Steel says, wrinkling his nose. His silver eyes look normal—as normal as silver eyes *can* look—his thin serpentine pupils round and human, disguised by his magic.

"I think we can get by with some new clothes." I tuck a yellow strand of hair behind my ear. I'm not sure of the fashions in France, or how rare blond hair might be here, but it's a simple thing to add to a description. If we can get hold of some vinegar, I can try to dye it.

"I passed a few shops on the way here," Steel comments. "We should be able to find something in the morning."

I nod. It's gone eight now, and the pub is starting to fill with people who would be at home on the dark streets of Whitechapel. I eye them, noting each furtive glance directed our way. Boulogne-sur-Mer is a small town. Even tourists stand out.

"Relax," Steel says, around a forkful of potato. "You'll draw attention, looking at people like that."

Chagrined, I drop my gaze. These are the kind of people I used to work alongside. The kind of men who'd walk me home as a child, just in case; the kind of women who'd spare me a shawl on the cold winter nights. Why am I so on edge?

The dream. My nerves have been tangled ever since that nightmare. My hand drops to my skirt, to the dark stain there.

"It's late, anyway," Steel says, placing his cutlery aside. "We should get some sleep. I, for one, could use it after being tossed around on the waves all day." He stretches as he stands.

We'd been lucky enough to benefit from a flat sea for most of the journey. I'm not sure if the exaggeration is for his benefit or mine, but either way, I'm grateful for the distraction.

The innkeeper is uncorking a wine bottle, and he greets us with a nod as we hover at the bar. "A drink?"

"Two rooms, if you have them," I say.

The man looks at us, a frown growing between his brow. "Two?" he repeats.

"One," Steel says, smiling. "My wife misspoke."

Wife? My brain catches up a moment later: an unmarried couple travelling together will draw attention.

The innkeeper's perplexed expression clears. He sets the wine to breathe and then fetches a key from somewhere under the counter. "It'll be five francs for the night."

That'll carve a chunk out of tonight's earnings; just as well it's only the one. Steel takes the key and we're directed to a narrow, poky staircase behind the bar.

"You speak French well," I say.

"Something else I can thank my father for," Steel responds. "He knew a lot of languages. Both my parents did."

In London, he'd said that his breed of demon, Dragons, held both the first and second Houses, the most privileged families in their class structure. Even if his parents had abandoned that structure, they would have come from wealth.

At the top of the stairs, we meet three doors. One matches our key and, on opening it, we find a small room with a small chair and an equally small cot. I'd been expecting it, but the sight still gives me pause.

"That looks comfortable," Steel mutters, eyeing the cot.

"Better than a coffin."

"You slept in a *coffin*?"

"Two pennies for a bench with a rope, four for a coffin." I'd only tried it once, after twelve hours in the workhouse when my feet were aching and I couldn't stand the thought of sleeping on a pew. "It gave me nightmares for weeks," I admitted.

"But your family...?"

"They had half a dozen other children to take care of and one room to do it in." Some of the children hadn't made it to puberty. I wish I knew what happened to the rest. But the wisp of a thought is merely that, insubstantial, and it evaporates in seconds. Those of my blood were never my family. "I slept in the workhouse, for the most part."

"What was that like?"

"It stank of lye and filth and we were packed so close together we could barely breathe." Half of us sick or diseased, all of us waiting to die. "At one point, my hands bled for three days straight and I lost two shirts to bind the cuts."

Steel is silent and I wish I'd been a little less communicative. He jerks his head at the chair. "I'll sleep there."

"It doesn't look much better." It's an armchair at least, but the upholstery is threadbare and torn in places, exposing cotton stuffing. "I can sleep there," I offer.

"I may be a demon," Steel says, "but I do have *some* sensibilities. I assume you can bear my unnatural presence for one more night?"

"Don't be ridiculous," I reply, before I see the upturned corner of his mouth. "That's not funny."

He chuckles.

"Thank you," I say, refusing to think about the fact that he'll be sleeping mere feet away. Propriety is of little use now. That ship, as it were, has sailed.

His mouth slants up, the last shreds of our previous conversation disappearing behind it. "Have no fear. Your virtue is safe tonight, Agent Locke."

"I appreciate that, Mr. Steel." It takes effort to add, "But it's just Locke. I'm not a member of the Agency anymore."

"Right now, it should probably be Mrs. Steel," he points out, settling into the chair with no apparent discomfort. "We're masquerading as a married couple, are we not?"

"Or perhaps it should be Mr. Locke," I counter.

He flashes me a grin, unperturbed. "If you prefer."

Jokes aside, it should be neither. "If the Agency does come looking for us, we should go by another name. None immediately spring to mind," I admit. Creativity was never my strength. I was the one who'd point out the logical fallacies in Eve's latest Penny Dreadful, making Jacob roll his eyes and complain: *It's a story, not a science lecture.*

"Lyr," Steel says, shutting down the memory. His eyes are closed, his head tilted against the back of the chair. "Lyr was my father's name." Nothing in his voice gives away how he feels about using it.

I scoot back on the bed until my shoulders hit the wall. "What about your first name?"

He hesitates and then replies, "Steel is fine."

The Blood Drinker in Whitechapel had declined to give her name. She'd said names weren't something that demons give out on a whim. Perhaps he'll tell me, someday.

I watch him for a moment longer. We can't go much further if I don't understand his case. "You need to tell me what happened." My voice falls into the quiet, only the faint reverberations from the tavern below its accompaniment. "I can't help if I don't know."

He lets out a long sigh and opens his eyes. "I suppose you're right. It's just...a painful memory." His voice radiates suppressed tension.

It had been easy for me to cut my heart's strings when I joined the Agency. I never thought much of it, but watching Steel struggle now, I wonder what might be wrong with me, that I could leave my family behind without hesitation.

I search for a gentler way to start. "You didn't have any shoes, when you were—when I summoned you," I correct. *I* was responsible for his predicament, not some twist of fate. "Or a jacket, for that matter. Did you leave them behind?"

His silver eyes flick to me. Their pupils are thin now, serpentine, the magic that controlled their shape discarded. He raises one knee and rests his arm on it. "I'd just been attacked," he starts, his voice even. "I ran into some copper class demons in Paris while I was searching. They hunt in gangs and I looked like an easy target. I fought them off, of course."

"Of course."

His mouth quirks, then falls again. "They were poisoned," he says abruptly, and it takes me a moment to realise he's talking about his family. "Did I tell you that? They poisoned the wine before they killed them."

"You didn't."

"It was the toast that was meant to celebrate their supremacy. Perhaps it was justice," he says, in a lilting, sarcastic voice. "Divine intervention."

"You weren't there?" I work to keep my tone from becoming detached. This is not just a case, this is family.

"I was there, but... Diamond favours pure bloodlines," he explains. "Keeps the magic in the House. My mother married a rogue Dragon, a demon with no name and no legacy."

"I take it this didn't recommend him to your family?"

"It did not. But after Revenants killed my father, my mother said we needed the protection of a House. She was going to beg them to take her back. And me, with her." He pauses and I wait, listening to the movement below us. "I was arrogant," he says. "Reckless."

"Was?" I ask, hoping.

It works; he barks a laugh and his posture relaxes a fraction. "Our House had these jewels—proof of their heritage," he continues. "One should have been my mother's. My uncle kept it in a vault underneath the mansion. I thought it would be fitting if I took it. I thought I could sell it, maybe, told myself we didn't need a House's protection if we had money. If I hadn't been such an *idiot*, if I had just stayed with her..."

"You would have been killed." I don't need to understand the details of what happened to know that much. "If these people murdered your family, it would have been a simple thing for them to kill you, too."

He sighs again, staring down at the floor. "When I came back with the stupid jewel, it was too late. They were gone, all of them, and my mother with them."

It must have been a potent drug to affect so many powerful demons. "How did you know it was in the wine?" I wince. The practicalities of the event call to me, but recollecting this is dragging out Steel's pain. I should be more empathetic. Also not one of my skills.

He replies instantly, though. "My mother's last words. The rest died with glasses still in their hands. They were—" He stops. The muscle in his jaw flexes. "They'd been beheaded, or their throats were cut. Whoever did it set the house on fire, too. Covered every eventuality."

"They were killed *after* taking the poison? So, the poison didn't kill them?"

"That's what it looked like."

With so many demons in one place, inhibiting their strength and magic would make the act of killing them easier. And Steel said he was the last. "How many people died?" I ask, forgetting to inject warmth into my voice.

Steel doesn't seem to notice. "About thirty, maybe. I didn't stop to count."

"So, they killed every member of the House, except you."

Steel stays silent as I mull it over. It wasn't just his immediate family they were after—they targeted the House. The second in thirty years to be eradicated.

There's something there, some shadow of a thought, but it's too indistinct to grasp. "We will find the people who did this," I whisper.

The hand that rests on his knee has curled into a fist. "Yes," he agrees, his voice distant, dark. "We will."

A wound like this cannot be lanced in one night. "Was there anyone who should have been there and wasn't?"

"Suspects, you mean?" Steel sighs and stretches out his bent leg, folding his arms over his chest. "No. None that I could tell. I thought it was the mayor, so I went there first."

"There?" I prompt.

"Oh, I didn't say, did I?" He shakes his head. "Florence. They lived in Florence."

"And what happened to the mayor?"

"He told me the wine came from the sommelier, that he hadn't touched it. So, I went to see the sommelier." Steel's head thunks against the back of the chair. His face could have been carved from marble. "He was a demon, though I don't know what class or breed. He was fast. And he wouldn't talk, at first. I had to get creative," he says, a light, affected tone to his voice.

This is another of his shields turned weapon, a deflection to keep me from seeing him. I meet his gaze. "He told you where the poison came from?"

"He said Paris. Just Paris, nothing else." Steel looks away, releasing me from the pin of his eyes. "I killed him anyway."

Only the slight jerk of my fingers betrays my shock. I exhale, and ask, "What then?"

"By that time, the mayor's people were on my tail and I had to flee."

"Why not go to another House and ask for help? Won't the First do something?"

"The First House won't act without proof." Steel taps his fingers against his arm, glaring at the floor. "They don't get involved in the petty disputes of other Houses. That's even if they'd agree to hear me. I'm a bastard son, remember?"

"I see. But you went to Paris."

"I tried asking around, figuring out who was in the city that could have had the power to arrange something. I'm not very good at that kind of work," he says, and his restless fingers grip the arms of the chair, make indents in the fabric. "Anyway, then I met the Stalker demons, and then your roses and anemones pulled me to London. And here we are."

"Here we are," I repeat, turning over his words. "Are you sure he was telling the truth about Paris?"

"I'm sure. Not that it helps, anyway—all I have is the name of the city and a label."

There are so many variables, so many ways that this could end. It's an impossible task. I don't let that thought show on my face.

"What will you do when we get proof?" I ask. "Will you reclaim your House?"

"I don't care about the House, or the power. I just want to see them pay for what they did. As violently as possible." This he says with the glimmer of a dark grin. "Do you still want to help me?" he asks. "Knowing all this? Knowing what I've done?"

The look he gives me is sharp, but there's a vulnerability behind his gaze. As if he's bracing himself for something. Perhaps, if he'd told me this three months ago, I'd have been more shocked, more wary of him. But I have blood on my own hands now.

"Of course I do," I reply. "Besides, I owe you a debt."

He shifts in the chair, resettling his limbs. "Well, Agent? What do you recommend?"

I take a moment to consider the size of the case, try not to let it daunt me. All we can do right now is work with the evidence we have: the wine. "We need an expert. A sommelier, or a vintner, someone who has connections in the industry. Someone who might recognise the label. There should be plenty of those in Paris."

He exhales. "All right. We can do that."

"Get some sleep, if you can," I tell him. "We'll need rest."

He nods, half distracted. I settle down, turning my back to him to mask my expression as I mull over the problem. I made it sound simple, and finding an expert may well be, but locating a single brand of wine in a city the size of Paris... Hope shrivels in my chest.

I hold myself still, staring at the wall. My brain begins its nightly rhythm, churning over every word, every action I took that day, searching for things I could have done differently, planning things to try tomorrow. Every time it leans towards London, I yank it back and cut the thought off before it can come to fruition. London is behind me. Paris is the future.

I close my eyes, try to shelve the problem for the morning. I count my breaths. Inhale. Exhale. Inhale. Exhale.

Steel's low breaths echo my own, a little slower, as loud as thunder in the quiet room. I realise that I'm slowing my breathing to match his.

My eyes pop open again. Holes pockmark the uneven bricks in the wall and a spider has taken root in one corner. Inhale. Exhale. Steel isn't a man. He's a demon. It shouldn't matter that he's in the same room. If only I was still exhausted enough not to notice.

"You're awake."

The words send a jolt through me. "I thought you were asleep."

"Seems neither of us are going to find sleep easily tonight."

Downstairs, the low hum of activity dwindles. The bar must be closing. "Steel," I whisper, to the spider and her web.

"Mm?"

I don't know what I want to say. "Your music was lovely," I reply, instead.

A mumble of goodbyes, then a door shutting. "Thank you," Steel murmurs back.

I shut my eyes. Inhale. Exhale. Wait for sleep to arrive.

Apprentice E. Wilson

Police fill the lobby when she returns to the Agency. Eve exchanges a glance with Jacob, who's sandy hair became a tangled mop about three hours ago and now looks ready to welcome a pair of starlings. His Reaper demon, Max, displays his own unease by etching a dent in his lower lip with one jagged tooth.

"Maybe we're about to be replaced," she says, aiming for levity.

Jacob shakes his head, the joke falling short; none of them are in the mood. She scans the room for a familiar face, finds Maia at the bottom of the stairs, shepherding policemen into the dining room.

Eve shoulders her way through the crowd, ignoring the disparaging looks thrown her way. "What's going on?" she asks the cook. "Where's Khurana?"

"She is upstairs, with the professor." Maia pushes back the kerchief tied around her hair. Fresh lines branch out from the corners of her eyes. "You had better go up, all of you."

That doesn't sound promising. Trying to ignore the way her stomach is falling to her feet, Eve jogs up the stairs towards

Monaghan's office. Dawn light streams through the Agency's windows, pale and thin among the creeping clouds.

"We lost too much time on the train," Jacob mutters. "If we'd kept searching..." He trails off. Behind him, Max stares at the floor.

"We don't know how many traps she might have laid for us," Eve replies. It was smart, to create a false trail by purchasing the train tickets, and Hazel might have set up any number of other distractions for them to follow. By now, she and her demon could be anywhere.

But *why*? That's the question Eve still doesn't understand, the question that stomps through her brain demanding an answer. Rayne had suggested that Hazel wasn't in her right mind and she'd certainly seemed out of it when she'd pressed a plate shard to her throat in a bid for freedom. Accusing agents of murder, though—*Khurana* and even Rayne—what could have driven her to that?

Her demon. He'd been acting strangely ever since Hazel had bonded him in the ritual. He could have been using her to get his freedom. Or to get her killed, which would have resulted in the same end.

They emerge on the first floor, where Monaghan's office stands open. He's speaking with a policeman in a blue helmet emblazoned with the City of London's arms. Monaghan's Reaper demon sees Eve first and clears his throat. The professor glances over.

"Please come in, Eve. Horner. Thank you for your assistance, Lieutenant." He shakes the hand of the policeman he'd been talking to and waits as the man exits. "Tiberius," he says, and the Reaper closes the door.

Monaghan's office looks the same as it had the last time she'd been here—shelves stacked with books, wide wooden desk—but something feels off. After a moment, it comes to her; the picture he keeps on his desk, the portrait of the girl he once loved, is missing.

"Well?" the professor asks.

"We couldn't find them." Anxiety makes her words short and sharp, though Monaghan doesn't react. His fair brows are furrowed and his normally clean-shaven jaw is shadowed with stubble. He looks at Jacob after she's spoken, as if to confirm her story, and Eve squashes her curl of irritation with the ease of habit.

"According to the cashier, a couple matching Agent Locke and her demon's descriptions bought two tickets at London Bridge train station," Jacob says, standing with his hands clasped behind his back. Even with the dishevelled state of his hair and the dirt on his suit, he looks every inch an agent. "We held the train and searched it, but they weren't there."

"It was bait," Eve interrupts. "She'll be halfway to Scotland by now."

"Scotland?" Monaghan's voice is as level as always, but his green eyes are keen. "Do you have reason to believe she would seek sanctuary in the north? Where are her family?"

Sanctuary? "No, sir. She hasn't spoken to her family in years, not since she joined. She has nowhere to go." And yet, she still left. "Sir, where is Khurana?"

"In her room." Monaghan takes a seat behind his desk, putting his hands on the wooden surface in the way he does when he's bracing himself to deliver bad news. Eve unconsciously widens her stance. "Agent Rayne is dead," he says.

For a moment, the meaning of his words doesn't register. Then, beside her, Jacob sways. Eve snaps out a hand to steady him but Max is there first, slipping an arm around him and propping him up.

"Dead?" Jacob croaks.

Eve winces. It was no secret that he'd been half in love with Rayne since he'd first set eyes on the man, personality not withstanding. The rest of them won't lose much sleep over his loss, but it's not often they lose two agents in less than six months. "How did he die?"

Monaghan rubs one hand over his mouth, hesitating, and that's what fills her with dread. "I have reason to believe," he says slowly, reluctantly, "that miss Locke and her demon killed him."

CHAPTER TWO

Glass crushes under my feet. Broken wine glasses, scattered among bodies—corpses. Silent stone statues loom above me, illuminated by flickering golden light. Everywhere is the scent of lemons. And blood.

Then—lavender and vanilla. I creep around a thick hedge and stop. For a long moment I can't move. If I don't move, I won't see.

But I need to see.

My feet slide over the ground. I sidestep a statue, brace myself—There. A body, curled protectively around another. My mother.

I kneel at her side. The world has gone blurry, indistinct, but my vision focuses on an unbroken glass still in her hand. Two more lie smashed on the grass, as if they'd been dropped. A bottle, disturbed by my movement, rolls across the ground. I pick it up. Black roses wind over the glass, prickling with thorns that spike into my hand.

A *whoosh* makes me flinch; I turn around, still holding the bottle—unable to let go—and find the building behind me in flames, blazing against a black sky. The heat needles my face.

The bottle shatters in my hand and I jolt awake. I stare at the dark ceiling, catching my breath. The dream was so vivid I can still feel the heat on my skin. Steel's story must have unnerved me more than I thought.

I rub my eyes and sit up. If the greyish light can be believed, it's not yet dawn. Steel is still asleep, tucked into the chair in a tangle of limbs. The noise of the locals setting up stalls outside drowns the sound of his breathing, but his presence so close makes me overly conscious of my appearance. We haven't changed clothes since we were locked up as murder suspects. Then there was the race through Whitechapel, then—then Rayne, and the ship... Our clothes are filthy and my skin prickles at every brush of cloth against my skin.

There must be a washroom around here. I creep out of the room without waking Steel—he must be exhausted—and find one down the hall, little more than a copper bowl and a jug. Still, the jug is full, and the water is cold but invigorating. I use the brush provided to scrub every speck of dirt from my body. Its bristles are hard and my skin reddens under each swipe. I scrub my hands the hardest, until they sting.

Putting my clothes back on makes me cringe. Nothing we're wearing is unique—Agency clothes aren't designed to stand out—but it can't hurt to find something else, in case anyone's on our trail.

Fresh from an icy bath and a decent night's sleep, the reasonable part of my brain objects to this plan. I'm overthinking this. Why would Monaghan come after us? He has everything he wanted, including me out of the picture. Following us would only risk his position.

And yet, I can't shake the rabbit-like fear in the pit of my stomach. Who knows what he'll do next?

I go back to our room and find Steel awake. A tightness to his expression eases as I enter.

"There's a washroom down the hall," I offer. "And we need new clothes."

"That is *one* thing I miss about your agency," he admits. "That and Maia's cooking."

I don't want to think about Maia's cooking; it'll just remind me of what else I've lost. "How many francs do we have left?"

"Not enough for clothes as well as the train tickets. Unless you want me to perform again?"

"There's no point." No one will be hanging around a tavern at dawn.

"Well, while you figure out what to do, I'm going to clean up." He ducks out of the room, and while I wait I tidy the bed, make sure we don't leave a trace behind. Paranoid, but I can't seem to help it. Turner taught me too well.

"So," Steel says, making me jump. He stands in the doorway, rumpled and creased, somehow managing to look artfully tousled rather than dead on his feet. "How are we going to get these clothes?"

I herd him out of the room and lock it behind us. "I thought we'd put your skills to good use."

His eyebrows arch up. "And which of my many skills would you be referring to?"

I give him a dry look. The innkeeper isn't downstairs, so I leave the key on the counter and follow Steel outside, glad when we're in the open street and can melt into the crowd. When we're absorbed by the city's early morning traffic, I say, "You're a thief, yes?"

"Ah. So, we're *stealing* the clothes?"

"*You're* stealing the clothes." As we walk, I scan the shops nestled along the side of the road. It's a big seaside town, a common stopping point for people going on to Paris, or elsewhere in France, so there are plenty of little stores and stalls.

"Right, *I'm* stealing the clothes. How, exactly? It's not like I can pluck a shirt off a man without him noticing."

"You'll have to grab whatever you can." I spy a small store offering cheap, secondhand clothes. Stealing from it is going to cost the owner and I fight a sudden qualm. I soothe my conscience by promising to return, even as I know the chances of that happening are slim.

The shop's sign swings erratically in the wind, a plywood board with a painted figure on it that could be a man or a woman. Its colour is smudged and faded, the paint flaking. Inside, old wooden walls are lined with plank shelving piled high with folded clothes.

There are a couple of women at the back of the shop, talking to a third who's wrapping something in brown paper—the owner. I wander over to stand close by, picking at a selection of worn calico dresses. Steel roams the displays near the door.

"Do you think it's true what they're saying?" one of the women asks, in a low voice.

"I don't know," the shopkeeper replies. "But it's worrying, isn't it? All those women, murdered that way."

"London is nothing like here," the third replies. "We don't need to worry."

I can't escape him even here. That rabbit-fear flutters again and I squash it. I can't afford to listen to fear, or to fall to grief. We have a job to do.

Once my stomach is cold and tight and my heart is quiet, I approach the women with a concerned expression, taking care to stand so they have to face me, their backs to Steel.

"Forgive me for interrupting," I say, hoping my English accent isn't too strong. "I just arrived in the city. What murders are you speaking of? When did they happen?"

"Oh, don't worry, they weren't *here*. They were in London. You haven't seen the papers?"

I shake my head. Steel drifts closer, after one of the dresses, and the owner turns at the sound of his footsteps. I totter forward with a soft cry and grab her arm. She makes a startled sound and the other women both grab at me, help me to stand.

"I'm so sorry," I say, making my voice tremble a little. "Just the thought of murder..." Steel sneaks out, the bell above the door chiming, lost in the moment, and I add, "Forgive me, I should go."

"Are you sure?" one of the young women asks. "You should sit down for a bit and rest."

"Thank you," I tell them, summoning a smile. It won't be long before the owner notices the missing clothes and remembers that Steel had entered the shop with me. I slide out of their grip. "Thank you, but I'm fine." I leave them with a quick *Au revoir*, and start walking towards the station.

Steel catches up to me a few streets later, the bundle of clothes tucked under his jacket. "It's a good thing we're leaving," he says. "I think someone saw me."

"They saw you? What about the police?"

"I was fast."

"We're cutting it close." The sooner we get to Paris, away from the coast and among a larger population, the better.

⁕⁕⁕

The train station at Boulogne is no more than a few tracks built directly into the ground, crowned by a large wooden pediment. We purchase tickets with the last of our francs, to an annoyed huff as the ticket seller counts out our collection of coins, and are directed to a waiting room. It's furnished with a few benches and smells of damp and cigarette smoke. Luckily, there are only a handful of people here; a couple of men in nice suits and a woman with three children and a lot of baggage.

A poster on one wall advertises a Parisian opera. Its central ballerina lifts one impossibly long leg, her auburn curls cascading over her shoulders, heart-shaped face and dancing figure drawn in lush curves. *Prima Ballerina La Sorelli*, the poster advertises. Above her, a woman in a huge golden wig sings to a lonely moon: *Prima Donna Carlotta*.

"Here," Steel says, handing the clothes to me. "Why don't you change and I'll find us something to eat?"

The station doesn't offer much in the way of facilities, but I find a room set aside for the ticket officers and slip in while no one's watching. I unfurl the bundle. A man's shirt and trousers come loose, along with a slightly frayed dress. The bronze skirt is designed to loop over a bustle and cascade down the back, but

I don't have a bustle, so I tuck the fabric up under my bodice to shorten the length and hope that will do.

My gaze catches on the scar marring my forearm. It's silvery-white against my pale, freckled skin. The last remnant of the spell that freed Steel. I tug my sleeve down, then transfer my warrant card from my old skirt and emerge to find Steel waiting outside. He holds up a croissant.

"Where did you get that?"

"Ask me no questions and I'll tell you no lies." He tears it into two and offers half to me, taking a bite out of his own piece.

"I suppose you're used to travelling like this," I say, accepting it.

"Needs must," he replies and disappears into the room to change.

I take a seat in the waiting room and devour the croissant. Its buttery, flaky pastry dissolves on my tongue. The woman is dealing out slices of bread and apples, dividing her supplies so each child has an even share. They look healthy. They don't look as though they know what it's like to go to bed with your stomach trying to gnaw out your insides.

Steel flops onto the bench next to me in his stolen clothes, kicking his legs out in front of him. "Is that enough?" he asks, nodding at the tail of the croissant in my hand. His is long gone. "My body can handle going without food for a while. I forget that humans need more."

I recall how voraciously he'd eaten while we were in London; he must have been famished. "I spent most of my childhood hungry." The memories are faint—I've folded them away, tucked into the time before the Agency, before Monaghan.

Thinking his name makes my stomach sink, an odd combination of guilt and horror. I peel a layer off my croissant half. "My parents had too much to worry about to concern themselves with anything except earning their livelihood. It was normal, for Whitechapel."

"And then you went to the workhouse?" Steel watches the other people in the room. It makes it easier to speak, not having his gaze on me.

"As soon as I was old enough. It freed up space."

"Do you miss them? Your family?"

"Not the one I grew up with." I hope they're doing well, but I have no desire to see them again. They were merely the people who raised me. It wasn't until I joined the Agency that I understood the kind of bond a family could provide.

"I can't imagine that." Steel keeps watching the woman with her children. "I only had my parents, growing up, and we stayed away from people—we had to, to be safe—but I never felt alone."

Perhaps it's just me who can sever my emotions so easily. But right now, that seems to be a benefit.

The whistle of the train is a relief. We join the small queue of people heading to the platform as it pulls in. White steam trails from the engine, adding depth to the pewter sky. As the train pulls up, the platform fills with a layer of smoke. The smell of hot metal and coal clings to my dress as we board.

Rows of red leather seats fill each carriage, deep and welcoming against walnut walls. For a moment, I'm transported to a world in which I'm travelling to Paris to nibble on macarons and waltz along the Seine. A version of the world in which all that awaits us in Paris is happiness. I take a seat by the window, watch the sea crinkle under heavy clouds. Steel sits opposite me and, as the train accelerates out of the station, the fantasy disperses with the smoke.

We're alone except for a gentleman who has fallen asleep with his mouth open. "This is the first time I've left England," I say, to fill the space between us. "I never stepped foot outside London, before. Never saw the sea beyond the docks."

"I lived by the sea, in Ireland," he replies, softly, as if he can read my intentions. "Someday, I'd like to go back."

"Perhaps you will," I offer and he hums.

The countryside flows past in shades of rust and honey. After a while, the *chug-chug* of the train on the rails becomes the *tick-tock* of a clock. Reminding me that our time is limited, that we have a case to solve.

"Is there anything more that you can tell me about the wine?" I ask, looking away from the rolling fields. "You mentioned the label. Did it have a name?"

"No," he replies, his expression hardening. "It had a symbol—a rose, I think. Black, with thorns."

Like my dream. My hands twitch with the urge to sketch it, and I remember that both my little notebook and Turner's journal are back at the Agency. I wonder if anyone has cracked her code.

"It's not much of a clue," I say, thinking aloud.

"I suppose looking for one bottle of wine in a city known for the stuff *is* a bit hopeless."

My first urge is to agree with him, but the vacant way Steel stares at his upturned palms checks my instinctive response.

"It's odd that it came from the city and not a winery," I say, grasping the only clue that I can discern from this kernel of a case. "It must have come from a seller, or a storage facility of some kind. We'll try asking a reputable sommelier."

Steel sits back, apparently relieved, and I turn to stare out the window. Sommeliers, at least, will be easy, but the case itself seems insurmountable. I wonder if we can succeed at all.

CHAPTER THREE

Paris is an artist's city. Green gabled roofs perch over narrow streets and each tall building is gilded with balconies, or shutters, or window boxes. Iron lampposts wrought like metal trees line the streets, their gas lamps glowing through the steam, and light streams from every window, rivalling even the stars. This beautiful golden city holds the key to Steel's past. Some-where.

"I can definitely smell demons," Steel mutters.

"What kind?" Passengers disembarking from the Boulogne train brush past me without even a *Pardon*, businessmen and families wanting nothing more than to be in bed. I search the crowd, but there's too many people, too much motion.

"Silver class, I think. No Reapers," he adds.

Reapers emit a distinctive kind of energy that warns other demons to stay away. They're strong enough to be a genuine threat. "That's something, at least."

"Let's find a restaurant," Steel says. "We need to get started."

I grab his sleeve before he disappears again. "Hold on. We can't just go running up to the first sommelier we find and start demanding answers."

He stares at me blankly. "Why not?"

I'm starting to see why he didn't get very far before. "One, because most people don't take kindly to interrogations," I begin. "Two, if this wine *is* poison, they're not going to admit to being familiar with it. Three, asking questions about it is going to draw unwanted attention, and we need to avoid that if we want to get this done."

"Oh." He glances at the people and carriages around us and I release his sleeve, wondering if he'll go anyway, ignore my advice. But he turns to me, his shoulders straightening. "So, what do we do?"

I exhale. The weight of responsibility is heavier than any case I've had before. Because this one is important in a different way, I realise. It's important to someone I—care about? *Do* I care about Steel?

"First, we need somewhere to stay," I reply. "Somewhere central that we can use in lieu of an agency headquarters." Somewhere with a library would be nice, but no hotel's going to offer the kind of books that I need.

Steel checks his pockets and holds out the francs we have left—not enough to cover his palm. "My musical talent isn't going to pay for a nice hotel. A lodging house, maybe, but that's assuming we can find another violin to play."

A lodging house will give us a single bed in a room packed full of people. Not the kind of place we can talk about demons and poisons. "Credit."

"I beg your pardon?"

I examine his clothes—a simple black suit and a white shirt. In the soft gas light, I can barely see the stains. "If you're rich enough, you can buy things on credit."

"We're not rich enough."

"You can pretend to be, *Lord* Lyr."

"Right. And what happens when they realise we're not? I can lift a wallet or two, but not a title."

"By then, we'll have the money. Enough to keep them from kicking us onto the street, at least."

Steel watches me, eyebrows lifted like he's both amused and fascinated. "And how are we going to *get* the money?"

"I haven't thought that far ahead," I admit.

He tilts his head and says, "It's been a while, but I'm a half-decent card player."

It's my turn to stare at him. "How will that help?"

"Gambling, mademoiselle. If we're going to create a Parisian nobleman, we might as well go all in. And you'd be surprised what you can persuade people to bet."

It'll be tricky, but establishing a presence as a minor lord among the aristocracy would give us access not only to their plump wallets but also to their wine cellars and personal sommeliers. And whoever orchestrated this assassination must have had money and influence to have arranged it so neatly.

"All right," I agree. "Then let's find a hotel and you can practise your impersonation of nobility, my lord."

"We spent enough time with Rayne that it shouldn't be hard."

I tense at the name and the air between us thickens.

Steel scratches the back of his neck and jerks his elbow at a road that leads away from the station. "It's not as if Paris will be sparse of hotels. Shall we?"

A few streets away, we stumble upon one that blends so well with the surrounding houses we wouldn't have noticed it if not for its tiny plaque. Inside, a fire chases away the evening draughts and brightens varnished mahogany floors and midnight blue wallpaper. There are no couches or chairs to encourage lingering, and the concierge regards our entrance with a single raised brow.

Perfect.

I hang back and let Steel approach the desk. "Good evening," he says, in a voice that hints at disdain. "I am in need of a room."

"For one night, monsieur?" Assuming that this young lord is looking for one night of passion with no questions asked is an assumption that will work in our favour, even if I have to fight a blush at the doubtful way the concierge looks me up and down. No wonder, I suppose. Most street workers tend to be built on less Amazonian lines; Aphrodites rather than Athenas.

Steel intercepts the look. "Well, I suppose that depends how the rest of the night goes." The demon leans over him, using his height and his sharp smile to his advantage. "Your discretion, of course, will be expected."

"Indeed." My estimation of this place seems to have been on the money; the concierge doesn't bat an eyelid at the request. He does not, however, move to accommodate it.

Steel makes a show of looking around the lobby. "Am I to be your only guest? Or have I stumbled into a bordel?"

The concierge wavers. "Your name, monsieur?"

"Lord Lyr. Here, I'll write it for you." He nips the man's pen out of his hand and scrawls a signature in the open ledger on the counter. "It should have been Earl, if not for the Battle of Flowers in 1786," he continues. "But I'll have my revenge; their lake is all trout, no salmon at all. Not even in the river, can you believe it?"

What on earth is happening? The concierge looks as baffled as I feel. Steel keeps talking, relating a series of battles that managed to kill off this mythical salmon population until the concierge thrusts a key into his hand and cuts him off.

"Is there a gambling house nearby?" asks Steel.

The concierge has been trained well, though, because he pivots into giving directions, though he speaks so rapidly I can't pick out the words.

Steel thanks him with a careless *merci* and strides across the lobby to me. "He said there's one not far from here," the demon says, in an undertone. "Take this. I'll be back in the morning."

"I'm going with you."

"It's a *gambling house*. They don't let women—they don't let *respectable* women," Steel says, "into gambling houses."

"Then I'll be a *disreputable* woman. What if something happens to you?" I add, as he goes to respond. "What if you get into trouble and don't come back?"

"Are you saying that I can't stay out of trouble?"

"That's exactly what I'm saying," I reply, in emphatic tones.

He eyes me. "Fine," he says. "But I've spent some time in gambling houses—"

"I'm sure you have."

"—and," he continues, ignoring me, "I know the kind of people you'd meet there. You'll have to do what I say. Follow my lead, I mean." He watches me with a cautious expression.

"You're the one with the gambling experience," I say. "What do you need?"

"Less clothing, for a start," he says, but it's uttered under his breath and I'm not sure I'm supposed to have heard it. "Just stay close," he adds, louder, and puts his hand on my back. "This way," he explains, herding me back out onto the street. I glance over my shoulder and find the concierge looking vindicated.

⎯⎯ ell ⎯⎯

The gambling den is an unremarkable townhouse, more genteel than the so-called "copper hells" of the East End, but a far cry from the elevated halls of White's or Almack's. Steel halts under an open arch that shelters an apothecary on one side and a narrow doorway on the other. The door cracks opens at our knock and we're greeted by a muscular bearded man wearing a suspicious look.

"Good evening, monsieur," Steel says, with a pronounced English accent, and his arm curves around my waist. I try to keep my expression unaffected. "Am I early?"

That makes the man blink. "For what?"

"My valet told me this was the place to come to spend some coin." He steps into the house with casual unconcern, pulling me in with him. "My French isn't that good, though. I hope I didn't misunderstand."

"Sir, you should—"

Steel pats him with a friendly, if vacant, smile. "My good man, I am remiss. My name is Lyr. Lord Lyr." He flashes a bill, tucks it into the man's pocket and winks at him. "Here, no need to announce me. Is it straight upstairs?"

The man blinks, shrugs, and waves at the stairs. "At the top on the right, monsieur. I hope your pockets are deep," he adds.

"As deep as the Thames, I assure you." Steel wanders up the stairs, weaving from side to side.

"La, sir," I say, for the sake of the man behind us, "you're still in your cups. Perhaps you shouldn't be gambling...?"

"Nonsense," Steel replies, in a voice that will announce his presence long before we get the chance, "I can beat any man who dares play against me."

"A little too strong, perhaps?" I whisper, as we near the top of the stairs. "And where did you get that bill?"

"His pocket," Steel whispers back. "To the tables, mademoiselle," he declares, throwing open the door and causing every eye in the room to turn on us. I go rigid, but Steel just tugs me against his side. "Which of you gentlemen can deal a hand of Faro?" he demands.

The men exchange glances and one jerks his thumb at a table in the corner. Steel expresses his gratitude in badly mispronounced French and snakes over to the table.

I keep him steady and seize the opportunity to glance around. The room is panelled in pale unvarnished wood, its furnishings of the same material. A number of tables fill the space, each occupied by members dressed neatly but not at the height of fashion. This is a den for self-made men, not the wealthy elite. Still, perhaps Steel can make something out of it.

He hones in on a man in a charcoal suit whose opponent is leaving with a great deal of muttering. "You know your way around the card table, monsieur," Steel says, taking the departed man's seat. "Deal me a hand."

The man raises his eyebrows. "Excuse me, monsieur?"

"I can see you're a man of trade," Steel continues, gesturing to his hands, which are calloused with uneven nails. The man draws them off the table. "I'm sure you'd like to match your wits against a real opponent."

That sparks something in the man's expression, a glint of anger at being classified as lesser. "And you consider yourself a 'real' opponent, I presume?" He starts to shuffle the cards and Steel relaxes into the chair.

"We English invented this game, monsieur," he drawls, instigating a furious debate across multiple tables over who created which card game, England or France. Partway through, Steel turns to me and chucks me gently under the chin. "Fetch me a drink, pet?"

My eyes widen and he hesitates. I hurry to regain my equilibrium. "Of course, my lord." He did warn me. "Don't lose too soon," I add, with a smile that's as coquettish as I can make it.

"Cheek," he murmurs and picks up the cards he's been dealt, an air of concentration dispersing the façade of the tipsy fool.

I drift to the side of the room. After a few curious glances, no one pays me much attention, too focused on their cards. Like Steel's opponent, most of the men here seem to be traders, businessmen on their way up the social ladder. It's not only men, though; a couple of women linger around the room, entertaining them or even hosting a couple of games. Those tables are more popular than the others.

Most of the players are drinking; some are well into their cups even though the evening has barely started. Someone here must know a good sommelier.

One of the women's tables has the most occupants. I drift closer. The game is Hazard and, as I watch, a player snatches up the two dice and rattles them.

"My play, Laurent. You can't win all night."

"The bank's winning, Hubert," his opponent says, with an obsequious gesture at the woman overseeing their table.

"We will see, monsieur," she says, honouring him with a charming smile. She leans over the table in a way that makes her black curls fall over the curves of her breasts, which are framed by a square-cut bodice. My own calico dress feels stuffy in comparison.

The man throws and the dice clatter over the table. A general cry of dismay.

"Your loss again, Hubert!"

The men bicker and the woman steps away from the table, grabbing my arm. "Cover the table for me will you?" she asks, in a new, crisp accent. "I need a break. That Hubert's been over me all evening."

"I don't—"

"You're new, right? It's about time they hired another girl—if we lose any more to that Austrian's new hotel, we wouldn't be able to open. Look, I won't be long," she adds. "And don't worry about Hubert. He's a pain, but he's not mean." She flounces off before I can protest.

"Mademoiselle, the bets?" the player asks, picking up the dice.

I waver. What I *should* do is explain that I don't work here and have them wait for the hostess to return. At the same time, these men might be able to point us towards the information that we need, and right now we have less than nothing to go on.

I'm moving into place even as I justify my actions. Smiling at the players, I dredge up my memories of the game. I never played much as a child. I was the eldest; I had to feed the others, make sure they survived long enough to get their own jobs and earn their keep.

The clinical nature of my thoughts seems suddenly unnatural with Steel's warm familial affection so close in my memory.

I sweep up the bets. "You are eager tonight, my lord," I say with a smile, flattering him with the title. "Your day went well?"

"Another venture came through, lucky sod," one of the other players mutters. "What's your secret, Laurent?"

"Damn good luck, I call it."

"Let's see if that luck holds."

The man throws, and the dice earn him the win to a chorus of groans.

I set the next bets. "Perhaps you should celebrate, sir. A better wine than the ones we have here," I say, indicating his glass.

The second player snorts. "He wouldn't know a good wine from swill. Champagne, that's what we need." He gestures to a server standing against the wall and I hide my disappointment. No sommelier here.

"There you are." Steel sidles up next to me, steering around an argument that's cropped up over a particular way of throwing dice. "You've made yourself at home, I see."

I glance over his shoulder, but his opponent is gone. "Finished already?"

Steel shrugs. "When I play to win, I win."

A Hazard player notices his presence and I recall our ruse. "Will you take a turn, my lord?"

"I never bet on dice, my love," Steel replies, breezily.

I fumble the bet. He's not paying attention, settling in at the table and eyeing the other players. It's a simple endearment, the kind any lord might throw his paramour. Certainly not something to take any notice of.

There's a commotion by the door and two young gentlemen stride in. The first, a dark-skinned man wearing a stern expression, sweeps the room with a hard gaze. The one behind him is a slender man with chestnut coloured hair and a serviceable sword dangling from his waist.

"Demon," Steel says, under his breath, then, "Perhaps I *will* make a bet." He arranges his limbs in a chair and tosses down a handful of coins. His position gives him a clear view of the newcomers.

I collect the dice, watching out of the corner of my eye as the strangers come closer. There's something familiar about them, though I'm sure I've never seen them before.

"Dumont," says Hubert. "What, going to try to shut us down again?"

"We have a licence," another player objects. "This is perfectly legal."

"I am not here about this," the stern man says, tapping the table, and I realise what's familiar about them; the way they hold themselves. The demon—for the man with chestnut hair must be the partner—is cautious, his hand near his sword, hovering at the other man's back. The one called Dumont stands with shoulders squared and hands loose at his side, steps cautious and deliberate, eyes keen. They're agents. I glance at Steel, but his eyes are on the demon, wary.

I curtsy, hoping the hostess returns. They spare me nothing more than a glance. The French agency, the Sûreté, only worked with London when it had to, when a rogue demon escaped over the Channel and one department saw fit to warn the other. As far as I know, neither agency is on real speaking terms with the other.

As far as I *know*, but Monaghan kept more than one card close to his chest. If he has connections here and they find out who we are...

"Hurry up and move on," Hubert says, scowling. "Police are bad luck."

"No doubt." Dumont levels the man with a direct gaze while his partner examines each player. He turns that gaze on Steel, who tilts his head in a careless greeting. "I'm investigating some missing d—people," the agent continues.

I note the correction. An odd mistake to make, for an agent. Demons hide in plain sight, and the world continues to turn because their presence remains largely unknown. Every agent is drilled in the necessary secrecy of their work from the moment they're recruited. Either he's new to his role, or he's foolish—and by the measured way he moves, I doubt it's the latter. New, then; his first case, perhaps.

The player responds with a scornful *bof* and says, "Around here? You'll not have much luck. They're probably in the Seine by now."

"Have you noticed anything unusual?"

The demon is still staring at Steel. My skin crawls with unease. "What kind of unusual, monsieur?" I ask, diverting their attention. Dangerous, but Steel, with his height, his unusual eyes and whatever scent demons produce, is more noticeable.

"Strange noises," Dumont says. "People where they shouldn't be. Servants acting oddly."

I shake my head. "I am sorry. We cannot help you."

The players seem perfectly happy to encourage the agents on their way. "Off with you. Let us play, for god's sake."

"You have an accent," the agent says, to me. "English?"

"Yes. I grew up there." I gather the bets, maintaining a cool expression, skirting the man's gaze. My palms are starting to sweat.

"Ah." He glances once more around the room and then steps away. "If you notice anything," he says, to the table at large, "you know where I'll be."

"Here, apparently," one player mutters. Another just waves him off. The demon glances back at Steel as they leave, an expression I can't read on his face, but then they're gone.

"Do they come around often?" Steel asks.

"Too often, for my liking, given they're supposed to be guarding those impoverished districts out by Père Lachaise."

"Not good for business," one mutters.

I meet Steel's gaze and see the same thought reflected in his face: this will have to be our only visit to this gambling hall. We can't afford to be identified.

Laurent gathers up his bills. "Too slow for me," he declares. "I'm going to try my luck against the Comte."

"The Comte's here?" another asks, craning his neck to see. "I might join you. He's on a lousy run of luck."

"The Comte?" I ask, following his gaze to see a man seated at one of the card tables. He's dressed in an impeccably well-made suit and a silk cravat tumbles down his chest in precise folds, making the other men at his table look downright shabby. His hair is a shade darker than gold and a tidy moustache crowns his full mouth. He looks the type to be twirling a young woman around a glittering ballroom, not dealing cards in a common gambling hall.

"The Comte de Chagny," the player explains. "Save your effort," he adds, to the man who'd stood. "The Comte doesn't have two francs to rub together."

"Then it'll be easy winnings." Laurent toasts the table and downs the rest of his wine. "Wish me luck." He strides away with a bounce in his step.

A count would be familiar with wine. At that moment, judiciously, the hostess returns. "Thank you so much," she murmurs, divesting me of my position with ease. The players brighten at the sight of her. I step away, veering towards the Comte.

"Perhaps another drink," Steel says. He takes my arm and walks me to the side of the room. "You have that look on your face," he murmurs. "Will you let me in on whatever it is you're thinking?"

"The Comte," I reply, turning my face away from the room. It's unlikely anyone here would be able to read lips, but it'll help to disguise whatever 'that look' is.

"What about him?" Steel leans closer, dipping his head so his voice is close to my ear.

"A member of the French aristocracy will know wine," I murmur back. "If he hasn't seen the label himself, he might know someone who's come across it."

He makes a considering sound, breathing against my ear. I feel abruptly unbalanced, as though we're back on the boat on an uneven sea. In London, the binding spell kept us tied to each other, but it also kept us apart. It defined our roles, and I had a responsibility not to abuse those roles.

But now Steel is free. He's no longer my partner. He's a handsome young man who I've seen devour two plates of Maia's cooking, and fall asleep in a corridor against a wall, and throw a desk across the room to protect us—

Danger, my mind says, alert in a way it never had to be before. Steel is a demon and once this case is done, he'll be gone. I reach for the cold, clinical part of my brain that I'd shied away from only moments ago.

Steel has said something. I ask him to repeat it. "How do we get that information?" he says, apparently not noticing my distraction.

"Play him," I suggest, glad that my voice is steady. "Play him and let's find out."

"I was hoping you might say that," Steel replies, with a chuckle, and moves away, towards the Comte. I take a moment, waiting for the lake of my heart to freeze, before I follow him.

Steel approaches the man with a swagger, his hands in his pockets, arrogance clinging to his expression. "Monsieur," he says. "I hear that you're a Comte. If that's true, I might have found someone worth pitting my talents against." He flips an empty chair and straddles it, offering a rakish grin.

Not bad at all.

The two other men at the table gape at him, but the Comte levels him with a cool glare. "May I help you, monsieur?"

"Lord Lyr." Steel inclines his head in greeting.

I find a servant at the edge of the room and ask him for a pack of cards. He hesitates, taking in my state of dress, and I add a stern, "*Now*," making him snap to attention and rush away.

"From what I've heard on the other side of the sea," Steel continues, "the de Chagny estates are sizeable—in their own way."

The Comte's mouth tightens.

"My own estates comprise nearly four hundred acres."

"Then what brings you to Paris?" the Comte asks. The other two men start a conversation between themselves, interested in the game of Faro at the next table.

"Better cuisine," Steel says, with a cutting smile.

The servant returns with a pack of cards on a neat little tray. I take it from him and approach their table. "Piquet, monsieur?" I ask.

Steel takes the pack. "What about it, Comte?"

The man hesitates and then nods. Steel starts to shuffle and I leave him to it.

There are no windows in this room, only wooden panelling, so I wander into an adjacent parlour where a cold supper is being served. Large arched casements reveal a cavalcade of tall windows, wrought-iron balconies and sloped green roofs. With a jolt, I remember how far from home I am.

I turn away from the view and go in search of the kitchen. As useful as the gamblers could be, it's usually the serving staff who know the most.

The kitchen is narrow and cramped, populated with a cook and a handful of servers. They ignore me, preparing what smells like roast mutton alongside thinly sliced potatoes topped with cheese. I ease to the side, close to a serving girl who's chopping vegetables with a bored expression.

"The men are getting a little forward," I explain, at her look of enquiry.

"Hubert again? He always gets too free with his hands after the first glass."

I hum. "How long have you worked here?" I ask and she shrugs with a brief, "Long enough."

"Do you often get men like the Comte de Chagny?"

"Oh, him? He's only here because he can't afford to play at the big tables."

"Does that happen a lot? Men coming here to gamble when they can't afford to play somewhere else?"

"Often enough that we can earn our bread." She glances at me again. "Are you new?"

"Relatively," I reply, changing tack. The last thing I want is to be remembered. "Do you serve wine? I might take him a bottle."

"He's not known for his drinking," she replies. "You might have better luck with one of the traders."

She thinks I'm trying to take advantage of him by getting him drunk. I don't correct her. "I'll take a bottle, anyway," I add, grabbing a Bordeaux from a nearby wine rack. "Thank you." I leave before she can do more than frown at me. Even if the wine is terrible, it'll help Steel direct the conversation where he needs it to go.

In the other room, Steel and the Comte are still playing, and a small stack of bills sits next to de Chagny's elbow. Steel doesn't seem worried.

"Wine, monsieur?" I offer.

Steel picks up on my cue and declines with a wrinkle of his nose. "I can barely swallow the watered-down slop you offer here. I thought France prided itself on its wine collection?"

To his credit, the Comte does not visibly react. "Perhaps you should try our vineyards," he says. "You may be pleasantly surprised."

"There was one, though," Steels says, as I linger, "that I have to admit was quite something. I can't quite remember the name... It had a black rose on the label, I think. Do you know it?"

"A rose? Can't say that I do."

"Pity. I'm sure I'd pay good money to find it again."

De Chagny regards his cards. "You might try Ménil-montant," he suggests. "Wine is cheap and there are plenty of *guinguettes*, although I can't speak for their quality."

Steel inclines his head. "My thanks, I'll do that."

They play for a few minutes longer until the Comte lays down his cards with a thin smile. "I believe that gives me the higher score."

"Too quick for me," Steel replies, tossing his cards on the table. "I shouldn't have let that spade go."

"Indeed." The Comte's composure is impressive, but as he gathers Steel's francs his mouth relaxes. "Will you play again?"

"No, I think not. I should be on my way. There's more than one club in Paris." Steel stands and I go to his side at the crook of his fingers. "Hopefully I'll see you here again, de Chagny."

The Comte nods, paying us no mind. I help Steel don his jacket at the door, under the watchful eyes of the front man, and we escape into the street, shivering at the chill.

"Ménilmontant," I repeat, as we draw out of view of the gambling house. "That doesn't help us much."

"I've heard of it," he replies. "It's a working-class district, for the most part. Saw a lot of fighting in the '70s." He's staring east, as if he can peer through the towering buildings by sheer force of will.

Sighing, I adjust my shawl and say, "Let's go, then. It's better if we move away from this place, anyway."

Steel's expression softens a little, something not quite a smile but nearly, and says, "After you."

I brace myself and follow his lead.

APPRENTICE E. WILSON

Her ears ring. Jacob and Max say nothing. "Sir," Eve says, when the silence starts to hurt, "that can't be true. Hazel's not a murderer."

"I'm starting to think that I do not know miss Locke as well as I believed I did," the Professor says. "As for her demon... He is a breed we've never encountered before, a member of their elite class. Rayne attempted to stop him and got in his way. How much of a role miss Locke played in Rayne's death, or in the other murder, I cannot say."

Jacob stirs. "What other murder?"

"A woman was killed last night. Her body was discovered in a building in Whitechapel, next to the square where Agent Rayne was found." He pauses, then says, "You have a concern, miss Wilson?"

Eve realises she's shaking her head and stops. "I don't know about her demon, but Hazel is not a murderer."

"It was miss Locke that accused Khurana of being that same murderer," Monaghan replies. "And when that failed, she accused Rayne. Miss Locke has always been...reticent. I fear she was hiding more from us than we could ever have guessed. You recall, Agent Horner, how she reacted at being confined. She and her demon broke out and escaped examination. That is not an indication of a sound mind."

"I…" Jacob blinks rapidly and swallows.

Eve thinks of Hazel staring at her wild-eyed, pressing a makeshift weapon to her throat, blood trickling in a thin line down her neck. She'd been desperate, that much was obvious. But a killer?

Someone knocks on the door. Tiberius opens it, stepping out of the way to let in Khurana and her Hound demon, Isis. Relief loosens the knot in Eve's stomach. "Khurana," she says, "what did—"

The agent taps the head of her cane with her thumb, three times in quick succession. *Be alert.* Eve cuts herself off, going tense.

"Forgive me for not being here earlier," the woman says, coming to stand beside her. Isis hovers at her side.

"Not at all." Monaghan gestures to her. "Please recount what you told me."

"I found Rayne's body in Miller's Court. He'd been stabbed once in the upper abdominal region. The weapon was found nearby: a shard of porcelain plate, roughly broken. Agent Locke and her demon were there, and both showed signs of a struggle. The former had blood on her hands. Agent Rayne's demon—Cassius—fled the scene when we arrived. He is still missing."

The sober description builds distance between her memories and reality, and Eve crawls into that distance to breathe.

"And the female victim?"

"Her body was inside an apartment on the ground floor of the court. The corpse was mutilated, in a similar pattern to the other so-called 'Ripper' victims." A flash of disdain at the name that had been popularised by the tabloids. Khurana never had much patience for the press. "This act, however, was far more elaborate than the others."

Isis shifts on her feet, as if she wants to take a step back. Her pale skin is wan, almost translucent. It must have been horrific. Even less reason to accuse Hazel of the crime.

A pause, as Monaghan lets the image that her words have conjured dissolve. "The police are here to investigate both murders," he says. "I have promised our assistance, of course. At least this gruesome act will mark the end of the Ripper murders."

Khurana stays silent, so Eve says nothing.

"I will give some thought as to how we will replace both agents. Khurana, you will need to give your testimony to the Inspector when he arrives, so please do not go far."

"Yes, Professor." Her voice is toneless. Unease tiptoes down Eve's spine.

Monaghan sits back, his expression weary. "You are dismissed."

Khurana doesn't hesitate, turning with a clip of her heels to march out of the room, Isis sticking to her like a faithful dog. Jacob has to be nudged by Max to follow and Eve goes last, casting a glance behind her as she leaves. Tiberius closes the door in her face, the Reaper's amber eyes dark.

"Agent," Eve says, hastening to catch up with Khurana's quick stride. "Did you really—"

"I appreciate that this could not have been easy to hear," the woman replies and her thumb taps again at her cane, "but the Professor needs your support. As with the San Paolo case on Church Street, a few years ago. You remember?"

"I remember," Eve says, keeping her voice steady.

"Good. Then go and get some rest. And don't forget to eat something soon. Before ten."

She nods and lets Khurana sweep ahead of her. The Hound demon throws her an unreadable look as she passes.

Eve watches them go. They never had a San Paolo case. Khurana wants to meet outside the Agency, in secret. Another ripple goes down her back. What the hell is going on?

CHAPTER FOUR

As we move into the poorer districts of Paris, the city's pretty façade starts to chip, her paint and perfume no longer enough to disguise the scent of rot underneath. The streets become squalid, piled with refuse, and every stranger we meet sizes us up as though we're a fattening calf and they're deciding how soon to eat us. I keep my stare cold, though Steel's glare seems to do more to head them off. Working girls linger in the alleys and drunk men lounge in doorways. Some of them mutter words as I pass, words I try not to hear so I can't translate them.

One leans out of a doorway, calling in a voice that I can't help but hear, "Beautiful mademoiselle, come, speak with me a moment." He says it with a leer and a laugh, in case I take him seriously. Another calls something less innocuous. At my side, Steel twitches. The city of light, it seems, casts a dark shadow.

We pass a few taverns, which must be the Comte's *guinguettes*, but they're already shuttered for the night. The streets have emptied quickly for a city so large. On account of the district, perhaps? Or perhaps the Ripper's infamy has extended even this far.

Steel stops. I trip on the uneven cobbles before I catch myself. "What is it?"

He tilts his head, listening, then he grabs my wrist and pulls me into an alley.

"What?" I whisper, peering into the street.

"It's our friends from the gambling house."

The alley is dark, untouched by the elegant lamps that light the main street. I press myself to the stone wall and peer at the street.

Two men appear from the other side, tracing our path. They pass under a lamp—the two agents from the gambling hall. By the way they walk and the way they scrutinise their surroundings, they're on patrol. The gambler had mentioned they guarded the poorer districts; this must be one of them.

"A Sentinel," Steel whispers, watching the demon. "Good senses, like Hounds."

I turn my face into the shadow to hide the pale glow of my skin. "Can you hear them?" I ask, as quietly as I can.

A pause and then he says, in the same tone, "They're not speaking."

If this is their patrol route, they must know the area; we could ask them for help.

I kick back the thought. Agents are no longer our allies.

Steel stands next to me, smelling of coal-smoke and something that makes me think of the air before a storm. Once the two have moved out of sight, he steps away. "They're heading west," he says.

"They must be looking for those missing demons," I say, as we take up our route again.

The street lights become few and far between as we move further from the affluent areas of the city, and we navigate by the scraps cast by lit windows. One or two people walk by, heads down, while others linger, chatting, in shop doorways. One group catches my attention; a young lady and two elder gentlemen. The men wear short caps and double-breasted jackets, twin rows of brass buttons marching up their chests. Truncheons dangle at their hips.

I catch Steel's arm. "Police," I murmur and he stiffens, trying to look while pretending that he's *not* trying to look. I sigh. "Over there, on the left."

I keep an eye on them, but they seem to be caught up in whatever business they're hassling the young lady with and don't spare us a second glance. I exhale as we leave them behind, only to bite down on a curse as we turn a corner and find a second pair walking down the street towards us.

"They must have increased the patrols after London." If they thought the Ripper was going to escape, then Paris, with all her nooks and crevices, would be the perfect place to seek refuge. They won't know that the Ripper sits in London like a fat contented cat, waiting to stretch out his claws.

"Or they're also looking for those missing demons." Steel guides us onto a side street. "They might be working for our agent friends."

"Wonderful."

We turn off the street onto another and the police presence evaporates. There are fewer people here, too, only an occasional woman squatting against the wall or a man trundling along, his barrow heaped with mugs and dishes for sale. It feels like a dead end, that we're wasting our time. I'm about to voice my thoughts when Steel pauses.

For a second his pupils fluctuate, dangerously close to revealing his true nature, before they flatten and he says, "I smell something."

I glance both ways down the street, which is empty. "A demon?" The Agency named Phantoms so because of their ability to vanish from plain sight. One could be following us even now.

"No," Steel replies. "It smells like—like burnt flesh."

"Flesh? Are you sure?"

His expression becomes grimmer. "Yes. This way." He strides towards a slim passage tucked between two buildings.

If Steel can smell it, so can that agent's demon. "Wait, Steel—"

But he's already squeezing between the buildings and out of sight. I follow him, glancing back over my shoulder at the empty street.

The alley feints left and cuts a jagged path around a series of tenement buildings. It's almost like being back in Whitechapel, hunting killers. I clench my fists, wishing I had a weapon. Then Rayne's face flashes through my mind and I feel the warmth of his blood on my skin. I shake out my hands.

Steel stops, scenting the icy breeze. On the other side of the street, a wall cordons off a large section of the district. It's too high to see over. A government building, perhaps?

"It's in there," he says and lopes across the road. I follow more cautiously. The wall forms a crescent, cut in half by a tall gate.

"Wait," I say, again. "We should come up with a—"

He kicks the gate open with a bang and vanishes inside.

"—plan," I finish.

I step inside after him. Within the walls are rows upon rows of graves. Some are small stone plinths or replica sarcophagi, others huge mausoleums with turrets and Gothic arches. And statues—everywhere are stone figures of angels or weeping goddesses or fallen heroes. In the silence, their looming presence feels as threatening as any demon.

Steel has paused, bemused. "Perhaps it was a cremation?" he guesses.

"At this time of night, with the gates shut?" I examine the graves, the large mausoleums. It's a city of tombs. "Someone could be hurt. Can you track the scent?"

"There's nothing else here to track, just moss and rot." He walks along a wide paved path that takes us on a tour of the cemetery. The wind drifts through a handful of trees that intermingle with the tombs, whispering through the leaves and moaning through gaps in the stone. If a demon wanted to hide, a graveyard would be an excellent choice.

We continue walking until the surrounding wall rises ahead; we've come around to its side. The scent of water draws my attention to a set of stone steps tucked against the wall and a metal door set at their base. From its positioning, it must open into an underground section of the cemetery. Maintenance on the crypts, perhaps.

"This way."

Steel turns off the path, slipping between the graves along a thin, overgrown trail. These tombs are ancient, the stone crumbling and broken, the gate rusted. Some contain small chairs or lanterns, others only a pile of shattered wood. None hold any flowers.

He stops, standing by what looks like an open grave. "Locke." Steel's voice cracks on the *k*.

I inch towards him. "What is it?"

He gestures at the pit. I look down and the reason for Steel's reaction becomes distressingly clear.

A body lies in the grave, curled atop a wooden coffin. My heart shudders and for a moment I'm in the small house in Whitechapel staring at a bed covered in blood. I blink the dream away, focus.

"She's dead," Steel mutters.

I crouch by the grave and examine the body. There's plenty of blood and even more bruising. Parts of the flesh are charred black. The coffin underneath her has partially rotted and holds no sign of burns. The dirt is freshly turned, piled on the side of the grave, waiting to be filled. The corpse itself is a woman, curvaceous but with toned musculature. She wears the scraps of a simple dress, too fine to be wool, though I'd have to climb down and touch it to determine the fabric. Her auburn curls are matted with blood and dirt, her heart-shaped face swollen on one side. Her legs are muscled and the knuckles of her toes swollen.

Something about her plucks at a chord of familiarity at the back of my mind, but I can't place what.

"She was beaten and burnt," I say. Her nails are filed very short. Some of them are torn. "She fought back." I look closer at her hands. They're not nails at all, they're talons, painted red to mask their peculiarity. "A demon?" I ask Steel and he crouches beside me.

"Must be one of the copper class breeds," he says. "I can't tell which. I can't smell much except the burning."

My gaze slips over her wounds. Copper class demons don't heal quickly, but they do heal. These must have been inflicted within a short space of time. And those burns. They don't look like the marks of a fireplace poker or a stubbed cigarette. What could have caused them?

"We should go."

I twitch, look at Steel. The moon has passed behind a cloud and he stands in its shadow. "Go?"

"There's nothing here and those agents are still in the district. We should keep searching."

Nothing. Like the woman lying dead at my feet is little more than a distraction. "She's been beaten, burned and dumped in a grave. We can't *leave*."

"You're not an agent, anymore."

I flinch and look away.

"I mean—We shouldn't be here," he says. "This is not our responsibility."

"It's not about responsibility," I reply, something cold and hard in my stomach. I remember Annie Chapman's corpse, laid out on a slab, the other working women who risked their lives on the dark streets of Whitechapel just to make a few coins. Something in me crystallises. I may not be an agent anymore, but the purpose that fuelled my hunt for the Ripper is still there: I want to help protect the vulnerable. "It's about doing what's right."

"You made me a promise, didn't you?"

The words are a shock of ice water. "What?"

"You said you'd help me," he continues, ruthless. "Don't you owe me that much?"

I suck in a breath, the question a solid blow. "Of course," I choke out. "Of course I do."

"Then we're leaving."

I dig my nails into my palm, seeking the cold clinical necessity to bury my soul in. *Not our responsibility*. "Then we should find a policeman and report it," I say, making my voice as hard as his. The least I can do is make sure *someone* investigates her murder.

The *very least* that I can do.

There is a long pause, then Steel says, "Fine."

I stand, tearing my gaze from the body. It alights on the gravestone, engraved with the name *RICHARD SOLOMON* and the dates *1795-1853*. It's not a recent burial, not an unfinished grave that would have been open and available. It must have been dug out specifically for this. I reach for the stone, pull at the vines that cling to its sides.

"Hazel—"

There. My hands go still. In the corner, against the naked stone, someone has carved a flower. "Is that it?" The words are so low I have to repeat them. "Is that the flower you saw on the label?"

Steel yanks away the vine in my hand, snapping the thin tendrils. The breath he draws rasps. "How—Why is it *here*?"

The symbol is rough under my fingers, its edges clean, unblurred by time and weather. It can't be more than a few weeks old. Less, maybe. And the way it's half-hidden, tucked into the corner... "It identifies the grave."

"For what?"

I look at Steel and we both look down at the body.

"But why?" he asks.

I examine the woman's face, hunting that vague sense of familiarity. Young and pretty, the kind of woman who could hold court with dozens of admirers—

"The opera," I realise, aloud. Auburn hair, heart-shaped face, muscular legs. "I saw her in that poster in Boulogne, the one at the train station. She's the *prima ballerina* at the Palais Garnier." The poster had included the dancer's name, but I can't recall it.

"Are you sure?"

"As sure as I can be from a painted likeness," I reply, but the longer I stare at her, the surer I become. Why, then, is the lead dancer of a famous opera house lying dead in a stranger's tomb? "Someone must be coming to fill in the grave," I add, scanning the cemetery. I have to admit, it's smart. The grave digger doesn't have to exchange a single word with the murderer. He only needs to know which tomb to uncover.

But that generates more questions. This is a *system*, organised in a way I've never known a killer to be. (*Monaghan*, my mind whispers, and I shut it down.) This won't have been the first time they've killed, nor is it likely to be the last.

Steel rises. "Someone's coming," he says.

I wait, trying to breathe soundlessly, listening.

"Two of them," he adds, frowning. "One is—*Shit*. It's the agents. I smell the demon."

Relief is the first thing that hits me. If agents find the body, they can start the investigation. The killer will be found. "They must have caught the scent of burning. This woman might be one of the demons they've been looking for."

He whirls on the grave and gouges out a chunk of stone with his talons, destroying the rose and leaving a small crater in its wake.

"What are you doing?"

"This is *my* case," he mutters and I feel an echo of similar words I'd said not that long ago, not that far away. "I'm not going to let them take it from me."

"But they're an agency. They can help us."

"Like yours did?" He grasps my arm and starts pulling me away. "What do you think they're going to do when they find us here?" he asks, a growl to the words.

"I don't—"

"You think they're going to give us a cup of tea and send us on our way? I'm a Leviathan demon and you're on the run from one of the most powerful agencies in the world. They're our enemies."

I remember the way the agent's demon had looked at Steel, the keen expression in Dumont's eyes. What would they do, when faced with the opportunity to capture a demon of Steel's skill? A demon with magic so rare and powerful he could re-shape an agency?

Footsteps ring on stone. The demon will smell us if we don't hurry. I lean into Steel's grip. He blinks, apparently not expecting me to capitulate.

"What do we do?" I ask.

"Run," he replies, his voice harried, and this time, I don't hesitate.

We rush through the winding paths, keeping to the soft grass, muffling the sound of our steps. We reach the gates to the cemetery, the door still wide open—that and the smell must have drawn them inside—and slip out. We find an alley to disappear into, then another, and another, growing the distance between us and the cemetery.

We duck into an alcove that turns into a courtyard strewn with sheets hung out to dry. Steel pulls me into a corner underneath a swathe of hanging clothes. I cover my mouth with my hand and listen for the sound of footsteps. But there's silence. If they chased us, we've lost them.

Steel leans his head against the wall, exhaling. "That was too close. If they'd found us, our descriptions would have been all over the Sûreté's headquarters by dawn."

The sky is mottled with clouds. I watch them sail over the flapping laundry as I catch my breath. "We have a lead," I say, once my heart has slowed its pounding rhythm. "If the murderer planned this, then he would have taken the time to select his victim. Someone at the opera might be able to give us information on the people she met, before she was killed."

Steel crosses his arms, and his fingers dig into his biceps, white at the tips. "And then we find the killer," he mutters, like it's going to be easy, but I nod, thinking of the strain in his voice as he'd said, *Don't you owe me that much?*

"And then we find the killer," I whisper, hoping it'll be that simple.

CHAPTER FIVE

Black and white squares stretch across the floor, gleaming with paint. The white squares cast a faint aura of light upwards, the only light in the room. Figures linger in the shadows, indistinct, hissing indecipherable whispers. I turn, breathing hard, and halt. Ahead of me, standing on a white square, is a woman.

Not a woman—a corpse. Her dark curly hair peels away from her head and drifts to the floor, marring the paint. Blood drips from vicious scrapes on her cheeks, her forehead. Her eyes are white, filmy, and—I flinch—grey loops of intestines spill from her gut and dangle against her legs. She sways, somehow still standing, somehow still staring at me.

Annie Chapman. It's Annie. Shuddering, I look down. Find a knife in my hand, dripping blood onto a black floor. Something tugs at my arm. I stumble, staggering across the floor onto another square. Pain shoots through my muscles. I drop the knife and grip my arm. My fingers meet string.

String?

The thread is taut, buried in my flesh. *No, no, no.* I tug at it and agony sears through my body. Another pull, this time from my leg. I feel down my thigh and find a second line of thread.

Then more; tiny tugs at my legs, my arms, my back, my stomach. My face. Sobbing, I reach up, scrabbling at threads embedded in my cheeks, my forehead, all wet with blood.

"Very good," comes a voice, behind me. "Next, the heart."

I look up and it's Steel in front of me, his eyes nothing but bloody sockets, his chest cracked open and scraped out. Dead, but still breathing.

I wake and can't move. Fear holds my body motionless save for the rapid beat of my heart. Dream. Just a dream. Steel is fine. He's fine.

I manage to turn my head. Dark hair and a huddled lump confirm it. I exhale, put a hand to my chest as if I can push my heart back inside.

These nightmares... I need to get a hold of myself. I should be stronger than this.

Floorboards creak overhead as another guest rises in the room above us. I push the sheets away. Sweat clings to my body and sticks to my chemise, turning my scent sour.

I wander to the basin and plunge my hands into the water. I rub until the sensation of the knife in my grip fades, but I can still feel the ghosts of threads where they plunged into my skin. I splash water on my face and wipe the sweat off with a towel, scrubbing until my cheeks feel raw.

Movement makes me turn and I find Steel awake, running both hands through his hair. His eyes gleam in the twilight of the room, shards of silver split by his unmasked pupils. I can see the moment when he recalls last night; his expression hardens.

I glance away, at the water. Clear. No blood. The skin of my knuckles cracks as I flex my hands.

"I need to dress," I say, "and then we can go."

He rubs his eyes with the heels of his hands, then levers himself out of the chair. "I'll...give you some space," he says and ducks out of the room.

Without letting myself think, I wash up and sponge down my chemise. It's damp when I put it on and I get dressed with a grimace. I'll have to ask Steel if we can spare the coin for another set of clothes.

The door opens and I think, in Eve's voice, *Speak of the devil*.

Steel's hair is wet, the longer strands slicked back and the shorter ones curling at his neck, damp. He takes me in and says, "Will the opera be open, this early?"

"Oh. Probably not."

We stare at each other for a moment, at a loss. There's no Maia here to make breakfast, no library to pillage for research. We have nothing except what we can beg, borrow or steal ourselves. I hadn't considered that.

"Food," Steel decides. "I can't think on an empty stomach. And you need tea," he adds, surprising me.

I *could* do with a cup of tea. I agree and we lock the room behind us, though there's nothing a thief would be interested in; the money Steel won last night is squirrelled away on his person.

I don't know what I'd expected from a morning in Paris—roses and perfume, perhaps—but the reality is the low babble of a working city and tight, winding streets that stink of urine more often than not.

My shoulders loosen. Just like home.

The hotel sits on a quiet street that bridges two longer roads, and we follow one until it broadens and flows into the river. The Seine's south side seems sparse, but on the north side a number of cafes are opening. Waiters in white aprons and combed moustaches attend to their personal crop of round tables.

I head for the nearest, but Steel walks past me, examining each until he finds one he approves of—a cafe tucked off the main road, with dirty tables and a waiter who's too busy lighting his cigarette to notice us—and tucks himself into a seat, his back to the cafe's glass front.

I contemplate a couple of wry comments and settle for dusting my hand over the table, giving him a look.

"The dirtier it is, the cheaper it will be," he points out.

"Charming."

"Not quite how you imagined your first time in Paris?" He's attempting to signal the waiter, who does an excellent job of ignoring him.

We're not talking about what happened last night, about the body. My brain prompts me to dissect the memory, to hash out possibilities with Steel over the small round table. To shatter this moment with the horror of our reality.

"Considering I never thought I'd get past the Thames," I say, instead, "I suppose this is an improvement."

He glances at me. "Never?"

"My job was to investigate the London area." I wonder why that surprises him. "There was no need to leave."

Steel gives up on the waiter, turning to me. "And you never considered what else you might do, afterwards? What about a holiday? Or a honeymoon?"

I snort before I can stop myself. "I likely would have been dead before the question of marriage ever occurred to me." Enough agents died in the line of duty that we learned not to dream too fiercely. Now, though, my future yawns open.

My skills might be more suited to chasing demons than keeping house, but they are, nonetheless, skills. Smaller police stations might take women as clerks, or secretaries. Or I could find a suitable post at a bank or an office to build references. Later, perhaps, with enough experience behind me, I could become a *real* investigator.

The idea is so new and so fragile that I turn away from it in case the attention inhibits its growth.

From our seat, I can glimpse the stone wall that keeps passersby from plunging into the Seine. I watch two women walk beside it leading a poodle and only as they vanish behind the corner of a building do I notice Steel's silence. When I glance over, I find him staring at the table, a faint furrow between his brows.

"What?" I ask and am interrupted by the reluctant appearance of the waiter.

"Coffee?" he asks, in flat English, and starts when I respond in French. After a quick exchange, he hastens away to deliver our tea and croissants.

"You thought you'd die?" asks Steel, once the man's out of earshot.

I tuck my heels together under my seat. "Well, yes." I wait for him to follow up with another question, but the pause drags on, and I start to feel defensive, uncomfortable. "You have to admit, the life expectancy for agents isn't long. Even Turner..." I trail off. Out of the agents I'd known, only Jacob's mentor had married and he'd kept his wife a secret from most of us. The other agents had dedicated themselves to the Agency. Or to their demons.

"That's a pretty grim outlook."

"Everyone dies. It doesn't scare me."

"It scares *me*," he mutters.

"I suppose it will be a while before you have to worry about dying. Of old age, I mean."

"Our ageing usually starts to slow once we reach maturity."

"How old *are* you?" I ask, marvelling that we're having a conversation that's not about a murder, for once.

Steel throws me a wry look. "How old do you think I am?"

"Judging by your normal behaviour? Twelve."

"I'm insulted," he teases. "I thought you'd say at least fifteen."

"Don't flatter yourself."

His laugh is a huff of breath that softens the hard edges of his face. The waiter chooses that moment to deposit our black tea and two rather stale croissants. Steel dunks the corner of his straight into his cup, making me look at him, askance. He grins, crunching down on it and scattering pastry flakes everywhere. I tear off a piece of mine and chase the bite with a mouthful of tea so hot it burns the roof of my mouth.

"I'm twenty-four," he says, brushing crumbs from the corners of his lips. "Only just started slowing. So, you don't have to worry; I'm not some decrepit old vampire a few years from dust."

Far from it, he's two years older than me. "Thank goodness for that." Across the pavement, a pigeon hops towards us, cocking its head at the sight of the pastry crumbs. "How long until you reach dusting age?"

"A hundred years or so. Possibly more." He watches the bird, too, something apprehensive in his expression.

"A long time," I say, gently. Long enough to watch the people you love die.

He directs a smile at the pigeon. "That's if I make it that long."

"Do you want to?" The question escapes before I can hold it back, my tongue lured into complacency by our easy conversation. "I'm sorry, that was—I shouldn't have asked."

Steel takes a long moment to reply. "I...don't know," he says, holding his cup by the rim, the steam from the tea warming his palm. "I suppose I haven't thought that far ahead. Besides," he adds, "given what happened to my family, the likelihood is that I won't *need* to think about it."

It's an obvious evasion, but I take it. "Florence," I nudge. "What was it like, the House? A real house, I assume?"

"A fucking mansion." The curse catches me by surprise and I dart a glance around us, but the street is empty save for us and the waiter. "It had a *vault*. That's where they kept my mother's necklace. My cousin wanted—" He cuts himself off, then drowns the sentence in the rest of his tea. "That's all that demon Houses are," he continues, his mouth twisting. "A collection of the richest and the most powerful of us."

"It must have been hard, losing your mother like that." I can't imagine the horror it must have caused.

Steel sets his empty cup on the table, spins it until it wobbles. "The sommelier was right," he says, deflecting my comment. "The person who killed my family is here, committing more murders."

Though all I want to do is keep talking about things that aren't murders, I let the desire slip away. We're not here for a fantasy. "Person or people," I say. "We can't discount the possibility that we might be looking for more than one suspect."

"Whoever they are, they have a taste for the wealthy as well as the innocent." He spins the cup so hard it topples off the table and smashes on the pavement. The waiter swoops in with a brush to collect the shards, pinning us with a glare as he flounces off.

"We've delayed long enough," Steel says, standing. "Let's go."

I hurry to pile enough francs on the table for our meal and follow Steel, whose long legs carry him towards the Seine at a brisk pace. The river curves like an old grey ribbon under delicate bridges. Despite the rancid smell and the noise, I think it pretty.

Apprentice E. Wilson

Eve walks slowly, toe first, and the faint drumming of rain on the stained windows helps muffle her footsteps. The priest's voice drones, causing the Latin words to bounce off the vast, gold-inlaid ceiling and echo among the colossal stone columns. Heads bob to each line of the prayer and she recognises Khurana's for its stillness. Isis sits in one of the empty rows at the back, a sentry.

Diamond shaped tiles lead her along the rows of chairs until she can slip in beside the agent. Khurana has both hands propped on her cane and her long braid is pinned up under a black straw hat draped with lace. Black is the theme of her outfit and Eve realises her own dove grey is too pale for this stage of mourning. Not that she cares to give Rayne that compliment.

As she takes a seat, the robed priest leads the congregation in the Lord's Prayer and she takes advantage of the noise. "What happened?" she whispers. "Truly."

"Truly?" Khurana replies, "Locke killed agent Rayne."

Eve reels back in shock. "How? Why?"

"Rayne was the Ripper. His demon must have been helping him—although where Cassius disappeared to after that, I could not tell you."

Amen ripples through the arched chamber, leaving a moment of silence undercut by the pouring rain. Eve waits, curling her fingers into her palms, until the priest ascends the wooden pulpit and begins his sermon.

"But Monaghan thinks Hazel was the Ripper." A woman a few rows ahead pivots to glare at her. Eve smothers the urge to curl her lip and glare back, and just ducks her head meekly. "Why?" she asks, lowering her voice.

Khurana hesitates and the unease that has taken root in Eve's stomach blossoms into nauseating fear.

"You haven't told him."

"It is...complicated."

"It doesn't sound complicated to me."

The agent cuts her a look, but Eve meets her glare. In the grey light filtering through the windows, Khurana's face is shadowed, her expression unclear. "We must be cautious," she says. "Locke ran. We must discover why."

Voices rise in another prayer and Eve pushes against the back of her chair, crossing her arms and hollowing her chest. The prayer grates and even the lines of the Mul Mantra that Khurana utters under her breath can't distract her. Life at the Agency, facing and fighting demons every day, has a tendency to grind faith down to the barest slivers of its bones. Khurana has somehow managed to keep hers intact.

Eve doesn't know when her own faith died, if it had ever lived. A god wouldn't have let her father leave her mother pregnant and alone without even the courtesy of his name to keep her warm. A god wouldn't let so many suffer and die if he had the power to stop it. There are no gods in England, only monsters.

Tapping her foot on the stone, she thinks about what Khurana has said. And what she *hasn't* said. "He's covering for Rayne," she realises and doesn't even lower her voice when the woman in front glares at her. "You would have told him if you thought it would help."

Khurana sighs. "Monaghan has been promoted to Shadow Commissioner."

The Commissioner controls every police force in London and can draw upon the entire country's military at a moment's notice. If Monaghan is *Shadow* Commissioner, then he can do all of that while standing in the dark, standing behind the man who'd take the blame should something go wrong. All the power to control England with nothing to stand in his way.

"Hazel wouldn't have run without a good reason." Could she have feared that Monaghan would prosecute her for Rayne's death? But if Rayne was the Ripper, no court in England would commit her, if it even got that far. Not to mention— "I still don't understand *how* she did it. Steel shouldn't have been able to leave her."

"That is something I can explain." For the first time, Khurana looks uncomfortable. "Later. First, find out what else Rayne was up to. We need proof that he was the murderer to have any hope of calling off this search. And Eve," she adds, "we must be cautious. Understand?"

Eve nods and doesn't wait for the service to finish. Ignoring the dirty looks thrown in her direction, she files out of the row and strides down the aisle, the click of her boots a reassuring rhythm under the sound of raindrops on glass.

CHAPTER SIX

A broad avenue trimmed with wrought-iron lampposts carries us to the Palais Garnier. Columns decorate the building's face and twin angelic figures flank either side. The statues are gilded and, as we approach, the gold shimmers in the daylight as if they're alive. Its roof is domed and fronted with a triangular stone pediment. A third angel crouches at its peak, not that it needs the extra decoration.

"Impressive," Steel comments.

The entrance is a long forum with a shining marble floor. I make my way towards a line of ticket booths at the side. Most of the booths are closed, except one, which is manned by a young man in a red jacket and cap. He peers at us through a golden filigree gate.

"Are you here to buy tickets, mademoiselle?" he asks, drumming his fingers on the counter.

"No, thank you," I reply. "We're here to ask you a few questions."

At my side, Steel folds his arms, glowering like some kind of thug-for-hire.

"Questions?" the man asks, frowning. "You don't want tickets?"

"No. Who is in charge here?"

His eyes flutter as if my words had momentarily blinded him. "I—The managers, mademoiselle. We will be reopening in three days, if you would like to purchase tickets in advance?" he adds, hopefully.

"Monsieur, I am not interested in—" I pause. "*Reopening?* What do you mean? There's no opera tonight?"

"N-no, mademoiselle. Tonight's performance has been cancelled."

"Why?"

The man shrinks behind the gate. "I—Forgive me, mademoiselle, I am not—You will need to speak to the managers, mademoiselle."

"Yes, fine. Where are they?"

Clearly, he hadn't expected me to agree; his eyes roll like a terrified horse's. "The—The new patron is here, mademoiselle. I do not think—"

"I'm glad to hear it," I reply. "Perhaps he can answer our questions."

Through an arch, I glimpse another pair of stone statues that flank an enormous staircase, the kind of thing that would be at home in a fairy-tale castle. None of the many sconces built into the walls and the statues are lit, but the shadows don't mask the figures standing at the top.

"Thank you for your help, monsieur." I whisk through the archway before he can do more than stutter.

Three men stand at the top of the staircase, two middle-aged gentlemen who must be the managers by their plain suits and the way they grovel towards the third figure, a well-built young man with golden curls and lightly tanned skin.

"Of course, Vicomte," one of the older men says, pressing his palms together in front of his waist. Nervous, I think, though nothing else in his bearing gives me that impression. "We'd be delighted to hear your thoughts on the performance. It is only—Given this upset, perhaps we should postpone..."

A movement catches my attention. On either side of the statues, more stairs twist down into a lower level. Half hidden in the gloom is a young woman in white stockings and a gauzy tulle skirt. A lock of glossy black hair has come loose from her bun and lies in a curl against her neck. She leans into the folds of a statue's robe, listening to the managers.

I glance once up the stairs, then walk closer to her, trying to mute the sound of my boots on the marble. "Mademoiselle?"

She glances at me and for a moment her eyes are hard, defensive, then her lashes dip and she's smiling, her lips a fine pink bow. "Are you looking for the ticket office, mademoiselle?" Her voice is clear and lilting.

"I'm looking for someone who can help answer some questions," I reply. "I understand that tonight's performance has been cancelled?"

"That's correct." She doesn't follow with an explanation and I find her eyeing me with the same guarded look I'm giving her.

I gesture at the steps that lead down to a round foyer shrouded in darkness. "Perhaps we could speak somewhere more quiet?"

"I—"

"About the lead dancer."

She pauses, her gaze sharpening. After a moment, she nods and glides down the stairs. The lower ceiling muffles the men's voices. "How can I help you, mademoiselle? Monsieur?" she adds, to Steel, with a bow. A quick glance from under her eyelashes sizes him up and I see her gaze linger on a stray thread dangling from his cuff and the scuff marks on his boots. She turns back to me. "You said you had questions."

"Why has the performance been cancelled?" I ask, first.

The woman raises a shoulder. "One of our dancers is missing."

"Aren't there understudies for that kind of thing?"

"There should be," she answers, unexpectedly acidic. "But there aren't. Not for La Sorelli."

"The *prima ballerina*," I prompt, thinking of the poster at the train station.

Her eyes narrow. "You know her?"

"I know *of* her. Are you sure that she's only missing?"

"What do you mean?"

I can't find any deception in her expression. "There's something I should—"

"And this is our rear entrance." The three men descend into the foyer, the two managers leading and the Vicomte trailing behind. "Indeed," one of the managers continues, ignoring us, "La Carlotta will soon be practising her aria. I'm sure she'd be delighted to perform for our newest patron."

The dancer gives them a graceful curtsy, but says nothing, keeping her gaze trained on the floor as they pass. I follow her example and draw back into the shadows. The Vicomte's gaze lingers on the dancer, his brows furrowing, but the managers draw him along on their tour.

"Perhaps we could speak to someone who knew her," I say.

"Who are you, mademoiselle?" Her words are pointed. "What could an English woman have to do with our *prima ballerina*?"

"She's dead," Steel cuts in. The words linger in the air after he's spoken and the woman's expression clouds over.

"I do not appreciate your humour, monsieur."

"It's not a joke. We saw our body ourselves. That's why we're here." I throw him a warning look, but he continues, "That's why the performance has been cancelled, I'd bet. Or didn't they tell you?"

Her fingers tighten. "It's not true."

"How long was she missing?" I ask.

It takes a moment for the dancer to respond. "Three days. She has been missing for three days."

The body had been a lot fresher than that. She must have been kept somewhere before she was killed. Somewhere that facilitated those bruises, the burns.

We're interrupted by a burly, middle-aged man in a blue shirt and tatty waistcoat, twine wrapped around his legs under his knees. Paint mottles his trousers and he carries a ladder on his shoulder. "What're you doing up here, Daaé?" he asks the woman. "Get backstage, with the others. And you," he adds, as the dancer drops a shallow curtsy and rushes away, showing none of the claws she'd flashed at me, "who are you? What are you doing, distracting our dancers?"

"Forgive me," I begin, watching the woman he'd called Daaé throw a dark look over her shoulder as she leaves. "We're investigating the death of a woman we believe to be La Sorelli. She was the opera's *prima ballerina*, yes?"

"Death?" he repeats, his jaw dropping. He could be considered handsome, but for the uncombed beard matting his cheeks and the stains on the muffler around his neck. "She's dead?"

"Yes. We're looking for whoever might have been involved in her murder."

"Well, that'll be the ghost, won't it?" He shifts the ladder, grimacing at the weight.

"Ghost?" Steel repeats. "What ghost?"

The man works his jaw and goes to spit, but then looks at the shining marble floor and swallows. "I seen him, once, without his mask," he says. "He's a monster. Don't let anyone tell you different. He's the devil."

"Surely, someone wearing a costume…" I reply, but he scoffs.

"I'm a stagehand. You think I don't know the difference between a mask and real flesh? No, that's the one that done for her. I'd bet my wages on it."

"What did he look like?" Steel asks and I frown at him. The man's taking us for a ride.

"Death," he says. "He looked like death."

Despite myself, a shiver runs down my spine.

He hefts the ladder again, holding it with two hands. "You want to know more, you better speak to the managers. They'll be upstairs in the bar when they're done hand-holding de Chagny."

"De Chagny?" I repeat, startled.

"Aye, the Vicomte. Our pretty new patron." He jerks his head at the path the managers and the Vicomte had taken. "Now, if there's nothing else, I got work to do." He strides off with the ladder, muttering to himself.

"The Vicomte de Chagny," I say, again.

"The gambler has a brother?"

"A brother who is the new patron of the opera house." Steel's looking at me with his *So, what?* expression, so I add, "If the Comte is on the verge of bankruptcy, then where are they getting the money?"

"I'm hardly an expert," he says, "but I don't think opening your new opera with a murder sets the right tone. Or earns you the best opening night."

"Perhaps you're right. It's a stretch." Though it's odd and, as we head upstairs, I file it away to consider.

CHAPTER SEVEN

Upstairs, we find the bar in a long narrow room decorated in elaborate frescoes that I have to crane my neck to see. Jacob would kill to draw this place.

My heart sinks at the realisation that I'll never be able to show it to him.

A gullible concierge gives us directions to the managers' office, but it's locked, so we wait outside for them to finish with the Vicomte. It doesn't take long until they appear, conversing in low voices.

"I thought you said you had it under control," says one, a slim man with a greying moustache. "Why isn't the understudy ready?"

"Because Sorelli was as bad as Carlotta for not preparing her," the other man shoots back. His complexion is red and uneven and flushes even further as he speaks. "She'll be in rehearsals tomorrow, we just have to change the *divertissement*." He looks up, sees us, and frowns. "Tickets are—"

"We're not here for tickets," I interrupt. "We're here to talk to you about a murder."

The man's eyes go wide. He laughs, stuttering, "A—a murder? What, here?" He glances up and down the corridor, as if he expects to see the killer lying in wait.

"Will you let us in?" Steel asks. "Or would you prefer to have this conversation out here? In public?"

"Of course, of course." He ushers us into the office. "This is Armand Moncharmin. My name is Richard. Firmin Richard."

The man takes a seat behind a desk painted blue and yellow. The office is spacious, with enough room to fit a second desk made of varnished mahogany. Instead of books lining the walls, there are paintings of people dressed in elaborate wigs and wide frilled gowns—women, for the most part. Singers and characters, I assume. The carpet is soft, luxurious, and a bottle of cognac stands open on one desk.

"The Sûreté, and now this?" Moncharmin asks, shutting the door with a pronounced click. "We run a respectable establishment—"

"No doubt you do," Steel interjects. He ignores the two uncomfortable-looking wooden chairs that sit opposite each desk and remains standing. Richard offers one to me but I decline, opting to do the same.

"There must be some mistake," the manager says, wringing his hands. "What do you mean exactly, a murder?"

"We found La Sorelli's body in a cemetery near Ménilmontant," I tell him. "She was killed."

"*You* found it?" asks Moncharmin.

"Luckily, the Sûreté weren't far away," I reply. "I assume Agent Dumont has already informed you?"

The two men exchange a glance at the name. Their eyes are still wide, their mouths tight. Richard rounds the desk and stands next to his colleague. "Are you working with the Sûreté?" he asks.

"We're private investigators," Steel says. "We want to find the murderer before he strikes again. Is there anything you can tell us that might help?" He's smooth enough that if I didn't know better, I wouldn't be able to tell that he's lying.

Another look exchanged. Moncharmin shrugs, spreads his hands. "What can we say? I very much doubt that any of our staff are here to murder each other. Perhaps you should seek out this victim's familiars. They may know something that can help you." Both managers keep a placid expression, but Richard cannot keep from wringing his hands again.

"One of your stagehands mentioned a ghost," I say, pretending not to watch them. "Perhaps you could tell us about that."

There is no look this time. In fact, the managers avoid looking at each other completely. "That's just Buquet," Richard says. "A mere rumour, madame. I'm sure you can understand that many of our dancers hail from the country—they are all very superstitious."

"Something must have given fruit to this rumour," I persist. "Some unnatural event? Buquet claims he saw something."

Moncharmin chuckles. He puts his hands on the desk. "I can assure you, madame, we have little in the way of such things, here." His fingers tremble.

"How odd," I say, "that such a rumour should come about." I flick a glance at Steel and he picks up on my unspoken cue without a word.

"You mentioned the Sûreté," he says. "They will of course need to investigate these rumours. The opera will have to be closed until their investigation is complete."

"Closed?" Richard bursts out. "For how long?"

"A few weeks," I reply. "More, if necessary."

"I cannot imagine that the Sûreté will be interested in spending so much time on such a minor case," says Moncharmin.

"Monsieur," I reply. "This killer may strike again if we hesitate. And even if they don't believe the story, no reputable police officer will leave a stone unturned in a murder case."

Richard bites his lip, glancing at Moncharmin. The latter slides his hands off the desk and into his lap. I wait, keeping my face expressionless. Finally, the man stands. "There is something that you should see," he says, his voice flat. He walks over to a cabinet and removes a small key from his jacket.

"Moncharmin—"

"You must understand," the man says, ignoring Richard, "that what you are about to read is not to be discussed beyond these four walls."

I look at Steel, who is already looking to me with raised eyebrows.

"There is nothing else we can tell you beyond what is in this memorandum." He lays a large book on the desk, gingerly, as though it's bound in chamois leather. We crowd closer as he opens it to a page in the middle.

The book is written in neat black ink, save for a short paragraph at the bottom of the page in a red, spiky hand:

THE MANAGER IS TO MAKE A PAYMENT OF TWENTY THOUSAND FRANCS, PER MONTH, TO THE OPERA GHOST.

"Twenty thousand francs," murmurs Steel. "I should take up a new profession."

I struggle to believe what I'm seeing. "You're saying that this amendment is, what, an act of vandalism from someone pretending to be a ghost?"

"This is no joke. The creature has been haunting this place for years."

I can't see any more red ink. "Are there any other requests?" I ask and Moncharmin nods.

"Box five on the Grand Tier is at his disposal for each performance. We let it to no one else."

"And he appears?"

Moncharmin hesitates. "Well... No. Not to us."

"Has he shown himself to someone else, then?"

"The boxkeeper, madame Giry." The gentleman is too well-bred to roll his eyes, but by the twitch to his lids I can tell that he wants to. "She claims he asked her for a programme. And a footstool, for his lady."

Behind me, Steel smothers a laugh. "A conscientious ghost."

Richard takes the book and shuffles it back to the cabinet. He brings out his own tiny key, a mirror to Moncharmin's, and locks it.

"Mademoiselle," Moncharmin says, drawing himself up, "we would not gamble our reputation, or the reputation of the Palais Garnier, on a jest."

The stagehand had seemed serious about what he saw, regardless of who or what he thought it was—perhaps it's not a ghost that has been terrorising the opera house, but a demon. I tap the desk. "There is a simple solution. We investigate box five and meet this ghost. Tonight."

"There is no opera, tonight," Richard says. "The orchestra will be using the stage for rehearsals."

"We have no time to lose." The Sûreté will be back. We need to confront this ghost and interrogate him before he's arrested and taken out of our reach.

"Very well," Moncharmin mutters. He sticks his head out of the office and calls to someone. A boy in a pillbox hat materialises at the door. "Escort these people to box five, on the Grand Tier."

"Box f-five?" The boy collects himself. "Yes, monsieur."

"Perhaps that will satisfy your curiosity," Moncharmin says and holds the door open for us to leave.

The boy leads us through the wide corridors, retracing our steps until we reach a curving hall. He walks us past a succession of wooden doors and stops at the end, next to a door that looks the same as all the others.

"This is box five," the boy says and takes off before we can ask any more of him.

I recall what Steel had said about demons earning a wage. "Do you think the ghost could have set this up to extort money from the managers?"

"It's an elaborate joke, even for twenty thousand francs," the demon replies. "And he could do that anywhere. There must be a reason he chose an opera house."

Box Five lies on one side of the Grand Tier, in perfect position to see all of the stage and all of the other boxes. It's small, holding four velvet chairs and a couch behind the curtain. It doesn't take long to confirm that we're the only people here. Nor are there alcoves that a ghost could hide in—not unless he truly is a ghost.

I lean over the balustrade, imagining the rows below us as a sea of feathers and glittering hairstyles. Now, the red chairs are empty and the boxes deserted. Music winds up from a pit by the stage, where a small orchestra play. The stage itself is filled with a handful of dancers, some practising, others stretching or talking. One glances at us, then the rest do, sending a ripple of silence through the enormous space. I swallow and a moment later the violins begin again, as if the theatre had only taken a collective breath and then exhaled.

"Can you smell anything?" I ask Steel.

"Perfume," he says and his nostrils flare. "Strong perfume."

"From a previous performance?"

"Perhaps. Or perhaps this box is kept fragranced to hide another scent."

I face the theatre again. Why the Palais Garnier? If this ghost is indeed real, then why haunt one of the most famous opera houses in Europe?

Below, the Vicomte de Chagny enters through one of the side doors. He moves down the row of chairs and takes a seat in the centre, flicking out his coattails with careless elegance. Once seated, he props his elbows on the back of the chair in front and rests his chin on his hands, intent on the stage. I search it for whatever has caught his interest.

"The Vicomte should be paying more attention to his wallet and less to my dancers."

"*Your* dancers?" I reply, then realise that the voice wasn't Steel's. I whip around. My partner has taken a seat in one of the chairs, his eyes closed, listening to the music. No one else is here.

My heart thrums in my chest. The violins tremble and fall, undercut by the low voice of a wind instrument I don't recognise. "Monsieur Phantom, I assume," I say.

The ghost laughs. "You sought an introduction," he says, "and I would appreciate the return of my box." The voice is deep, melodic, and speaks with a rich lilt that wraps his words in unintended sensuality. Or perhaps intended.

"I apologise for the interruption." It sounds as though the voice is coming from my right side, near where Steel sits. But there's no one there. I want to reach out and feel the air, to see if this voice belongs to a cloaked demon, but I keep still. "We wish to speak with you, Monsieur Phantom."

"So I gathered, mademoiselle Lyr."

Cold sweeps over my body, pebbling my skin. "How do you know my name?"

The voice doesn't reply. A woman dressed in an emerald mantua draped over wide panniers takes the stage. Feathers spring from her towering wig. She raps out an order to the conductor, who lowers his baton, halting the light melody the orchestra had been toying with.

"No, no!" she calls, loud enough that her voice travels to our box. "Play *O patria mia*! I want *O patria mia*!" She claps a fan against her hand with each word.

The conductor shakes his head, but stirs his musicians. The woman begins to sing and her voice barrels through the theatre.

Below us, the Vicomte jerks back, propelled into his seat as though by a strong wind.

"Tch. An aria needs emotion like a rose needs water." The ghost, again.

Steel sits up, dragged out of whatever daydream he'd fallen into, and frowns at me.

"Who *are* you?" I ask, holding up my hand for Steel to wait.

"You spoke of murder," the voice continues, ignoring the question. "What murder?"

He must have been in the office with us, somehow. "A young dancer was found dead near Ménilmontant."

"A dancer?" the voice repeats, a thoughtful hum to the words. "And you seek to interrogate me?"

"We wish to confirm your whereabouts last night."

"Here, of course. I am a ghost. This is my place of rest."

"A ghost," I say, "or a demon?"

A pause and when he next speaks his voice comes from the open air in front of me. "What I desire is to be left alone."

I can't disguise my startle and I hasten to respond, "We will leave you in peace once we have concluded our investigation."

"You and your companion?" Another laugh. "I doubt he will be able to help you. He couldn't save his own family, could he?"

Steel goes stiff. "Who are you?" he demands. "How did you know that?"

"I see many things," the voice replies, in arch tones. "And in Paris, rumours spread like embers on dry wood."

My gaze goes to Steel's eyes, which are fluctuating, his control shaken. "Steel—"

"You know nothing of my family."

"I know that your family are dead. But not you." The voice makes a considering sound. "Did you kill them, I wonder?"

Steel's chair topples back with a thud that causes one of the violins to squawk. Heads turn in our direction.

"Not so loud—"

"You don't know me!" He prowls around the box. "Show yourself!"

A laugh, low and mocking, then silence. Steel flicks back the curtain that separates the box from its entrance, examines the small couch there and even turns over the other two chairs, but finds no one. Unless this ghost can move through walls, he isn't here.

The *prima donna's* voice had continued throughout the conversation and I'd tuned it out, but now it cuts off with a croak. I rush to the balustrade and lean over: has the ghost appeared? Has someone been attacked? Is it another murder?

But there's no sign of the ghost. The prima donna clasps her throat, opening and closing her mouth. No sound comes out. There's a moment of shocked silence and then she's swarmed by people.

"It was the ghost!" Buquet emerges from the wings. "I heard his voice!" That sends the entire theatre into uproar.

Steel makes an annoyed sound. "Time to go hunting," he mutters and ducks out of the box.

APPRENTICE E. WILSON

As she hangs up her cloak, Eve lists the things she'll need to do to prove Rayne's guilt: search his rooms; interview Miller on the agent's last cases; re-examine the evidence for each Ripper murder. It'll be long, tedious work, and she won't have long to do it.

She makes it halfway across the lobby.

"Eve," Maia calls, her sleeves rolled up to her elbows, dusty with flour, "Professor Monaghan wishes to see you in his office."

"Already?" she blurts out and Maia frowns.

"Is something wrong?"

"No, nothing." Eve envies Hazel's ability to hide her expression; she has to look away to conceal her own unease. "I'll go right up."

Each step winds the tension in her body even tighter. Monaghan could have had someone following her, or Khurana. Someone in the church could have been spying on them.

Which isn't a problem, she tells herself. All they would have heard was that Hazel was innocent. The Professor is a reasonable man. He wouldn't act rashly.

She walks a little quicker.

His office, when she reaches it, is full. Monaghan stands beside his desk, Tiberius an ever-present figure behind him. Standing at attention in front of him are two fresh-faced young men, too plump in the cheeks to be orphans or slum rats.

"You called for me, sir?" Eve asks, hoping this will be over soon.

"Apprentice Wilson," Monaghan says, "allow me to introduce you to Agent Berry and Agent Parker."

She dips in a curt bow, amused when they struggle to mask their consternation at being presented with a woman—and a woman with much darker skin than theirs, no less.

"Phantom agents?" She lets a flicker of scorn slip out, making their spines straighten.

"Indeed. I was delighted to find two men with such excellent, varied experience."

If they could puff out their chests any more, she'd be worried they'd crack their ribs. "Oh?"

"They were Lieutenants in the Metropolitan Police force before agreeing to join us."

"The police?" The Agency has always taken its recruits from the poorest areas of London. It's an easy way to find children eager for a job and parents desperate enough to give them away. The 'recruits' are more malleable, more willing to believe in the supernatural than those raised to think the world belongs to them. If it's now recruiting straight from the police force...

Monaghan's expression gives nothing away. "We will perform the ritual this evening."

Eve eyes the two men. "I thought only those with a direct connection to the Houses of Parliament know our true purpose."

"That is still the case. For now, at least. This will be something of an experiment." The faint crescents under his eyes that had been almost blue the night Hazel left are now faded to insignificance.

"I see." She doesn't see. Half the police force are idiots and the other half only signed up for the pleasure of wielding a truncheon. If more of them find out that demons live in secret alongside them—many with the power to crush a man's skull with their bare hands—there will be uproar. Police will target anyone who looks or acts outside of social norms, regardless of whether they're demons or not. Not to mention the likelihood that some will use the discovery as an excuse to carry out their own petty revenge.

She tries to figure out a way to put that into words, into a protest, but Monaghan speaks first. "It is beyond time that you received your dues," he tells her. "Tonight, you, too, will receive your demon."

Her breath catches and escapes in a surprised laugh. "My own demon? I'll be—I'll be an Agent?" She's smiling stupidly wide.

Monaghan looks pleased at her reaction. "Yes. You've demonstrated skill, dedication, honesty, loyalty—All the traits that make an exceptional agent."

Loyalty. Eve struggles to hold on to her smile. She's not so dizzy that she can't recognise the strings attached to that word.

For a moment, she doesn't care. She deserves this. She *earned* this. It doesn't matter what the strings are—if Monaghan's using her, then she's going to use him back.

"I trust that you have both sourced your ingredients for the ritual?" he asks the two new agents.

"Yes, sir," they answer, almost in tandem. Whatever he told them about the Agency, it appears to have been enough to convince them that this is a significant promotion.

But even she can't subdue a flutter of excitement. Ever since she'd first met Isis and understood what being an agent meant, she'd dreamt of choosing her own demon. Someone full of courage, and ambition, and intelligence. Someone who can keep up with her and, most important of all, will *want* to.

Monaghan smiles at her. "Agent Wilson," he says.

Wilson was the name her mother gave her to help ease her way in a world that didn't want her. Over the years, it had become her own. And now, hearing it come after the word *Agent*—a word that will open doors all over the world—her heart soars towards the stars.

"I have taken the liberty of sourcing your components for you."

She comes crashing back down to earth. "Sir?" she asks, wondering if she misheard him. She'd never written down her components, but maybe Khurana had given him some idea of what she wanted, or Jacob.

"Ordinarily I would promote you as a Hound agent," he says, "and although we do need one to replace miss Locke, I believe that another investigative agent would be of more use. Therefore, you will summon a Phantom."

A Phantom agent. A *Phantom agent*. "We've never had a woman as an investigative agent, before," Eve says.

"That's true. You will be the first."

Despite Khurana's warning, she can't halt the thrill of delight that shoots through her.

"What's more," he continues, "we cannot afford to lose an experienced demon."

"Wha—Who do you mean?" There are no demons with Agency experience. None that still live. None except—

"You will summon Rayne's demon. Cassius."

CHAPTER EIGHT

By the time we get downstairs and find our way backstage, the shock has transformed into chaos. We wind through narrow corridors among a confusion of walking props, shouted orders and flouncing costumes. I avoid one stagehand and almost collide with a woman carrying a heap of tulle.

Loud voices draw us to a cluster of men standing by an open door. Through it, I glimpse a dressing room strewn with costumes and hair pieces. The dancer we'd seen earlier, Daaé, stands in the doorway.

"Are you certain you know the part?" one of the managers asks her.

"Yes, of course, monsieur," Daaé answers. "One moment and I will be ready."

"Christine." The Vicomte is here, too, and he tries to push forward to get close to her. "Christine, is that really you?"

The woman looks at him with a flat expression. "Monsieur, I require a moment, please."

The Vicomte falters, then rallies and says, "Surely, you remember? The little cottage by the sea?"

Something passes through Daaé's expression. She smiles, close-mouthed. "Of course I remember, Raoul."

The mere sound of his name sends the Vicomte into transports of delight, as if he'd seen the sky after years underground. "Christine—"

"But I must have a moment," she interrupts, firmly. "My teacher—" She stops, sends a swift glance over her shoulder at the empty room, so swift I might have missed it if I hadn't been watching so closely. "I need to practise."

"Of course, forgive me. We will wait for you." The managers go to protest and the Vicomte draws them away, letting Daaé close the door between them.

"Messieurs," I say, drawing their attention as the managers begin to argue. "Did something happen to Madame Carlotta?"

"Only a catastrophe!" Moncharmin cries, throwing up his hands. "How on earth are we supposed to open now, with no *prima ballerina* and no *prima donna*?"

"Peace, Armand. We can at least try."

"We'll be a laughingstock! Maybe we should sell our souls to the devil, at least it would be a quicker and less painful death."

De Chagny keeps one eye on the door. He stands a few inches shorter than Steel, but his black suit makes the most of broad shoulders and muscular arms. A man who's done more with his body than lounge around as an aristocrat.

"Vicomte, our name is Lyr." I introduce both myself and Steel at the same time. "We are private investigators looking into the disappearance of mademoiselle Sorelli."

He's collected enough to bow and offer us a smile that shows off twin dimples in his cheeks. "A pleasure to meet you," he says, more cordial than his brother.

"Perhaps you could tell us what happened? We heard someone mention a ghost?"

"I know nothing of a ghost, mademoiselle," he says, shifting from foot to foot, gaze drawn again to the door. "The *prima donna* could not sing. But Christine—" The words burst from him as if he had been struggling to hold them back. "Christine has the voice of an angel! She will sell out every stage when she performs!"

The cut of his clothes and the broad line of his jaw had made me think him older, but it's clear he can't be much more than twenty.

"Do you know mademoiselle Daaé?" Steel asks, in his deep, cool voice, blanketing the man's enthusiasm.

"We met as children," the Vicomte explains readily, eager to speak more of the woman. "Her father was a great violinist. He used to play for us, at their little house by the sea in the summer. I had no idea she was in Paris." He trails off, turning towards the door, a flower drawn to the sun.

Steel drops his voice, murmurs, "I doubt we'll get anything useful out of this one."

I nod. "Where's Buquet?" I ask the Vicomte. "Did he pass you?"

The man looks confused. "Buquet? Is that one of the workers?"

"The stagehand?" Moncharmin asks, overhearing. "He went into the cellars. Useless man, disappearing just when we need extra hands. I've half a mind to turn him off! Pestering our dancers and now this?"

"Pestering dancers?" I repeat.

The man seems to recollect that his audience includes the Vicomte. "Ah, well, we've only had a few complaints. And his work is adequate, so." He stops, as if that settles the matter.

"Where are these cellars?" Steel asks, impatient now.

Moncharmin gives us directions which take us to a flight of stairs at the end of the passage, tall and wide enough that any manner of set pieces could be carried through them. They lead down into darkness.

"If this ghost is getting twenty thousand francs a month," Steel says, as we descend, "I don't understand why he'd put that at risk by killing their leading ballerina."

"Perhaps he's not the perpetrator," I suggest, "just a facilitator." That still doesn't answer the question—why risk it at all?

We emerge in a vast room filled with colourful backdrops and gigantic statues. The scent of dust and old paper permeates the air. I duck around a helmeted warrior with a red crest and find Buquet crouched next to a tapestry, struggling with a lantern.

"Monsieur Buquet."

The man jumps. He peers at me and Steel. "You two again. What are you doing here?"

"We're looking for your ghost."

He stands, casting a shuttered glance at the shadows that lurk just out of the lantern's reach. "Well, I don't know about that. Could have been I was mistaken. Could have been the old rat-catcher, he works down here sometimes."

"But you said you heard a voice," Steel presses. "When the singer lost hers, you said it was the ghost."

Another darted glance. "You hear things all the time, in this place. The building's old."

"Where did you see this...rat-catcher?" I ask. "Was it here?"

"Further down." He lifts the lantern and directs its light towards another set of stairs. The opera must run deep underground.

"Could you show us?"

He hesitates, the lantern swaying. Shadows curl around the abandoned sets.

"It may be someone playing a trick." Steel folds his arms, looking rather fed up with the situation. "The sooner we find him, the sooner we can arrest him."

Buquet examines Steel's tall frame and capable build. "You'll arrest him?" the stagehand asks, then adds, without waiting for a response, "Aye, he *should* be arrested. He needs to be brought to justice. Watching me, all the time," he mutters and his hand tightens on the lantern.

"How do you know he watches you?" I ask, but the man is caught up in his fixation, a stone rolling down a hill.

"Good-for-nothing bastard. Aye, I'll take you there." He starts picking his way towards the stairs. "It was in the third floor cellars that I saw him."

I should have brought a weapon. My hand twitches with the ghost sensation of Rayne's blood and I flinch away from the thought.

"At worst, it's a Phantom demon," Steel says, evidently reading my thoughts on my face. "I can handle it."

"Right." Still, I think of the burns over the girl's body and my determination twists into doubt.

In the golden glow of Buquet's lantern we descend lower into the Opera House. A second cellar passes, crammed with false marble gods and wooden palaces. We keep descending and only the tap of our footsteps follows us down.

"So," Buquet says, as if the silence has become too much to bear, "how are you going to catch a ghost?"

"Let us worry about that," Steel replies. He carries himself with confidence, head high and gaze alert. I take comfort from his apparent ease.

The lantern bobs and then halts. Buquet steps off the last stair and plants it on the ground. "It was in there that I saw it," he says.

'In there' being a near-black room filled with the faint shapes of objects. "What's in there?" I ask, unable to see a wall. "More sets?"

"The cellars all have four rooms," the stagehand says.

I glance at the lantern, but Buquet's grim face dissuades me from asking for it. "Can you see?" I ask Steel.

"Well enough," he replies. "Stay in the light."

I'm not leaving Steel. "I'll follow you. We're looking for his location, not a fight," I say, when he looks at me sceptically. "We can't afford that kind of attention," I add, under my breath.

He sighs and holds out a hand. "As you wish."

My stomach gives an odd twist. I grip the sleeve of his jacket instead. "You'll need your hands free if something happens," I mutter and then wonder why I'm making excuses.

"Suit yourself." He advances into the cellar and the glow of the lantern fades, leaving us in darkness.

I keep my other hand out, trailing it over velvety tapestries and firm wood. "Can you smell anything?"

Steel moves slowly, letting me find my feet, picking a path free of obstacles. "I smell *something*," he says, "but it doesn't smell like any demon I've met before."

"What does it smell like?"

"Death." The tapestry under my hand ends and I meet emptiness. "We're in another room," Steel murmurs. "Buquet said there were four."

Anything could be in the room with us. Could be behind me, right now.

I take a deep breath. It's just darkness. Nothing to fear.

"Here's the third." Steel changes direction and I tighten my grip.

"What do you see?" I ask him.

"Paintings. Mannequins. Not much detail—my eyes aren't *that* good. Just a lot of stuff covered in dust."

"Any other doorways or openings?"

"Only the ones leading to the other cellars."

A scuttling noise rushes past me. I jerk forward and grip Steel's wrist.

"A rat," he says, softly.

I clear my throat. "Buquet mentioned a rat-catcher. There must be a lot of them." We're whispering and the sound strains to lift the silence. Not even an echo returns to us.

"Here's the last room." Steel's voice is tinged with relief. Perhaps the darkness is getting to him, too. "This one's emptier than the others, but I can't see anything to show that there might be a demon living down here."

I haven't let go of his wrist. I can't quite bring myself to. "Buquet might have been mistaken," I admit. "He could have seen one of the set pieces and thought it a ghost. Heard the rats, maybe."

"That's starting to sound more likely," he says. "No one would *choose* to live down here. Especially not if they have twenty thousand francs a month. Even in Paris, that can get you a better bed than this." Steel stops walking. His wrist shifts in my hand, as though he's clenching his fist. "Whatever Buquet saw, it's not here anymore."

Damn it. I'd been hoping... Biting the inside of my cheek, I shake my head at myself. I thought I could solve the case in one night. Murders aren't that simple.

"Buquet will be waiting," I say. "Let's go back."

"Perhaps this ghost knows exactly what we're doing and is laughing at us," Steel mutters, turning. He walks in what feels like a right angle direction to the way we came. The four rooms must be laid out in a square, each one connected to the other in a huge grid.

We move sideways for a few steps and then dim light spills over the ceiling. It had been hidden by a large background stacked against a huddle of chairs. We cross through an open doorway and back into the first room, the glow of the lantern growing stronger with each step. I release Steel's wrist, the light becoming bright enough to pick out my path alone.

"There must be hundreds of props here." I gaze at the collection of odd pieces, all covered in dust. "But the opera house was built a few decades ago. It can't be old enough to house a *real* ghost." The words are only partly in jest. Part of me wonders if such a thing could be true. If demons walk the earth, why not ghosts?

The path opens up, revealing the dim staircase and the lantern. No Buquet.

Halting, I gaze at the empty space. "Buquet?" I call.

Silence answers.

"Could he have returned upstairs?" Steel asks, toeing the lantern.

"Alone, in the dark? He looked pretty terrified."

"Perhaps he came after us."

The suggestion is thin. "Why leave the lantern, in that case?"

"I had better check the rooms again," he says, grimly. "Stay here."

"But—" The tail of his black coat disappears into darkness.

The noise of his movement fades as he travels deeper into the cellars, leaving me with only the props for company.

"So, you ignored my suggestion, mademoiselle."

I blink, exhale, and ease the rush of tension out of my body. The props and a ghost. "Good afternoon, monsieur," I reply, in an even tone. How far away is Steel? Can he hear my voice? "You ended our conversation rather abruptly. We came to look for you."

"Did you?" The rich tones of his voice lilt with delight. I can't tell if it's false. "I am flattered. What have I done to earn such a visit?"

"I think you know." Unable to help myself, I peer over my shoulder at the stairs. They are dark and empty. To all appearances, I am alone.

"Enlighten me."

"A woman has been murdered, monsieur," I say, a bite to the words; part anger, part fear. "A dancer from *your* opera house."

"Is it mine?" the voice wonders. "I thought I was a guest."

The words are so deliberately mocking that I clench my hands against my skirts. "Let us not play games, monsieur." I glare at the dim shadows of the cellar. "You know why we're here."

A pause and then his voice drifts from the shadows to my left. "As I said, I desire to be left alone."

I turn to confront him—and meet nothing but empty air. "Show me your face," I demand.

"I would, mademoiselle," the voice murmurs, this time from behind me, so close I swear I feel his breath on the back of my neck, "but I fear it would drive you mad."

I spin around, but there's nothing there. Of course there isn't. "What are you?"

No answer. Only dust motes, floating through the air like dandelion fluff.

Then: "Hazel!" Steel calls, from deeper in the cellars.

I snatch the lantern and rush in that direction, stumbling over chair legs and broken statuettes. "Steel? Are you all right?"

"Over here."

I follow the sound to the third cellar room, holding the lantern high. Its glow lights up Steel's face, the taut slash of his mouth. "What is it?"

He gestures at something just beyond the reach of the light. "Look."

I lift the lantern higher. Its glow climbs over a low table and up a faded tapestry, then further up, over black shoes, wool trousers. With a sinking feeling, I lift it even higher. A plaid shirt, then a face: Buquet, his head at an unnatural angle, a rope tight around his throat.

"Dead," I say, swallowing my horror. "Suicide?"

"In the short time we were gone? Unlikely."

"Hold it there."

The words cuts through the cellar like gunshots. We turn, coming face to face with the two officers of the Sûreté, the same men that we'd run from after finding Sorelli's body.

And one has a pistol. "My name is Sebastien Dumont. You are both under arrest."

CHAPTER NINE

I raise my hands. To my right, Steel flexes his claws, his gaze on the gun. "I don't understand," I begin, aware of my every movement. "You say you're from the Sûreté?"

The agent's demon glances between me and Steel, his fingers curled close to his sword. The one called Dumont scrutinises me. "And you are under arrest," he says.

"There must be some mistake. What are you arresting us for?"

Dumont reaches into his pocket and pulls out a familiar leather wallet. "For the murder of the opera's *prima ballerina*, mademoiselle Locke."

My warrant card. I must have dropped it at the cemetery. *Careless.* "Monsieur, I can explain."

"You can explain at the station." Dumont gestures and his demon steps forward. Immediately, Steel moves to intercept.

"Wait!" I say, to both of them. "Let's discuss this like agents. Or does France not extend its hospitality to other agencies?"

Steel twitches and I can practically hear him think, *Bad idea.*

But the pistol drops a fraction. "British agents do not lurk in the cellars of an opera house, *mademoiselle*."

"We could not attend the Sûreté for fear our presence would be detected." That causes the pistol to drop a little more. "Perhaps we could go upstairs? To talk?"

The two exchange a glance, and it's easy to read the demon's reluctance to let us go and Dumont's silent calm response. "The manager's office," he decides. "After you, mademoiselle."

"Monsieur Buquet—"

"We will notify the authorities. The body will be collected." He doesn't take his eyes off me as he says it.

"Thank you, Agent." I gather my skirts in one hand and glide to the stairs, projecting confidence, holding the lantern aloft so it casts enough light that they can follow without stumbling.

We go up in strained silence, stopping for Dumont to exchange a few words with a stagehand about the body. The man blanches and hastens to take care of it.

The opera house has calmed somewhat since we left it. We pass someone sweeping dust from the glossy marble floor, while another balances on a ladder, trying to reach a single strand of cobweb tucked into a high corner.

Richard opens the door to the manager's office, staring in blank surprise. "Uh, monsieur Dumont? I'm afraid Moncharmin is with the orchestra—"

"We require the use of your office, monsieur," Dumont says, with admirable command. "If you would give us a moment, please."

Richard is manoeuvred out of his office into the corridor and Dumont's demon puts his shoulders to the door, preventing any escape.

"Do you know the managers?" I ask, coming to stand in the middle of the room.

Dumont ignores the question. "What is your purpose here, mademoiselle? Why did we find a British agent with one dead body in the cellar—" He lifts my wallet. "—and a second in Père Lachaise Cemetery?"

"Are cemeteries not where you put bodies?" asks Steel.

The agent stares at him, apparently unprepared for a facetious rejoinder.

"My name is Hazel Locke," I say, "and this is my partner, Steel."

The demon throws me a piercing look at the sound of our real names, but there's no point in lying; the warrant card has already given us up. Besides, the Sentinel demon would have recognised Steel's scent from the cemetery.

"I—we," I correct, "are no longer members of the British Agency."

Dumont pauses. "Oh?"

"We left to become private investigators."

The man's demon scoffs.

"René," Dumont says, and the demon shoots a disgruntled look at the back of his head. "Private investigators, you say."

"That's right."

"Why?" His expression gives very little away. I have to admit, I'm impressed.

I consider a handful of replies and discard them. Instead, I meet his eyes and say, "Progression within an agency is limited, for women. I have more options in the private arena."

"And yet you still hold on to your identification."

"Sentiment," I reply and my voice hitches unintentionally on the word. The error seems to play into my favour, though, as the line between his brows softens. "Our client hired us to track down an old business partner of his, with the idea to recoup some lost profit."

"What partner?"

It's not an outright rebuttal, at least. "Without permission from my client, I cannot disclose the exact nature of the business deal."

"Then why do I find this at a crime scene?" he asks, waving the warrant card.

"We were investigating the last known location of his partner. The trail led us into the cemetery and we arrived a few moments before you did, finding the young lady as you saw." I spread my hands, slide a rueful twist into my smile. "When you arrived, monsieur, I'm afraid we panicked."

The demon called René makes a derisive noise. "You expect us to believe that?"

"I know how it must look," I reply, my pulse thrumming. "But why would we be here, investigating, if we were the culprits?"

"I'm sure you can appreciate how outlandish this sounds," Dumont says, but slowly, as if he's looking for a reason to believe me.

I suppose there's only one thing for it. I'll have to give him a reason. "Perhaps we can work together," I suggest.

"Pardon?"

"We believe this 'ghost' may have connections to our client's business partner." Jacob would be proud of how quickly I'm weaving this fiction. And here I thought I had no talent for the arts. "I assume that you're investigating those missing copper class demons?" I wait out his silence and he finally answers, "Yes."

"Was Sorelli one of them?"

"No." He sheathes his pistol. More promising. "We were not informed that she was missing," he adds, his mouth going pinched. "But a colleague was able to identify her body. As she is also a copper class demon, I theorised that she might be connected to my case."

And now they're here, on the ghost's trail, the same as us. "Perhaps we can assist each other. And, of course, we would take no credit for any part in solving the case. That would be entirely yours."

His impassive expression flickers. Ah. I was right—new to the role and eager to prove himself.

"How do we know *you're* not the killers?" René asks.

"If you arrest us and you're wrong," I say, "can you live with the consequences should the murderer kill again?"

There's a moment of silence. I don't look at Steel.

Dumont holds out my identification. Relieved, I reach out to take it. He flips it up, out of my reach. "This does not mean that I trust you," he warns.

"Then tell us how to earn your trust." There must be a way. Everyone has a weakness.

"The Vicomte de Chagny is holding a soirée tomorrow night to launch the new *prima donna*. Given how familiar the ghost is with this place, it's likely he has some connection to the people who work and perform here. Perhaps he'll even deign to attend."

"And four against one gives you much better odds," I muse.

"Exactly."

Steel says, in a repressive voice, "We're not equipped to go dancing."

"Your client hasn't given you an advance?" Dumont gives me a thin smile. He'd have fit right in at Monaghan's Agency.

"It's our first client," I say, making the words sound bashful. "We're covering our expenses from our own pocket."

Dumont examines me and then sighs. "Tell me where you're staying. I'll see what we have in storage."

"Thank you." I pen the hotel's details on a card I poach from the manager's desk. "Where is this soirée going to take place? Here?"

"At the Vicomte's estate. His brother's estate, rather. We will meet you there."

We exchange information and I hope I haven't gotten us into more trouble than we can handle.

Dumont opens the door and we emerge into the corridor to meet a bleak procession. Guards carry a stretcher between two lines of observers, their faces drawn with sorrow. Buquet's corpse is covered in a sheet, but his prone form is obvious. Whispers stalk the cloaked body through the opera house.

"Should never have talked about the ghost," one man behind me mutters. "Was only a matter of time before he took exception."

"Good riddance," snaps a woman. "He'd try it on with the new girls all the time. We're better off without him."

A few other women nod. Did the ghost know that?

That's ridiculous, why would the ghost murder one woman and protect the rest? His reluctance to be seen must have spurred him to kill Buquet. He'd said it himself, in the cellar, his face is inhuman. Perhaps Buquet's description was closer to the truth than I'd suspected.

We wait for the procession to pass before I curtsy my farewell to Dumont and his demon. As we leave, I feel their gazes bore into my back. Confusion tempers my resolve. He can't be so naive as to let us go this easily.

As we walk, I glance sideways at the windows of a store, searching the reflection. Some thirty paces behind us, a boy with a mop of thick curls bobs between people, keeping us in his line of sight. As we turn off into a side road, he cuts across the street to follow. I halt to peer into a shop window and he mirrors my hesitation. So, Dumont's not as naïve as I thought.

"Don't look, but we're being tailed," I murmur.

Steel immediately cranes his neck to look.

"I said *don't* look."

"How can I know who it is if I don't look? We need to lose him somehow."

"We're not going to lose him."

"Excuse me?"

"Losing him will only make us look more suspicious. Walk a little slower," I add and he obediently checks his pace.

"So, you *want* him following us? Isn't that going to cause problems?"

"He won't have anything to do. We'll go back to the hotel and wait to see if Dumont can find us something to wear."

"And then go to a party," Steel says. "I thought the idea was to stay *away* from the authorities." His look burns the side of my face. He's not talking about our agreement; he means the identification card.

"I didn't realise I dropped it."

"Why did you still have it?"

Because I hadn't been willing to let go. If I'd kept it, if I could convince myself that I was still an agent, perhaps someday... "I wasn't thinking," I reply. "It was a mistake."

Steel sighs and runs his hand through his hair. "Well, there's not much we can do about it, now. I just hope this doesn't come back to bite us in the ass."

Me, too.

AGENT E. WILSON

Torches force shadows into the far corners of the underground chamber, limning the agents in gold. Monaghan had wanted to squeeze all three summons into the same midnight hour, so when the first Phantom demon appeared, bemused and visibly shaken, they were hustled aside to make room for the next. It didn't take long, and the fire of the second has already turned white.

The black silk bag bulges between Eve's fingers, the eagle's talon inside digging into her palm. Cassius' components were exactly as she could have guessed; a laurel leaf for ambition, thistle for nobility, yellow poppy petals for wealth, and an orange orchid blossom for pride. The only thing missing is a white feather for cowardice.

Jacob has been drafted to help with logistics and, when it comes to Eve's turn, he tosses dirt onto the last few flames to smother them. With Max's help, he tips the urn's contents into a pile at the edge of the room and returns it to its stout tripod. Both men move away, stepping out of the intricate array of glyphs painted on the ground, leaving room for her and Khurana.

Eve's seen enough rituals to know what to do. She takes her place in the primary loop while Khurana crouches to set and light the kindling. Time seems to slow under the *scratch, scratch* of the matches. Eve bounces the silk bag in her palm. Only the London agents are here, standing by the columns in a loose circle, but it could be an arena full of people for how heavy their gazes feel. And she, the entertainment. The first woman to become a Phantom agent in the history of Her Majesty's Paranormal Investigation Agency.

Standing, Khurana shoots her a neutral look. She and Isis hadn't seemed surprised at the news of Eve's promotion, just wary. They'd been prepared for Monaghan's guile.

The flames glimmer over the faces of the other agents and their demons. Eve holds out the bag and mutters the ritual words under her breath, her vision blurring until the heart of the fire obscures everything else. Then she upends the bag, giving it a hard shake to disperse the thistle, which catches on the silk. It tumbles into the urn. In answer, the rusty glyphs at her feet light up and the flames turn white.

She closes her eyes for a moment so she doesn't have to see what she's summoned. Then—

"What the hell is this?" Cassius' voice is little more than a growl. When Eve opens her eyes, she meets his glare over the dying fire.

"You know what it is," she shoots back. "You're my partner."

"I am not. I *will* not."

"Come," Monaghan says, interceding. Tiberius clamps a hand on Cassius' shoulder. "It is time to be tested."

"No!" Cassius tries to shake off the other demon's hold, but Tiberius does not budge. "I will not be *tested* like some *school-boy*—"

"Khurana," the Professor interrupts, "take the other new agents upstairs and begin."

The agent hesitates for long enough that Isis looks alarmed. Eve drops her chin in a quick nod, and Khurana tucks her cane-sword under her arm and sweeps away with the others, leaving the four of them to stare at each other.

"Get your hands off me," Cassius demands.

"Not so fun when you don't get to pull the strings, is it?" Eve snaps, anger boiling through her veins.

The Phantom demon draws himself up as best he can under Tiberius' iron grasp. "I have no idea what you're talking about."

"You—"

"Enough." Monaghan's too controlled to show exasperation, but fatigue burdens his voice. "It is your agent's choice whether you submit to the test. What is your decision, Agent Wilson?"

"Fine," Eve says. "He knows what will happen if he steps out of line." She glowers at him, just to be clear that it will be *her* hand on the hilt of the blade if he tries anything.

"Very well. Take some time to acclimate, then come and see me. It should be unnecessary to say aloud," adds Monaghan, "but in case it is not: Tiberius will be close by."

Cassius mutters a curse, running a hand through his red hair. The Reaper demon releases him, and he and Monaghan take the tunnel up to join the others at the testing.

Eve crosses her arms, looking her new partner up and down. He wears the same rich brown suit that she'd last seen him in, but the cuffs are tattered and the legs are soiled with mud. The shirt collar is missing buttons, his cravat is nowhere to be seen, and even his talons are ragged and torn.

"You look like shit," she says, not in the mood for pretence.

He stares at her, then tips his head back and laughs. "Of course I do," he says. "I've been running for two days."

A glimmer of macabre curiosity strikes her. "How far did you get?"

"Holyhead," he admits, after a moment of narrow-eyed assessment.

From there, it would be a short ferry ride to Dublin. "Ireland?"

"And then the Colonies."

"You think you'd do better in the Americas? What, no Baron's sons that you can manipulate into doing your killing for you?"

He sneers. "Whatever Rayne did, he did of his own free will. And those are strong words from you," he adds, before she can cut in. "You seem perfectly happy to tie me to the end of your leash."

"You think I *want* this?" She marches for the entrance and Cassius swears again as he's forced to follow. "I dreamt of this for years," she continues, spitting the words into the darkness, uncaring if he hears her or not. "I wanted a *partner*. I wanted someone who'd fight alongside me and instead—" Her rapid stride brings her to the door. She stops and turns to glare at him, at his curling, disdainful mouth, at the arrogance in his ice-blue eyes. "Instead," she says, low and hard, "I get a spineless, manipulative cur who can be bought by a handful of shiny baubles."

Cassius gives her a slow smile, baring sharp canines, and takes a bow. "Delighted to meet you, *Agent* Wilson."

Eve spins on her heel and walks away.

CHAPTER TEN

Dumont makes good on his promise to send clothes to the hotel: we receive a tailcoat and trousers for Steel, along with a satin red dress for me that has capped sleeves and unidentifiable stains at the hem. Hopefully no one will notice. We're not going as guests, after all.

That's what I tell Steel when he finds a frayed buttonhole as our cab trots along the river towards de Chagny's estate.

"*I'll* notice," he grumbles. His fingers keep twitching over the loose threads at the edges of his tailcoat.

"Are you all right?"

He hesitates before he replies, so I know to disregard the "I'm fine," that he responds with.

I try to turn his attention to something practical. "If the ghost is the murderer, then the new *prima donna* could be his next target. He might be going after the leading actors."

"The ones with talent," Steel says. "But what if he's only targeting the dancers?"

"I'll stick close to them. Or Dumont can," I add, remembering that we have allies, that we don't have to spread ourselves thin.

"Assuming this isn't a trick to arrest us," Steel replies.

I have the cab drop us off a few streets away in case it is, and we stalk a handful of guests as we move closer, letting us assess the situation before we're seen. But Dumont and his demon are waiting, alone. He must be desperate.

The Vicomte's dwelling is a pretty white townhouse with delicate balcony railings outside each window. Two aggressively clipped trees guard the front doors. Dumont and René stand in the small cobblestone court just outside. Both are dressed in formal black suits, Dumont with a blue cravat and René with a dark caramel one the same shade as his hair. Looking closer, I see wear at the knees and unfinished stitching at the collar.

Dumont greets us with a nod. "I'm glad you decided to attend," he says, as if we might have absconded into the night.

"Do you have a plan, monsieur?"

"Just Dumont." He examines the building, which emanates music and laughter. "I suggest we find the Vicomte first. We will need his support to conduct our investigation."

"In that case," Steel adds, "I go by Lyr in these circles."

Dumont arches a brow, but does not comment. I say nothing, hoping the Vicomte's brother doesn't recognise me from the gambling den.

We're greeted at the door by a staid-looking man who betrays what he thinks of our second-hand attire by only a twitch of his eye. Sparkling white stone paves the entrance, so clean someone must have spent hours on their hands and knees scrubbing between the tiles. Music drifts out of one of the nearby rooms, and the sound of voices comes from every direction.

"Where is the Vicomte?" asks Dumont, and the servant directs us up a curving staircase.

Upstairs, one room is packed to the brim with guests dressed in everything from frothy pink bustle dresses to full brocaded ball gowns; Parisian nobility. At their centre stands Carlotta, gesturing wildly with a fan and mouthing silent words that are given voice by a grey-haired woman at her side. Over in a chaise longue at the side sits her male co-star, surrounded by his own crowd of sycophants. He tugs at his thick moustache whenever he manages to squeeze a word in edge-wise: even without her voice, Carlotta dominates the conversation.

We pass a couple lingering in the corridor. "There is a new hotel on the square," the man tells his coquettish partner. "I will take you there. I hear the entertainment they provide is quite extraordinary."

Steel bumps into the woman as we squeeze past, uttering an apology with a smile that has her blushing and the man working his jaw.

"Let's not get into any fights," I whisper, ushering him after Dumont.

"Certainly." We slide into a room next to René and Steel shows me the diamond bracelet cupped in his palm. "Just making sure we can pay our bills." The bracelet vanishes into his pocket.

This room is large, with a polished wooden floor intended for dancing. Women in sweeping silk dresses steer their bustles around gentlemen in black suits. Light from a dangling chandelier casts a warm glow over plush chairs and smooth mahogany panelling. An ornate mirror lines the far wall, multiplying the number of guests tenfold, as well as the freckles scattered over my cheeks and the mess of a pinned braid I'd forced my hair into. My fingers flutter over the fabric of my dress.

"Don't be nervous, miss Locke," Steel murmurs. "It's just a party."

"How could you tell?" I ask, ruefully stilling my hands, only to find, when I glance over, that he isn't looking at me at all.

"I—" He does look at me then, an odd expression crossing his face. "I just knew."

I raise one eyebrow. "We've been spending too much time together, monsieur."

"That must be it."

"There's the Vicomte," Dumont says. The man's golden hair is arranged in delicate curls and his suit is pristine. The Comte stands next to him, hair a little duller and skin a little paler.

I click my tongue. The chances that he'd recognise me are slim; very few men of wealth pay attention to their underlings. Still.

"You distract the Comte," I tell Steel. "I'll speak to his brother."

"As you wish."

Dumont and René are already making their way around the dancers towards the pair, so I slide into the path they've carved out. As we get closer, the Comte's voice becomes clearer.

"—ink you understand the expense," the Comte's saying. "An orchestra? *Fifty* bottles of champagne?"

"The musicians all work at the opera," the Vicomte replies, his golden brows inching closer together. "And what did you want me to do? Serve them sparkling wine? We're *de Chagnys*."

"And that's another thing," the Comte continues, following his brother's gaze. "If you think I'm going to allow you to throw yourself away on an opera dancer, you are very much mistaken."

That draws the Vicomte's attention. "Singer," he corrects, stone-voiced. "Mademoiselle Daaé is a *prima donna*. Her voice will draw crowds from all over France."

I glance at the woman in question. Daaé stands with her back to the wall, resplendent in white and silver, besieged by guests.

"She's little more than a penniless waif. I let you return from the navy because you promised me you would settle down, Raoul. You need to marry an heiress."

"I don't care about *money*," the Vicomte replies, curling his lip.

"Oh, I know that already, I can tell by the way you spend it." They glare at each other.

Dumont sidles closer, having stopped out of range of the argument. "Monsieur Comte? Vicomte?"

The older man jerks at the bottom of his embroidered waistcoat. "Monsieur," he says, a little cold. "You have the advantage of me."

Released, the Vicomte strides over to Daaé, extracting her from her flatterers.

"Comte," Steel says, with lazy charm. "This is Agent Dumont and his partner. I ran into them at the opera house, while I was looking to meet its new patron. Seems there's been some trouble."

The Comte looks startled at being addressed so casually and examines Steel with narrowed eyes. "Have we met, sir?"

I leave Steel to explain and follow the Vicomte, narrowly avoiding a waltzing couple. The effort to dodge pushes me into a stench that makes me first think I've stumbled onto the water closet. But the scent seems to be emanating from a plate of thick sausages cut into rounds and drizzled with a creamy yellow sauce. The plate and its waiter have attracted a throng of devotees; it must be one of those French dishes that tastes better than it smells.

"Your venture is attracting a lot of interest, Marquis." The voice belongs to Moncharmin. I sidestep the godawful sausages to see him speaking to a man in a blue military tunic who has his back to me. "I am certain that our patrons would be eager to explore what your hotel has to offer. Perhaps, in return, your guests might enjoy a night at the opera."

"A night at the opera?" the other man repeats, chuckling. His accent is clipped, not native to France. "I do not think so. Let me say only that my guests have less...sophisticated tastes. Good evening, monsieur." He walks away without a bow and disappears into the crowd, leaving the manager gaping like a suffocating fish. I hurry to catch up with the Vicomte.

The nobleman reaches Daaé and bends solicitously over her hand. "Are you all right?" he asks, in a low voice.

The way she looks at him is tinged with both affection and exasperation. "Still trying to rescue me?" she replies and perhaps it's only me who hears teeth in the words, because the Vicomte grins with a sheepish, boyish air. But it seems to work; Daaé laughs. "Oh, Raoul! I should have known I wouldn't be able to say no to you."

He kisses her hand, all sincerity. "I hope your teacher will not rebuke me for stealing you away. You'll have to apologise to him for me."

A shadow crosses her face and Daaé bites her lip. "I shouldn't stay for long. He doesn't like me to leave the opera house."

"Nonsense. You are no prisoner."

I'm about to interrupt them to introduce myself when someone snatches my hand and wheels me into a dance. "Monsieur!" I protest, trying to pull my hand free. His hold is inescapable.

"Mademoiselle," the man says, in a voice as soft and smooth as melted butter, and I trip over my own feet.

"Ghost." The man's face is covered by a pale mask and shadowed by a wide-brimmed pipe hat. Only his lower lip and his jaw are visible; the former thin and straight, the latter angular, skin a shade darker than the mask. "A pleasure to see you in person," I manage, as my brain catalogues the information.

"Is it?" he says, with humour. "Perhaps I am losing my touch."

He sweeps through the steps of the dance with ease, steering around the other couples. I don't have the grace of the women who've practised these steps all their lives, but there's a pattern to the dance that feels like a code, easy enough to replicate. I have to tilt my head a fraction to meet his eyes—or where I assume his eyes are; the shadows beneath his hat disguise them.

"Has something drawn you out of hiding?" I ask, flicking my gaze around the room. No one seems to be paying us any notice. More than one man is wearing a hat, and the mask is so close to his skin tone it would be difficult to notice unless you were close. As I am.

"I could ask you the same," he says, pushing me into a turn. His frame is thin, and I can feel the hard bones in his gloved fingers. "Allied with the Sûreté, now? I am surprised they did not hang you for murder."

I stiffen. "They are intelligent enough to recognise that *we* were not the murderers."

He hums. "Pity."

We've moved along the length of the space set aside for dancing and I realise that he's manoeuvring us so that he always faces one direction. "Do you have business with the Vicomte?"

The ghost's hand tightens on my own. I suppress a wince. "Oh, I believe that I do," he says, in foreboding tones.

"Not an admirer of your new patron?" Needling the ghost—demon?—may not be my wisest idea, but it seems to be a fruitful one. "Is he refusing to pay you?"

"The managers handle my salary. Or, they will, once I bring them to their senses."

What, then, could cause that tone? I try another approach. "Your *prima donna* looks lovely this evening, does she not?"

His head ticks towards me and for a second I glimpse twin sparks among the shadows under his hat, as if his eyes were pools of fire. Then he looks away, concealing the flames.

My brain points out the danger in this line of enquiry. I forge ahead. "What is mademoiselle Daaé to you?"

"She is the moon," he answers, so promptly that the words must have been circling his head for days. "As beautiful and as mysterious."

"And the Vicomte?" I ask, a flower of sympathy blooming in my chest.

The ghost does not answer at first, and when he does, it sounds like the words have been dragged from him, rough and unwilling. "He is the sun."

"So, what does that make you?"

"Me?" He laughs, a sound that makes me think of pain long suppressed. "I am the starless, soulless night that wants nothing more than to swallow them whole."

Alarm sings in my blood. "You won't hurt them, will you?"

The response comes quick and savage. "I would die before I hurt Christine."

"And the Vicomte?"

"If he gets in my way, I will remove him."

"I thought he was the sun."

"I do not favour the light."

I take in his mask, the fine twill and satin lapels of his suit. "But you yearn for it," I say, tentatively.

The ghost is silent.

The music comes to a stop, the small orchestra settling while they prepare for the next piece, and we halt with the other couples. I glance over at the Vicomte and Daaé. Under the radiance of the chandelier, his golden hair and skin look as perfect as if he had stepped from Michelangelo's ceiling. Beside him, Daaé's dark hair and pale colouring are the perfect foil.

"Mademoiselle," the ghost says, bowing over my hand.

"Wait." I clutch his bony fingers. "Did you murder House Leviathan?"

He pauses. "Why would you think that?"

Is that actual surprise in his voice, or is he evading the question? "There was a rose carved into the tombstone where we found La Sorelli's body."

"That seems to be a tenuous connection, mademoiselle."

"Then answer my question."

"I have had nothing to do with the Second House," he replies, obligingly. "The machinations of the diamond class are beneath my notice. You will need to look elsewhere for your murderer, mademoiselle."

Before I can retort that I've already found a murderer, even if he wasn't the one I was looking for, he disentangles himself and vanishes into the press of bodies. I hiss. It was foolish to ask him; he wouldn't have told the truth, and now he knows what we're searching for.

A French gentleman steps up beside me, offering his arm, and I realise that I'm standing in the middle of the floor.

"Oh, I—"

"Forgive me for keeping you waiting, madame wife." Steel materialises between us and the gentleman excuses himself.

"Wife?" I ask Steel, in an undertone.

"I could claim that you're my mistress," he says, "but I thought you'd prefer to avoid any scandal."

"How thoughtful," I reply, dryly.

"You should have some champagne before your tongue shrivels."

"I think I'll manage."

A few of the couples glance at us. One lady covers her mouth with her hand, eyeing my simple braided hair and my second-hand kid slippers, and titters. Instinct curves my shoulders inward as I do my best to shrink through the gleaming hardwood floor.

Steel offers his hand, smirking. "Will you do me the honour, madame wife?"

"No," I blurt out, without thinking.

"I beg your pardon?" His smirk becomes a grin of delight. "Are you *rebuffing* me, my wife?"

"Please stop calling me that," I whisper, desperate to prevent any more disconcerting words from coming out of his mouth.

"Dance with me, then." One of his canines is crooked and the glow from the chandelier picks out the fine lines that his grin draws out. *Danger*, my brain whispers.

After a brief hesitation, I take his hand. My own is clammy and I'm careful to touch him with just my fingers. A thin scar lines his palm from Khurana's sword, from where he'd grasped her blade when she'd tested him. He must have a similar scar in his shoulder, where she'd stabbed him.

It's my fault he was injured, my fault he'd undergone that test in the first place.

"People are looking, my wife."

"*Fine*." I slap my other hand onto his shoulder, fighting the way my stomach tightens. "You needn't look so happy about it."

"This is a party. It wouldn't kill you to smile a little."

"We're in the middle of a murder investigation. I don't see much reason to smile."

"Now you're just being contrary."

Steel draws me into a position that mirrors the surrounding couples, his right hand cupping my waist. We start to move, taking slow, easy steps. I stare at the folds in his cravat. The months he'd been tied to my side had taken him away from his search, might have even given the murderer a chance to get away. How can I repay him?

Steel squeezes my hand. "What are you thinking about?" he asks, frowning as he tilts his head down. Strands of black hair fall out of their pomade. "You look like you've swallowed a lemon."

"I met the ghost."

He misses a step. "What, here?"

"We danced."

"You *danced*?" Steel exhales a gust of breath that fans my face. "At least you're making more progress than I am. Where is he?"

"He disappeared. But I don't think he'll leave, yet." Daaé is still speaking to the Vicomte. They've moved apart from the other guests.

"Oh? Why not?"

"He's in love with Daaé."

A pause, then he says, "I suppose that would explain why he stays at the opera. So, he took out Carlotta? Made Daaé the *prima donna*?"

"That would be my guess." I hesitate, before adding, "He said he had nothing to do with what happened to your family."

"You *asked* him?"

"I'm not saying that I *believe* him, I only thought—I wanted to see his reaction."

"And?"

"He seemed surprised." I shrug, awkwardly in the midst of the dance. "He could have been acting. He's still our best lead, given the incident in the cellar," I say, mindful of the people surrounding us.

"Dumont and René are with the Comte," Steel says, after a moment. "Apparently he didn't know about the Vicomte's decision to patronise the opera until this morning. And he can't afford it."

I tuck that information away in case it proves useful. "Can you detect any other demons here?"

He wrinkles his nose. "All I can smell is bad perfume and stale cigarette smoke. And some kind of meat that smells like it went rotten three weeks ago."

"That'll be the sausages."

"I don't think I want to know."

"We should stay close to Daaé," I decide. "The ghost might show up again. He doesn't like the Vicomte."

"I see."

I chew the inside of my mouth. The ghost won't confess. We'll need to investigate the opera house, search for other links to the murders.

"You're thinking again."

I frown at him. "I'm always thinking."

"Yes, I know," he says, with half a smile. "Perhaps you should stop."

"Stop thinking?"

"Not every waking thought needs to be about the case. It won't kill you to think of something else, for a change."

What has gotten into him? "We need to focus on survival."

"Surviving is not living," he says, quietly. "But then, I suppose I should be grateful. If you'd chosen living, you wouldn't be helping me."

"Of course I would. I owe you," I reply, my voice colourless.

We turn together in silence, stumbling behind an old, white-haired couple who seem to float across the floor.

"Did I ever tell you," Steel says, in a measured voice, "that I once tried to pick a lock with wine?"

I blink. "What?"

Steel glances down at me and then away, scanning the room. "I'd slipped out of the house to visit our local tavern," he says, his tone so compelling I can't help but listen. "I had a little too much to drink and my control was slipping—my eyes," he explains. "Home was a few miles away, which might as well have been a few thousand. I found a barn, decided to stay there for the night. But the door was locked."

"What did you do?"

"Well, obviously I'd taken a bottle for the journey."

My mouth twitches. "Obviously."

"And I figured—wine's mostly water and I can move water, so why can't I use it to pick a lock?"

"And?"

"And...the farmer found me unconscious outside his barn, covered in wine." I laugh and Steel's mouth curls up in a smug, feline smile. "Sometimes I forget that you can laugh, you do it so infrequently. No, no," he says, as I open my mouth to respond. "Don't tell me; we're on a case. Laughing is prohibited."

"This is *your* case," I protest. "We're here for *you*."

"And perhaps that makes me a hypocrite." His fingers flex as if he wants to clench his hand but thinks better of it. "Still, there are times when the last thing I want to think about is my case. London helped with that, in a way. It...distracted me, I suppose."

"I'm glad it was good for something." I watch a young man spin his partner. Her gauze skirt flares out at the hem.

"That looks like fun," Steel says.

"Don't you dare."

"I'm going to try it."

"Wai—"

He whips us around and the words are lost in a gasp as I try to keep up. We level out again and I feel like a sparrow caught in a hurricane.

"That was too fast," I manage.

"Hmm. Let me try the other direction."

"No—" Too late.

When we stop spinning, I clutch at his shoulder until the dizziness fades. "How much wine did you drink?" I ask his chest, fighting the laugh that swells in my throat.

"Champagne," he corrects. "I like the bubbles."

We've fallen into the steps without treading on each other's toes. The spinning might have helped. I don't tell him that.

"You're not a bad dancer," I admit, after another few minutes of successful navigation.

"Nor you." He spins us again, slower this time, and the glitter of lights and colours blur around us. For a second I wonder what my life could have been, if I were a woman of wealth, able to choose my own lot, and he a human man, free from thoughts of vengeance. If we'd met at a ball, one night, and he'd asked me to dance.

The music peters out with a single, resonant note. We come to a stop and Steel releases my waist. I glance over his shoulder and find that Daaé has vanished.

CHAPTER ELEVEN

I weave through the other dancers to reach the spot where she'd been standing. The Vicomte is on the other side of the room, armed with two flutes of champagne. He's been intercepted by a woman in a wide, old-fashioned hoop skirt with a frilled bodice. Daaé is nowhere in sight.

Steel reaches me and indicates a door tucked into the corner. It stands ajar. "She might have gone to use the lavatory."

"I'd rather be certain."

Through the door we find a modest parlour, which is empty, and beyond that a larger drawing room. Its balcony overlooks three other townhouses, their windows just visible in the darkness. Cold air sweeps in through the open doors.

Daaé stands on the balcony, both hands on the railing, surrounded by soft clinging shadows. One, in particular, seems much more solid than the rest.

Relief wars with fear. He said he'd never hurt Daaé, but love can drive people to actions they'd never normally consider.

As I approach, the noise of the ballroom fades and I hear the ghost's voice; he's singing. His voice is too low for me to make out the words, but the sound is... It makes me want to sink into the nearest chair and close my eyes, forget everything else so I can let the song wash over me.

Beside me, Steel inhales through his teeth. "Now, I understand why he chose the opera," he whispers.

Shaking off the sensation, I step closer. "Mademoiselle Daaé?" I call.

The ghost's voice cuts off and Daaé swings around, her face drawn. "Mademoiselle." Her eyes dart towards the corner, where the ghost lingers. "I was just...practising."

She's hiding him. "You know the ghost?"

"Ghost?" Daaé asks.

It's Steel who replies, "What would you call him?"

"She calls me angel," the ghost interjects, sardonic, and Daaé flushes, "but I can tell she knows better."

"Angel?" Clearly there's some story here that we're not privy to.

Daaé straightens, squaring her slender shoulders as if the ghost might need to take refuge behind them. "Whatever his nature, he is my teacher."

"Is that why you removed Carlotta, ghost?" asks Steel. "So your protégé could take centre stage?"

"And you agreed to this?" I ask the woman. "Taking lessons from a killer?"

Her mouth twists. "I can't tell you what he is or what he's done," she replies. "Only what I've had to do, to get here. And I can't go back. I won't."

That irritating flower of sympathy unfurls another petal. I turn to the shadow. "What about Buquet? Why did he have to die?"

"He attacked my dancers," the ghost retaliates. "The man was a rat and I will not suffer vermin in my opera."

"If you want to protect the dancers so badly, then why kill Sorelli?"

The shadow writhes, though the ghost doesn't yet step into the light. "Kill our *prima ballerina* days before Christine's debut? Are you mad? Why would I do such a thing?"

"You tell me."

"I may not spend much time in the city, but even *I* can tell that I am not the only demon in Paris."

"Demon?" says the Vicomte.

"Shit," Steel mutters, taking the word right out of my mouth.

Not only is the Vicomte standing behind us, still clutching his two flutes of champagne, but he's also brought along the woman he'd been speaking to earlier, and *she* has brought a young Asian woman in a forest green gown who watches us, expressionless.

The first lady cups her elbow in one hand, the other holding a lit cigarillo. Smoke curls from its tip, filling the room with a strong, woodsy scent. Her nails are long and painted scarlet. "Well," she says, in an accent I don't recognise, "this is interesting. Is it not, Mei?"

"Very," the other woman replies, in prosaic tones.

"Christine?" the Vicomte asks. "Who were you talking to?"

"Raoul." Her eyes dart to the shadows and back. "I was speaking to my teacher."

The Vicomte's gaze focuses on the shadow, his grip tightening on the glasses to the point that I brace myself for the shattering of glass. "What manner of teacher calls himself a demon?"

"I call myself nothing," the ghost replies, audibly amused, "it is others who give me names. Christine has many for me." This with a purring undercurrent that makes the Vicomte's golden cheekbones flush rose-pink.

"The name I would call you is not to be uttered in front of a lady." He spits the words as though the unspoken curse is bound up among them.

"I believe there's more than one of them in the room," Steel adds, an impertinent grin tugging at the corner of his mouth.

"Not you, too," I whisper.

"Oh?" the ghost continues. If he's deliberately fanning this flame, I wonder to what end. "Do not fear to curb your tongue on Christine's account, Vicomte. After all, she has tasted much worse."

The champagne flutes smash on the floor as Raoul lunges at the shadows. The ghost steps out of thin air and seizes one of the Vicomte's arms. He twists it behind the man's back and pivots so it's the Vicomte that faces us, drawn close against the ghost's body, the ghost himself shielded behind him.

"How impolite," the ghost drawls, drawing back against the balcony, his face in shadows. Daaé flinched away when Raoul had attacked and she stands nearby, hands clenched as if she wants to intervene. Or to hit one of them. I can't blame her for that urge.

Raoul struggles, but his strength is no match for a demon's. "Unhand me, cad," he bursts out, his flush burning down his throat.

The ghost's other hand winds through the man's hair, black glove stark against the golden curls, and yanks his head back into an uncomfortable arch. The Vicomte's stretched throat bobs. "He *is* lovely," the ghost says, contemplative. "Does he sing, too?"

"Don't you dare," Daaé snaps, dropping all pretence. "Raoul is too good for you."

"But you are not?"

Daaé swallows and says nothing.

The Vicomte makes a sharp, wounded sound. "Christine..."

"What the hell have we walked into?" mutters Steel.

"Perhaps we should fetch help," the Vicomte's guest suggests, tapping cigarette ash into a nearby vase. "Mei, would you go and find the Comte?" Her companion pivots for the door, but almost runs into someone entering; the Comte himself.

"What is going on here?" he demands, pushing past the young woman. His gaze falls on the Vicomte, still restrained by the ghost. "Raoul! Unhand him, fiend!"

The Comte darts forward, balling his fists. His brother is released and pushed towards him, making both brothers stumble. The ghost vanishes, his form disappearing into thin air. At the same time, Daaé grabs the vase, hefting it like a weapon and pressing her back to the wall, while Steel yanks me behind him, his other arm held out like he's bracing for an attack.

We all take a breath. The woman called Mei has also taken up a defensive position in front of her companion, but the older woman hasn't moved. In the sudden stillness she takes a long drag from her cigarette.

"Well," she says, blowing out the smoke in a thin stream, "to think that I almost stayed at home this evening. Mei, help the gentlemen to their feet."

The Comte glares at the woman as she goes to help them, rising and dusting off his trousers where he'd gone to one knee. She hefts the Vicomte up with one hand under his arm and the man shakes his head, cupping his wrist.

"How...?" he wonders. "He was so strong."

"Someone call the police," the Comte says, tucking his brother into his side.

"We're here with Sûreté agents," I speak up, stepping out from behind Steel. "That man was a criminal that we're pursuing. Please accept our apologies, monsieur, for the disruption."

Daaé puts down the vase, stepping away from it as though to hide the fact that she'd reached for a weapon. "Raoul, are you hurt?"

"It's nothing," he says, wincing.

"I'll call for a doctor." The Comte glares at the singer. "As for you, mademoiselle—"

"Philippe," the Vicomte interrupts. "The guests."

The woman in the old-fashioned gown curtsies gracefully, if shallowly. "Oh, don't worry about us. I've seen a great deal of unusual things, in my time." Her gaze flicks to me, to Steel. "Madame Bellemeure, at your service. This is my companion, Chang Mei."

We make our bows. "Madame. Mademoiselle."

She gestures at the room behind her with her cigarette, wafting a thin curl of smoke in her wake. "The Marquis von Tier is in the other room, Comte. Perhaps I should tell him to return at another time?"

The Comte inclines his head. "I would be grateful if you would, madame. Thank you."

"Not at all," she replies. "I would caution you against waiting too long, however. His new hotel is attracting a lot of attention and if you wish to invest, you should make your bid soon."

De Chagny nods, though the words seem to make his expression gloomy. "Thank you, madame."

"If I can offer further assistance, perhaps Mei and I can disperse the other guests?"

"I could not presume—"

"Do not be foolish, Comte. The pleasure is mine, I assure you. I've not had such an interesting evening in quite some time. Come, Mei." She sweeps out of the room, leaving a trail of reeking smoke. Chang Mei follows her.

I do my best not to inhale too deeply. "We'll find the Sûreté agents and make our report," I offer.

"See that you catch that monster," the Comte says, walking his brother out of the room. "And while you're at it, escort mademoiselle Daaé back to the opera house, where she belongs."

Daaé presses her lips together and looks away, even as the Vicomte cranes his neck to see her. When they're gone, I listen for a moment to the music dying, to the sound of conversations turning into whispers. My gaze falls on the balcony.

"Is he still here?"

No comment comes from the shadows, and the ghost does not reappear.

Steel marches to the rail. "If he is, he's doing a better job of hiding than I'd give him credit for."

The jab goes unanswered. Perhaps he *has* left. "Are *you* all right, mademoiselle?"

"Please, call me Christine." She makes a move as if to rub her hands over her face and then pauses and instead pats the skin under her eyes with her middle fingers. "Thank you for your assistance."

"You said he was your teacher," Steel responds, cutting past any necessities of etiquette. "What does that mean? What was he teaching you to do?"

The look she gives him is shadowed and weary. "If by that, you're asking if he was mentoring me in some dark art, then my answer is no. He helped me sing."

"Did you need his help?" I ask.

"To sing well enough to become *prima donna* of the greatest opera house in Europe?" She lets out an inelegant snort. "There is no other teacher who could have put me there."

"No other teacher would have attacked your competition," Steel counters.

"I wouldn't be so sure. Besides, Carlotta lives," Daaé says. "I'm sure she will recover."

Steel's brow quirks. "The opera is a cut throat business, it seems."

"Has he ever talked about other demons?" I persist. "Any mention of the name Leviathan?"

"Demons," she says. "You said that before. You can't seriously think that he is one."

"You thought he was an angel," I point out. "Is it so different?"

"I was mistaken. He is simply a man."

"With the ability to vanish from thin air and to disable a grown man without effort." I flick my hand, conscious of the minutes ticking past. "It doesn't matter. We need to find him. Question him."

"His ties are to the opera," Steel says. "What would he have to gain by the fall of my House?"

"If he didn't do it, he might know who did." He'd told us he wasn't the only demon in Paris—he'll just have to tell us where these other demons are. "Where can we find him, mademoiselle?"

"Christine," she corrects, a harder edge to her voice.

"Christine," I repeat, obediently.

A long sigh and she slumps against the wall. "I don't know. Only that he sings to me from behind the walls of my room, or the chapel. He can find me anywhere." She seems to realise how disturbing that sounds and hurries to add, "He has never hurt me. Not once."

"Not yet," I reply, colder than perhaps is necessary. For a moment I'm not sure why and then I realise; he reminds me of another Phantom demon. A demon who delighted in the opportunity to cause harm.

"Promise that you won't kill him," she asks me, as if I have the power to grant such a vow.

"We'll take you back," I say, instead of answering, and her expression turns wintry.

"That won't be necessary, I can make my own way, mademoiselle." She strides out of the room before I can stop her.

I turn and find Steel eyeing me. "What is it?"

"Have you considered that he might *not* be our suspect?" he asks. "He might just be trying his best to survive."

"Murdering innocents is trying his best?"

"I wouldn't call Buquet an innocent."

I think of Annie, again, and of the women who'd died because I wasn't smart enough or fast enough to catch the Ripper. "That doesn't make it right."

"Perhaps he was trying to protect Christine. He does seem to care for her."

He'd described Christine and the Vicomte as the moon and the sun, and himself as the hungry night. "That's not love, that's obsession. Why are you defending him?"

He raises his hands. "I'm not. I'm considering all the options. You used to do that, too."

The words cut, deeper than he may have intended. "I used to be an agent," I say, with a bitterness I try and fail to suppress. "I'm not anymore."

Steel lapses into silence and I go to find Dumont.

AGENT E. WILSON

They put her in Hazel's old room and Cassius in Steel's. Eve locks the door between them and falls into the single chair, unable to think of sleep even though fatigue saps so much strength from her muscles that she wonders if the ritual pulled more from her than just words.

Rubbing thin fingers over her face, she tries to forget the demon just next door. Did Hazel feel this way, that first night when Steel joined her? She should've asked. She shouldn't have been so quick to dismiss her concerns. If she'd tried talking to her, maybe Hazel wouldn't have run.

Eve stands, examining the room with fresh eyes. It's stripped to the essentials: a bed, two wardrobes and a chest of drawers, with only a copper bowl as decoration. She goes to the drawers first.

Every agent has a journal. Most use it to make notes on their cases, but some, like Khurana, rely on it to untangle their thoughts. Hazel's thoughts never seemed to need much untangling, but looking over her case notes might give Eve an insight into why she ran.

But the drawers are empty. Even the wardrobes are bare.

Monaghan should have shared Hazel's journal when he promoted Eve. He should have passed on anything that might help her understand what happened. Instead, Hazel's room has been picked clean.

If the Professor's right and Steel *was* involved in the murders—

Then Hazel would have turned him in. Eve knows better than to think that her friend would try to protect a killer, even one she might have grown some affection for. The law is the law, and the Agency upholds the law. Hazel would never have disobeyed it.

Unless the law itself was unjust.

Suspicion prickles under her skin. Those last few days, Hazel had suspected Khurana of lying about her whereabouts. She must have been on Rayne's trail, too. She must've seen, at the end, that Monaghan would choose to protect his memory—and the Agency's reputation—rather than reveal Rayne as the killer. So, she'd run off with her demon.

Eve paces the length of the room, her cheap cotton nightgown swishing around her ankles. Something about that theory sits ill. That Hazel would choose a man over her work, perhaps, however unnaturally handsome the man. Or that she'd leave without even a word to explain herself, reduced to a thief in the night.

Eve's hands ache for a weapon, for something as simple and true as her blade. All this theorising makes her head spin like a ball full of pebbles.

She has to be patient. Wait for Khurana to come up with a plan.

Eve flops onto the bed. She hates being patient.

Luckily, sleep takes her once her head hits the pillow, and it's just after dawn that she gets up to dress, banging on the adjoining door to wake the demon. Monaghan had said to take some time, but he didn't specify how long, and she wants to be ready for whatever his orders are.

She expects Cassius to be grumpy and sleepy when he emerges. While he is the former, his eyes are keen and his bearing straight.

"Good morning," he greets her. "How do you command this lowly cur today, my lady?"

She tells him exactly what he can do to himself today and his smile glints, smug as a cat over teasing a reaction out of her. He follows her to the kitchen, chortling, and only at the doorway does he hesitate.

"What," she says, "too good to eat with us lowly folk? I don't have any delusions of grandeur, like Rayne. You'll have to get used to the kitchen."

"Like a dog," he mumbles.

Maia is already up and surveying her kingdom. Her raised eyebrows ask a question Eve isn't sure how to answer. "I did not expect to see you until this afternoon," the woman says.

"Couldn't sleep," Eve answers.

Cassius, having taken a seat beside her—closer than neces-sary—puts both elbows on the table and folds his hands under his chin. "What do we have for breakfast this morning, good woman?" he asks, with drawling contempt.

"If you wish to eat," says Maia, "you will cage that tongue of yours."

The demon smirks.

Maia gives them each a plate of curried fish. On Eve's sit two peeled hard-boiled eggs, perched on the rim like ears. The cook winks at her as she goes back to the sink and Eve swallows a sudden pang of grief. Her mother would cook eggs in nearly every meal when she was a child. The other children used to laugh at her for eating them with her hands, biting into the tip and then swallowing them in a single gulp. Now, she crushes them with her fork before piercing the chunks with the tines.

The weight of his gaze draws her attention to Cassius. Watching her, the demon slides his own fork between his lips, attempting an expression that she assumes is supposed to be seductive. Interesting; she would have given it at least another day before he tried such a move.

"You have herring on your lip," she says and is rewarded with a hastily veiled look of consternation.

Jacob chooses that moment to enter, saving her from any more attempts. He does a passable job of pretending that Cassius doesn't exist, while Max greets the demon with a cordial nod.

After helping Maia serve two more plates, Jacob takes a seat. "So," he says, through a mouthful of fish, "did he give you a case?"

Eve experiences an odd moment of dissonance when she waits for Hazel to tell the man to swallow before speaking and the pause only stretches. "No," she replies, recovering. "He said to go and see him once we've adjusted."

"Don't you find that odd?" Cassius asks. "He must want you for something. He must want *me* for something."

"He probably didn't want to catch you roaming around causing trouble," Eve snaps.

"I am offended, Agent Wilson. I certainly wouldn't be *caught*."

"How long will it take for you to acclimate?" Max's quiet voice cuts through the conversation as easily as if he'd shouted.

It's successful in diverting Cassius. "You're an agent now, are you, Reaper?"

Max stiffens, his large frame drawing back. "It is not wrong to want to help others," he says.

"Do yourself a favour," the Phantom demon replies, "help yourself first."

Eve picks up her plate, standing. "Come on. We can spar, or we can play cards. And I'm not in the mood for cards."

"It's not as though I can fight you, is it? Or is the plan for me to stand there and let you prick me to death?"

She drops her plate into the sink with a clang. "Fine. Cards then. But don't cheat."

"It's no fun if you don't cheat."

If Monaghan doesn't give them a case soon, she's going to kill him herself.

CHAPTER TWELVE

When we'd emerged from the room, we'd found that madame Bellemeure had ushered out most of the other guests. A handful lingered in the entrance hall, speculating as to what had cut the night short. Dumont and René had been monopolised by their questions, and had greeted us with relief and the story of the ghost's attack with anger. By that time, Christine had been long gone and the servants were cleaning up behind us. Dumont hadn't wanted to finish there, although all four of us had agreed that bursting into the Palais Garnier with no plan was a mistake. So, Dumont had taken us to his headquarters at the Sûreté. Refusing would have triggered questions that we wouldn't be able to answer, so we hadn't.

Standing in front of it now, I wonder if we should have. The Sûreté building squats among a dozen townhouses, big and stark and grey, as intimidating as a building can get. Guards flank the entrance, armed with three different weapons that I can see.

Dumont strides past them without a second glance. I take a deep breath, careful not to look anywhere except straight ahead, and follow. The guards eye us, but Dumont's presence seems to be enough to let us through.

Steel stays on my heels the entire way. He'd barely left my side all night and when he had he'd stayed within about twenty feet or so. The same distance that the ritual had forced him within.

I shoot him a look and he grimaces, mutters, "Later."

The big door lurches open and the young man who'd shadowed us last night appears, a navy jacket thrown around his shoulders over a tattered white shirt. His round cheeks are ruddy and as freckled as mine.

"Sebastian," he says, with an impish grin. "Uh—I mean, Agent Dumont," he corrects, his eyes landing on me and Steel and widening. "Please, come in."

My mouth turns up. He reminds me of Doyle. "Monsieur Dumont's apprentice, I presume?"

"*Agent* Dumont," the boy says, his blue eyes flaring. Loyal, then.

"My apologies."

"This is Jacques," Dumont introduces and then says, in a harried aside to the boy, "I told you not to wait up. It's late."

"But I need to take down your report," he protests.

"In the morning. Go to bed and get some sleep. *Now*, Jacques."

He pouts and steps back, letting us pass. As we move into the building, I glance over my shoulder. Jacques wavers, torn between obeying and following us. Then René makes a shooing motion, smiling. Jacques flushes, ducks his head and scurries away.

"He's still learning," Dumont says, his bearing rigid as though I might cast aspersions on his teaching style.

I make no comment and we move on.

The Sûreté's interior is papered in cream and gold, its windows framed with draped curtains the colour of buttermilk. A stark contrast to the Agency's narrow dark hallways and dim grey parlours. Despite the hour, a low buzz of conversation drifts from open doors as we're marched through the building. I catch glimpses of young moustached men in three-piece suits, police officers in helmets and full uniform, the occasional maid-servant in plain dress and apron.

"I didn't know the Sûreté was this big," I offer, an opening.

Dumont doesn't look around. "We oversee the country from here. France is quite a bit larger than England."

I smother a smile. "Yes, of course."

We head up a series of staircases. The oil lamps become sparser and the furnishings cruder, until they drop away completely, revealing bald stone walls. This is more what I'm accustomed to. The tiny, austere study we end up in feels so familiar that my spine relaxes without conscious thought.

Dumont leans against a simple pine desk—little more than three planks nailed together—and asks us to describe what happened. We'd given him the broad strokes of the ghost's movements earlier, but this time as I recount the evening I spare no detail, watching his brows lower and his mouth twist.

"Attacking a Comte and the patron of the opera house," he says, when I've finished. "This demon is causing us more and more problems."

"If he murders an aristocrat, Auguste will have our hide," René says, referring to someone I assume is a Sûreté leader.

"Do you still think he's involved in your case?" I ask.

Dumont stares at the wall, his gaze clouded. "I do not know. I cannot see a motive, not yet. But he has the means to have murdered the opera dancer. And he has murdered since, so regardless of whether he's involved in the abduction of other copper class demons, he is still a criminal." He looks at René and something unspoken passes between them.

"You have a concern," I prompt.

"It is nothing."

"The Sûreté will not support us." René's words are blunt. "They consider the activities of the lower demons to be beneath them—they don't even allow their agents to summon copper classes."

"But..." I trail off and Dumont answers my implicit question, "René was a mistake."

The demon makes an insulted sound.

"The *summons* was a mistake," Dumont corrects, with audible exasperation, as though it isn't the first time he'd been chastened. "I was told to try for a Reaper, silver class, but I was nervous. I mixed up the components. An advantageous mistake," he adds, with a softening around his mouth, "even if you *are* a no-good troublemaker."

"Hah, more like a very *good* troublemaker." Pacified, René adds, "But you see how they will not be troubled by the fate of a few copper class demons. And if we proceed with an investigation into what is considered a jewel in Paris' crown, a favourite haunt of the elite..."

"The Palais Garnier is an institution. I might as well suggest we remodel Notre Dame," says Dumont. "At best, they could pull us off the case. At worst, they might dismiss us entirely."

I look from one to the other. No wonder they were so quick to trust us; they had no one else to turn to. "Yet, as you say, the ghost is still a criminal. What will you do?" I ask, although I already know the answer. They've come this far with the full awareness that their agency might turn its back on them. They won't withdraw now.

"We continue." Dumont's voice is composed and René, when he looks at the man, cannot hide a smile. "What of your case? Is he your suspect?"

"We still need to find out," I reply.

Steel shifts. "The question is, how? If he's living behind the opera's walls, we'll have to tear down the place to find him."

"The ghost spoke to us twice already, I'm sure he'll do so again." Spoke to *me*, specifically. Because I am a woman or because he thinks me vulnerable? Either way, we can use that to our advantage. "What if I try to lure him out?"

Steel's head swings in my direction. "*What?*"

"There must be a reason that he spoke to me alone," I say. "Perhaps I can find out what that is."

"No," Steel says, but Dumont seems to be considering it.

"It might work." He glances at René.

"Better her than us," the demon replies with cheerful uncon-cern, and Steel glowers at him.

"I suppose it is better than all four of us turning the place upside down," Dumont says. "It is worth trying."

"Absolutely not." Steel jerks at the top button of his shirt, yanking open his collar. "If this ghost is the murderer, you're putting yourself in danger for nothing."

"Not nothing. If this ghost is the murderer—*our* murderer—then it'll be worth it."

"Worth risking your *life*?"

"The cellars are full of props that you can hide behind. It's not as though I'll be alone." His mouth purses and I hurry to speak over him. "And even if it doesn't work, we'll be no worse off than we are now."

"Agreed," Dumont interjects, earning a fierce glare from Steel.

I pick at a stray cuticle on my finger, suppressing a wince as it tears and a tiny bead of crimson wells up beside my nail. "I will need a weapon," I say, in a measured voice.

Steel raises his chin as if he's been personally insulted. "You have *me*. I'm all the weapon you need."

"Dramatic, aren't you?" the other demon mutters, rolling his eyes.

I wipe the dot of blood on my skirt. "You're not a weapon."

"Same risks, remember?" he says, throwing me back to another conversation on the streets of London.

"I think it's best you stay out of sight," I reply. "If something goes wrong, you're more likely to catch him."

That rankles him. "What do you mean, *if something goes wrong*? What are you expecting to go wrong?"

I wave my hand vaguely. "It's best to plan for the worst." Perhaps I should be scared of what I'm suggesting, but the absence of fear is a hole in my stomach. Somehow, I don't think the ghost will kill me. I don't think the ghost has any interest in me at all.

The three men watch me with expressions raising from curiosity to aggravation. I ignore Steel's hot glare and direct my next words to Dumont. "Not a knife, though." My hand flexes and I shake it out. "I notice you wear a pistol. Your agency doesn't prohibit it?"

"Not in exceptional circumstances," Dumont replies. "Do you know how to use one?"

I shake my head. "Can you teach me?"

He considers me, his face neutral, no doubt performing his own calculations. "Very well," he says, after a moment. "You can use my old revolver. I was going to put it back in the armoury, but we have enough weapons."

"Armoury?" Steel asks.

"For the agents."

"And the test," René tells him. "You do have a test in Britain, I assume?"

"I still have the scars."

I wince before I can stop myself.

"I would offer you a derringer," Dumont says, "but they only give you one shot before you must reload."

"Why a derringer?" I ask.

"They're small, easy to handle, favoured by ladies."

It seems some things are the same in every country. "I see."

Dumont clears his throat, shifting. "I'm sure that you can handle the Lefaucheux model. However... Most of our agents go out of the city to learn, but we don't have the time. I'm sure you won't object to a demonstration here?" He catches my look and smiles. "I can show you how to load and clean it. More than that, I'm afraid you're on your own."

"Thank you."

Dumont takes a silver case out of one of the desk drawers. Inside lies the revolver. It has a slender, blueish cylinder, engraved with a faint pattern of leaves, and a plain wooden handle. Dumont loads the gun for me, pointing out its cylinder and trigger mechanism with calm efficiency.

He hesitates before he hands it over. "Are you certain this is the weapon you'd like to use?"

I nod. I will not handle a blade again, not for this.

"Very well."

Steel's irritation bubbles like a living thing. I cast him a quelling look. "When do you want to make the attempt?" I ask Dumont, taking the gun. I go to slip it into my pocket and the agent makes a stifled sound.

"No—Not in your pocket," he says, his hand spasming as though he wants to snatch the gun away from me. "Hold on." He goes to a chest tucked against the wall and digs through it, discarding heaps of gleaming fabric. This must be where our clothes for the soirée came from. He turns and hands me an off-white muff. "Use this, if you must hold onto it."

"Thank you." As soon as I get the time, I'll find somewhere out of town to practise. "Tomorrow, then?"

"Tomorrow." He closes the chest with a decisive thud. "We will meet you at the Palais Garnier, when the curtain rises. If he does not appear in box five, we will search the cellars."

Where Buquet was murdered. From there, we can work our way through the building. On impulse, I offer the man my hand. "It's a pleasure to work with you, Agent."

Dumont hesitates, as if no one has extended this courtesy to him before. But he takes my hand. "Agent," he acknowledges, caution in the tentative way he grips my fingers.

I can feel Steel's annoyance ratchet up a notch. "Tonight, then," I say, hastily, and scurry out of the room before we get a chance to destroy this precarious alliance.

We escape out of the building and into the cold grim day, and my muscles loosen, letting go of a tension I'd grown so used to that the relief of its loss takes me by surprise.

"Bait?" Steel says, practically fizzing, and my body tightens again. "This demon has already killed one person that we know of, maybe more. Putting yourself in danger to lure him out is a terrible idea."

"I'm not saying that I should wander into the cellars by myself. You and the agents will catch him. I'll just draw him out."

"*Just*," Steel repeats, with audible scorn. "You'll *just* lure out a murderer."

"This is no different from Whitechapel." My voice is too loud, but no one seems to be paying us any attention. "I put my life on the line to catch the Ripper every time we went into the East End. This is the same."

"It's *not* the same," he says. "You're not an agent anymore. I'm not your demon."

I press my lips together to disguise how much that hurts. "You're right," I say, instead. My death back then would have meant his freedom. Now, it'll just be an inconvenience. "Be honest. Can you think of a better idea?"

He scowls. "That doesn't mean I have to like it."

"I trust you to have my back."

"Do you?"

"Of course. Even if you're not my demon anymore, you're still…" I hesitate, reluctant to put a word to whatever we are, reluctant to create an *us*; as soon as I build an *us*, I risk losing it. "You're Steel," I end up saying, "the best gambling demon in Paris."

There's a pause and then he says, grudgingly, "Maybe the only gambling demon in Paris."

"Maybe not the *humblest* demon in Paris." I see the line in his cheek that precedes his smirk. Success. I don't examine why that should matter so much. "Come on," I say. "We don't want to be late."

CHAPTER THIRTEEN

The managers allow us into box five after Dumont threatens them with another, much larger, investigation. Steel and I wear the same outfits the agent had sourced for us for the party, while Dumont and Rene wear another set of simple black suits. No doubt the Sûreté also has a tight budget. I tuck my hands deeper inside the muff Dumont provided, my grip tightening on the pistol.

We stay out of the way of the other guests and slip into box five just after the orchestra strikes its first notes.

It's empty. Even though I'd expected it to be, disappointment makes my heart drop. Disappointment and fear. Regardless of what I'd said yesterday, part of me is reluctant to go through with this plan.

In the theatre below, the guests seat themselves and faint notes from the orchestra twine with the sound of excited voices and laughter. Some of the seats at the back have been sold to people in cheap suits and secondhand dresses, filling out the stalls. Less than half of the boxes are full. Word of the new *prima donna* isn't quite enough to attract a crowd.

"Well?" Steel asks, taking one of the chairs and leaning back so its front two feet tip off the ground. "How do you expect to find him in here?"

René shoots him a narrow-eyed glare. "You could start by *looking*."

Dumont is already examining the walls, smoothing his hands along the creases and corners. "Keep an eye out," he says, absently. "The ghost may be watching us."

"If he is, he'll be a fool not to make himself scarce."

"It's Christine's debut," I add. "Wouldn't he want to be here?"

Steel makes a sweeping gesture towards the stalls. "Somehow, I don't think this is the audience he had in mind."

"What makes you say that?"

"He has an ego," he says. "This isn't going to be good enough. It's no better than a dress rehearsal."

I make a thoughtful noise.

"That's if he hasn't seen us and gone into hiding," Steel adds, letting his chair thump back down.

"But what—"

The swell of the orchestra cuts me off and the curtain rises. The light dims. Electric bulbs around the theatre go out, leaving a handful to illuminate the doors at the back of the stalls. Our attention falls to the stage.

A figure appears in front of a pastoral backdrop; Christine, almost unrecognisable in a tall wig and glittering gown. Then she sings.

The entire theatre gasps. Her voice spills over the edge of the stage and flows through the theatre, soaring and falling and captivating every soul that hears it. If not for the deep breaths that she snatches between notes, I would swear that an angel had descended from heaven to grace us with its presence.

An odd shiver crawls down my spine; a wave that starts at the crown of my head, travels over the nape of my neck and dissipates at the base of my spine. My hands twitch for no reason, reaching for something. The music strums at my heart like the string of a lyre.

Blinking, shaking off the sensation, I glance at Steel. His hands are curled, his eyes heavy-lidded, directed towards the stage but focused somewhere else, somewhere distant. The beat of drums resounds in the hollow of my chest, enduring long after the individual sound has been swallowed up by the rest of the orchestra. It's hot, in the box, and I watch a tiny bead of sweat form at Steel's temple. It detaches from his skin, a minuscule floating bubble caught on a wave of his peculiar ability to control water.

"Steel," I whisper and catch it with my finger, smudging it out of existence.

Steel's gaze slides lazily to me, then his chin dips as he comes back to himself. "My apologies," he rasps. "I got carried away."

"With the music?" I ask, keeping my voice soft. Dumont and René are still studying the room for any sign of the ghost.

"With magic," he replies, in the same tone. "It's always had a similarity to music, to me."

The song continues and Christine holds the entire theatre in sway. "Is that normal, for demons?"

He shrugs. "My mother never told me more than what I needed to know. The rest I sought out myself, rumours and legends that pieced together into something real."

"What does it feel like?"

"Like the lilting call of a brook, or the thrum of a deep lake." He speaks haltingly, as if the words take all his concentration to process. "My mother's felt like a wide, slow-moving river. Graceful."

"And your father's?"

He pauses. "My father never used his magic, not where I could see. He said it was tempting fate. And then he died, anyway."

We fall silent, letting the music steal the words away.

"He's not here." Dumont's voice makes me jump, tearing me from the quiet, liquid place I'd slipped into. "If he lives in the walls, then I can't find a way in—if he was ever here. "

René's examining the curtain that divides the main box from the entrance. A small couch huddles behind it, out of sight of the stage, for no apparent purpose that I can divine save for illicit trysts. The demon lets the curtain fall. "He could be watching us right now," he says, "and we would be none the wiser."

I move away from the balustrade. "Then shall we try the cellars?" I ask in low tones, conscious of the audience below us. "There might be an entrance of some kind." Christine had mentioned her mirror, but backstage will be chaos as the opera moves through its various scenes.

Dumont agrees and, as we leave the box, Steel tells me, "I still think this is a terrible idea."

"Noted." I tighten my grip on the pistol, my hands warmed within the white fur muff Dumont gave me. As long as I keep my hands tucked inside, I can keep the weapon out of sight.

René is armed with a rapier and he keeps his hand on its hilt as we walk. One stagehand opens his mouth to say something and a harsh look from René has him bustling away. My mouth is too dry to attempt to break the heavy atmosphere lying over our heads, so I don't bother to try.

We reach the stairs to the cellars. Dumont came prepared; he lights a small lantern and descends without hesitation. Steel catches my elbow before I can follow him.

"Are you certain about this?" he whispers.

"Of course," I reply. "We might be able to prevent any other murders."

He releases me and I follow the others, trying to ward off a surge of doubt. If this ghost is as smart as he seems, why would he fall into this trap?

The third floor cellar seems eerier than ever. I squint at the gloom that lingers at the edge of the light. If I close my eyes, I can still see Buquet's body, hanging from the ceiling.

Dumont hands me the lantern, making the light swing over a carved silent warrior. "Over to you, agent," he whispers.

"Hide," I tell him.

The man clicks his tongue at René and they both disappear behind a tapestry. Steel hesitates until I give him a look, and then he sinks into the darkness, disappearing between a bust of Augustus and a painting of the Seine.

I advance into the first room. Perhaps this *is* a stupid idea. The ghost could've been watching us all this time—maybe even while we were coming up with the plan.

I don't have any choice now but to commit.

"Monsieur Phantom," I call into the dark. "Are you there? I would speak with you."

A low scuttling sound comes from somewhere in the dark—one of my companions, or a rat?

"Unless you have another engagement," I add, louder, trying to ignore the eyes on me. "Another Joseph Buquet, perhaps?"

Something crashes. I jump and pivot to stare in the direction of the sound. Steel appears at my side. "The other room."

"We'll go," Dumont offers, the light flashing on his face for a brief moment before he vanishes.

"Stay here," comes René's voice, already moving away. Their footsteps tap across the room and fade into the dense, absorbing silence.

Joseph Buquet, body so still he wasn't even swinging. "Go after them." My voice is a harsh whisper. "It might be a distraction."

"And leave you?"

"They're no safer alone than I am."

Steel makes a *tch* sound, but he leaves. I heft the lantern above my shoulder. Better sight should make the place less intimidating, but the light picks out craggy shadows among the set pieces and draws sharp faces in the gloom.

The lantern sways a little. I swallow and steady my arm.

"This is becoming tiresome."

I shy from the sound on instinct. "Do you regard human life as tiresome, monsieur?" I snap back, scrambling to regain my equilibrium. "Is that why you prey upon the defenceless?"

"I would not call the stagehand defenceless."

"Then please explain to me why you killed him."

"I can do better." His voice drifts away. I follow it. "I can show you."

"What do you mean?"

"Your passion is admirable, Agent. But I can't help but wonder why you are wasting your time with me."

A dark opening yawns in front of me, a doorway to the second room. No—the second room is to my right. This door lies within the wall itself. A room we missed? I hesitate, tightening my grip on the pistol.

"Perhaps if you would refrain from speaking in riddles," I reply, "I could understand what you're saying."

"Come, then, and see."

I stare at the opening. On the other side, the walls are stone, the ceiling swathed in cobwebs. This is how he's moving around the opera house. He's not a ghost at all.

I open my mouth to call for the others and the creature speaks again.

"Perhaps not. Farewell, mademoiselle." His voice grows faint, retreating through the open doorway.

He can't get away now, not when we're so close. I plunge through after him.

The opening leads to an empty corridor, more stone and cobwebs. No sign of the ghost.

A scraping noise fills the silence. I whirl and find the doorway shrinking. The wall is closing. A trap.

Suddenly, a figure fills the tightening space and wriggles through with a muffled curse. Steel falls into the corridor with me just as the opening grinds shut, sealing us both in the space between the walls.

"You had to investigate, didn't you?" Steel mutters, pulling himself up and wincing. "You couldn't have waited for the others, instead of stepping into the *obviously dangerous* corridor?"

"It's a corridor. It was hardly going to eat me."

Steel gives me a look.

"I didn't *expect* it to eat us," I amend. Now, Dumont and René are on their own in the dark and we're...wherever here is. I lift the lantern, examining the wall. "It didn't move of its own accord. There must be a trigger, or a handle."

Dutifully, Steel puts his hands to the stones, digging into their edges. I mirror his movements on the other side. This section of wall looks the same as the rest, and the moment I take my gaze from it I struggle to remember which part moved and which was just wall. How had the ghost discovered this?

"This wall is newer than the one behind us," Steel says, on the same train of thought. "It must have been built after the opera was constructed."

"Someone added a secret corridor? Why?"

"Perhaps we should ask this ghost, when we find him."

I squat and check the edge where the wall meets the ground. It feels like wall. Whatever triggered the thing to close, I can't locate it. Not from this side.

"What if it can't be opened from this side at all?" I ask, stealing a glance at Steel.

"Then I suppose we had better shout for help." His mouth twists, as though he finds the idea beneath him.

"Monsieur Dumont!" I call, without waiting for him to lower himself to the effort. "René! Can you hear us?" I nudge Steel, and he sighs and joins his voice to my own.

We pause, listening, but the only sounds that come back to us are the rapid puffs of our breathing.

"The wall is too thick," Steel says. "No doubt he built it so."

"*If* the ghost built it."

"Who else?"

At this point, I have to agree. A neat way to extort the managers while hiding from them in their own opera house. And an easy way to prey upon its inhabitants. Exhaling, I stare at the wall.

"I don't see we have much choice," I say. "We can't get out and they can't get in. We'll have to find another route."

Steel lifts his gaze to the gloomy passage that stretches onward. "You mean go in there."

"We're in already. There must be another way out. The ghost wouldn't leave himself without a second escape route."

"You speak like you know him."

"I'm making an assumption."

A picture is forming, though, an image of the kind of man he could be. He dispatched Buquet silently, making it look like a suicide. He planned and constructed this secret corridor, and who knows how many more. He deigned to speak to me in his box, and then in the cellar, just to lead me into this trap.

The one element that doesn't fit is Sorelli. His quiet, methodical approach with Buquet seems incongruous with the signs of rage imprinted in black and blue on her body. If this is only one side of the ghost that we're seeing, what, then, did Sorelli do to earn his rage?

"Well," I say, making my voice brusque, "there's nothing to do about it now, except find the murderer." I drop the muff on the ground and slide the pistol into my pocket. Forget what Dumont said, I want my hands free. Then, lifting the lantern to shoulder height, I start down the long, empty corridor.

AGENT E. WILSON

"The library?" asks Cassius, with every appearance of scorn. "You want to play cards in the *library*?"

It's quieter up here than the last time she'd come, desolate without the scratch of Hazel's pen. The other woman's desk is bare in a way it had never been while she was on a case. Despite that, the orderly bookcases and the smell of musk steal into Eve's chest and start to unwind the thorny emotions tangled there.

"I know *you* were never here," she replies. If Cassius had ever done any grunt work, she'd never seen it. "That won't be happening on my watch, by the way. We do our own research."

"Once a Hound agent, I suppose."

It's politer than some of the other things she's heard about women agents with Hound demons, so she ignores it and walks to the far end of the library, the end that leads to the ingredient room. The stuffed animals with their perpetually snarling jaws had scared her when she'd first joined. Now, she barely notices them.

She *does* notice the dark head bent over a stack of books in the corner.

"Clara?" she asks, bemused. Even after she became Hazel's apprentice, the maid had rarely stepped foot in the library. "What are you doing here?"

The woman looks up. Her curled auburn hair is pinned into a simple twist and her unlined blue eyes assess Eve. "Agent Wilson. I didn't realise you wanted to use the library." It's said with cold politeness.

Eve returns the tone. "We can go somewhere else, if you need the space." She feels a flash of disloyalty for talking to the woman at all, but their relationship had never contained the same friction as Clara's relationship with Hazel. And even if Eve didn't employ the more feminine techniques that Clara favoured, she admired the girl's ambition.

"Not at all." The woman shuffles her papers together, taking care not to flash the words in Eve's direction. "I was just finishing up." She gathers her notes before gliding past them.

Cassius watches her go. "Hmm."

"What?" Eve examines the books Clara left behind; texts on the history of the summoning ritual.

"Nothing. Just admiring the line of her dress."

"I'll bet." With Hazel gone and Eve a Phantom agent, Clara must be preparing for the order that'll come to summon her own Hound. The Agency will need more of the tracking demons soon; Isis and Khurana can't handle the whole of Britain alone.

Eve leaves the books where they are and digs out one of the card decks she'd hidden among the stacks back when she preferred playing cards to reading reports. Well, that hasn't changed, she's just a bit more disciplined about the reports.

Taking a seat in the chair Clara had vacated, she shuffles the cards from one hand to another. Then she catches Cassius staring.

"Problem?"

"Did you learn to play in a brothel?" he asks, cuttingly. "No one shuffles like that."

Oh, right, she'd forgotten there were rules about things like that. "Half the world shuffles like this. Just not the half you're from."

There's no way she's going to tell him that she *had* learnt in a brothel. The women there had taken care of her while her mother had worked, and from them she'd learnt the meaning of the words *auntie* and *sister*. The one who'd taught her to shuffle had beautiful straight black hair and large doe-like eyes. That and her nut-brown skin had made her popular as an exotic, and she'd had the luxury of turning away clients, leaving her with more time to look after Eve.

Eve wonders if she ever made it out of the brothel. Wonders if she should have gone back after her mother died, to help them the same way they'd helped her.

"What game?" she asks, throwing those thoughts back into the murky den they'd crawled out of.

He sits in the chair opposite, unbuttoning his jacket as he does, as prim as Monaghan. "Old Maid," he replies, destroying the image with a smirk.

She deals for Rummy. He takes his hand and spends a few moments reordering it, while she leans back, propping her cards on her stomach. "You were with Rayne for years," is her opening gambit. "You must have known him well."

"As well as he let anyone know him. Which is to say, not very." He picks up a card and discards a jack.

She collects it, exchanging it for the four of clubs. "What was his story?"

Cassius gives an elegant shrug. "A Baron's youngest son, too ambitious for his own good."

Monaghan's tendency to recruit people with no future didn't incline agents to share their past, but Rayne had made no secret of the fact he came from wealth.

"How did he end up here?"

It's common for demons to have elongated canines, but when he smirks, Cassius reveals a pair that look more like daggers than teeth. "His sister drowned."

She tries to recall a time when Rayne had seemed melancholy and can't. "He didn't spend much time grieving."

"Which was enough reason to worry that another of his siblings might be next. Particularly his eldest brother, the next Baron."

"You can't be suggesting that he killed his own sister!" Eve exclaims.

The demon draws another card and then discards it with a tut. "I am merely relaying what I learnt of his past."

"I doubt he told you all this himself."

"He told me nothing," he says, terse all of a sudden. "I had to read his letters to learn anything about him."

"You *read* his *letters*?"

"Of course," he replies, sounding faintly surprised. "How else could I have done my job?"

"If you read any of *my* letters—"

He tuts again, at her this time. "So violent."

If he'd read Rayne's letters... "You would know, then." He arches his brows and she adds, "If Rayne was the Ripper."

"Rayne was a selfish brat," Cassius says. "Don't tell me you think he could murder so many women and get away with it?" He laughs, as if the very idea is absurd.

"You could be lying to spare yourself."

"From what? I'm bound to you, now. If the Professor was going to string me up for murder, he would have done it."

Her stomach sinks. "So, he's right, then? Hazel *was* involved?"

"If she was, she's a much better actress than I gave her credit for," he says. "By the way she fought us, you'd think the last victim was her own sister."

"So, she did fight you." Just as Monaghan had said. "She—Did she kill Rayne?"

Cassius regards her over the crest of his cards. "Stabbed him with her own weapon," he says and she winces. "Which freed me, of course. And if you hadn't brought me back—"

"Yes. I know." Eve tosses her cards onto the table, no longer in the mood for games. She walks out without waiting, half-hoping that he'll grumble and snap, but he just chuckles under his breath and pads after her.

Eve is tempted to go back to her room and sit alone in silence for the rest of the day, but all that will do is make her tense and short-tempered, so she goes downstairs, hoping to find Jacob.

Three tall, silent guards stand in the lobby. At the door, saying his farewell to the Professor, stands a mostly bald man in a frock coat. His beard is thick and crawls up the sides of his head, as if trying to compensate for his lack. It's the beard that she recognises—the Prime Minister. She shrinks back, overcome by an instinctual urge to hide. Monaghan is Shadow Commissioner now. He'll be dealing with the Prime Minister regularly, perhaps even with the Queen.

"Damn," she hears, whispered, and glances at Cassius. His face is frozen in sudden stark shock. But as she opens her mouth to query him, he masks the expression. "You said you were good with a sword," he says, his voice cool and easy. "Let's see what you can do, hmm?" And he leads the way to the training room without looking back.

CHAPTER FOURTEEN

The corridor seems never ending. The walls remain unchanged and the only sign of our movement is the vibration of gossamer webs that cloud the corners. No sound reaches us, nothing to distract from the hollow ring of our footsteps on stone. I use the toe of my boot to scratch a crescent in the unbroken dust along the edges of the ground.

"What's that for?" Steel's voice is dampened by the stone surrounding us.

"So we can find our way back." Assuming we don't find another way out. Which we will. "Just a precaution."

"Right," Steel mutters. "They don't need our corpses adding to the stench."

All I can smell is sour rot and dust, but it doesn't take much to imagine our skeletons propped against the wall.

"Dumont and René will come looking when they can't find us," I say, not sure if I'm trying to reassure Steel or myself. "They won't believe we just vanished into thin air."

"I don't have the same confidence in our companions that you appear to do."

I eye him sidelong. He hides it well, but there's apprehension in the line of his jaw. Or perhaps that's the voice in the back of my head, whispering to me of his fear. "They'll let us go after this."

"You don't believe that any more than I do."

I shift the lantern to my other hand, shaking out the ache in my arm. "This is the only lead we have, and we needed their help. It was a calculated risk."

The passage slopes downward and the air thickens, turns musty. Moisture gleams on the stone. We must be under the cellars. A soft scratching sound comes from up ahead. I still, holding my breath to hear better. It comes again. Footsteps?

Steel has gone tense, his shoulders hunched. I point down the corridor towards the noise and then hold my finger to my lips. His nostrils flare. He makes a pushing gesture with his hand; me, behind him.

Holding my arm in front of the lantern to block the glow, I inch down the corridor, ignoring the gesture. Steel lets out a harsh breath and hovers beside me.

We creep along the passage. I'm careful to place my feet softly on the ground, keeping the weight out of my heels.

Scratch, scratch. Then silence. Is it a trap?

Without the light from the lantern, darkness clings to our toes, folding back only as we step into it. Each small slice of corridor reveals nothing, and nothing, and nothing. But the sound continues.

Then the light reveals an edge to the wall—a corner. The scratching comes from the other side. I stop, plunging my hand into my pocket. The handle of the revolver is snug in my palm. I draw it out, my thumb on the hammer, my forefinger along the barrel. Holding it at my waist, level, I dart around the corner.

Something squeaks and a tiny furry body scampers away into the shadows. Neither a monster or a ghost.

"A rat." Steel crosses his arms. "Are you going to put a bullet in it?"

I drop my hand, scowling at him. "Possibly," I retort.

He doesn't snap back with a response, so at least I've diverted his annoyance. The tension in my body still seethes and I hoist the lantern, putting the pistol back in my pocket.

"This can't go on forever," I whisper, moving forward. My ankle catches on a thin line of pressure. I tug and the pressure vanishes. Halting, I lean down. A strand of wire lies on the floor, stretching from one wall to the other, a clean break in the middle where I'd snapped it.

"An alarm," I say, over the thud of my heartbeat. The light trembles over the walls, makes the shadows dance. I grip my arm with my free hand to steady my hold. "If he didn't know we were here before, he does now."

"And I have even better news," Steel mutters. "It's a dead end."

"What?" But when I step around him and raise the lantern, I find our progress blocked by a forbidding stone wall. "It can't be."

There must be a way out, a way through. How else can the ghost move around the building? I put the lantern down so I can feel along the edges of the stones with both hands.

Sighing, Steel leans against the wall beside me, crossing his arms. "I'm surprised we haven't found any bones," he says. "I guess ours will be the first."

A rapid series of clicks makes me flinch back. Have I tripped something? But the stones don't move.

"What was that?" Steel asks. At his side, a thin line is travelling up the wall, as if it's cracking under his weight.

Not a crack, a *seam*.

"Watch ou—"

The wall opens behind him and he falls backwards, an almost comical expression of surprise on his face. I reach for him. His sleeve brushes my fingers.

Without pause, I hurl myself after him and we both tumble into the darkness.

I slam into hard ground, smacking my elbow and hip. Then I'm skidding, rolling sideways, Steel tangled with me. There's one horrifying, heart-stopping moment when the ground vanishes and we fall through empty air, nothing to stop us—then we slam into a floor. No, Steel hits the floor, and I hit Steel.

Something above us goes *snick*. A lock turning over.

"Ow," Steel mutters. He lies half-sprawled under me, one of his arms around my waist. My head is on his shoulder, my legs stretched out beside his. I gather the information gradually, focusing on the touch-impressions my body sends back. It's pitch black.

"What happened?" I ask, my mind blank and bewildered.

"This ghost just signed his death warrant," Steel says. "That's what happened."

I wriggle a little to bring up my arms, pressing one under Steel's to lever myself upright. "Where ar—"

Steel's hand clamps around the back of my head and there's a sharp crack.

"*Ow*," Steel says again, aggrieved.

Mortified, I sink back down. "I'm sorry! Are you all right?"

The weight of his hand disappears. I hear a few faint ticking sounds and a rustle, and I picture him flexing his fingers.

"No permanent damage," he says, his chest vibrating under my other hand.

"Can you see? Where are we?"

He pauses and a rising sense of dread fills my stomach. "I could be wrong," he begins and the dread ratchets up, "but it looks like we're in a coffin."

"A what?"

"A coffin," he repeats, not at all helpfully. "As in, where they put the bodies."

I drop my head, taking care to touch him as little as possible. "I'm aware of what a coffin is." That night I'd slept in one, the lid had been off and I'd fallen asleep to the sound of a dozen other people snoring and snuffling, but it had still given me nightmares for weeks. This is so quiet and so dark we could be buried alive.

"Ah." Another pause. His body shifts. "It appears to be locked," he adds, after another moment.

God. I inhale through my teeth and think only about the facts. The ghost led us here. Deliberately. "It was a trap."

"It seems so."

Cautiously, I explore the surface under us. It's wood, not stone. My hand reaches a little beyond the width of my shoulder before it encounters a wall. A box. Not at all a coffin. Just a box.

A long, thin box.

"I could try breaking it," Steel suggests, before I can drive myself to hysteria, "but I don't have a lot of leverage." He shifts, again, and something creaks. "Definitely not enough leverage."

I curl my arm underneath me to take some of my weight. This is a trap to take care of would-be trespassers—like us—but the same end could be served by some other device. The ghost has already proved that he'll kill. He left Buquet's body dangling from the ceiling; he doesn't need coffins (*boxes*) to hide his corpses. Unless he chose this one because of its nature, to fill its victims with horror before they starved to death.

Steel taps the back of my head gently. "You're thinking too hard."

I huff. "How could you tell?"

"Even if I couldn't hear the cogs whirring, that frown is going to damage your face."

I consciously smooth my expression.

"Now you look like you're plotting a murder," he says, with a breath of laughter. "If it's the ghost's, I'd like to volunteer my assistance."

That wrangles a smirk out of me.

"Better." He moves again, this time to make himself more comfortable. "So, what's the plan?"

"Why does he have a coffin?" (*Box*, my brain protests futilely.)

"You're asking me?"

"I mean, where would he get one? He's hidden away in an opera house, it's not as though he can ask for one to be delivered. So, what resources does he have access to?" My mind puzzles over the question as I speak.

"The things that are already here?" Steel hazards.

"Are there any operas that would require the use of a coffin?"

"My knowledge of music is restricted to what they play in taverns and at festivals. So, unless they put on a lot of puppet shows..."

"If it is a prop," I say, "there should be a mechanism to open it from the inside. In case someone ever got stuck."

Steel makes a doubtful noise. "Are you sure they thought that far ahead?"

"Not really, no," I reply. "But *I* would, if there was a chance I'd fall into my own trap."

"Let's hope the ghost is as sensible."

I start with the seam where the wall of the box meets the floor, poking my fingers into the crevice to feel for any bumps or cracks. It feels like a regular seam. The wall itself is smooth and unmarked.

"There are scratches here," Steel says, doing the same on his side. "I, uh—I don't think they're a mechanism."

"No?"

"I think they're just scratches."

"From what?"

"Fingernails."

I suppose I should be grateful we're not sharing the coffin—*box*—with the bones of whoever was in here before us.

Steel has moved onto the panel above us, his arm brushing my shoulder. I strain to reach the far end, beyond our heads. My fingers brush over a smooth surface and then a raised bump.

"There's something here." I try to explore the pattern, but my shoulder aches. "I can't reach it."

"Here." He grasps me by the waist and scoots me forward until my palm smacks flat against the surface, then holds me there.

"Is that—comfortable?" I ask, desperate to say something to keep silence from descending, overly conscious of my expression.

"It's fine." His voice is a little strained. I resolve to act as fast as I can.

The raised bumps are not bumps but small engraved handles. I map the contours with my hands, wishing my eyesight was as good as Steel's. There are two, each in the shape of a creature that I can't identify, perched on the wall like door knobs. The material is cold—a metal of some kind.

"Two figurines," I tell Steel. "I think I can turn them."

"Excellent. Then let's figure out which one."

That's the question. One of them could be another trap. I hesitate, propping one hand on the floor to ease the burden on Steel. "It's too easy," I say, aloud.

"What?"

"Why would you put a key where your prisoner could find it?" I continue.

"But there are two of them, right? Only one of them can be the key."

"That's still a good chance of getting the correct answer." The darkness is making my eyes water. I blink a few times, then give up trying to see anything. I think of my profile for the ghost: quiet, methodical, intelligent. He must have had this prepared for some time, in case he was ever found out. He led us here to die, slowly, where no one can hear us. Why would he give us such an easy way out? "It's a distraction."

"From our impending doom?"

"From the correct answer."

I flatten my hands on the wall again, searching for some other clue. Apart from the two figurines, the surface is flat, unmarked. Then my fingers hit a small indentation along the juncture where the wall meets the floor of the box. Just enough space for the pad of my thumb. I press lightly, and a shallow vibration runs through the box. Something above us clicks.

Steel moves so quickly that I'm rocked to the side and topple off of him. A shaft of dull grey light spears into the box, alleviating the darkness.

"Sorry," he says. He's holding the box open with one hand. "I wasn't sure if it would lock again."

"Be my guest." I gesture at the lid and he heaves upwards. It falls backwards and clacks into an open position, shedding enough light for me to make out the shape of it: a sarcophagus, the outer casing shaped like a man, gilded with blue and gold paint.

I lever myself out and clamber over the side. My breath comes out in a rush as the space around me broadens.

"A coffin," Steel points out, sitting up.

"Please get out," I implore.

He leaps out nimbly and pulls the lid closed. Above the box lies a dark open shaft. That must have been where we fell through. The ceiling swoops down around it in triangular formations reminiscent of ancient churches. An old chapel, perhaps.

"What is all this stuff?" Steel asks, turning on the spot.

"Old props, I would guess."

Dozens of items surround the sarcophagus. A small table overflows with costume jewellery in every shade, holding every kind of gem. Elaborate, frilly gowns lay stuffed into chests alongside rich woven capes. One tapestry covers an entire wall, depicting mounted knights streaking across a golden desert. Red blood runs under the horses' hooves.

Most of the room, though, seems to be dedicated to music. Instruments lie propped against chair legs and are tucked into the arms of mannequins. Sheet music crinkles under my boots as I move towards a grand piano sprawled in one corner. More sheets sit on the piano's rack, hand written and chaotic with notes. Other papers in the same spidery hand are scattered over its lid.

"How did he bring all this down here? We must be at least three floors beneath the opera."

"He must have been here for years," Steel comments, picking up what looks like a sketch of a grand palace. "Squirrelled away like a rat."

"Must be lonely." No wonder he fell in love with a beautiful woman with the voice of an angel.

"I think this is a way out." Steel investigates an arched opening that leads into another corridor. A cluster of candles set in an iron sconce provide the thin light, casting a glow down the passage. "Shall we?"

I grasp for my revolver. It's still in my pocket and I grip the handle tightly, feeling the grain of the wood imprint into my palm. "I'm ready."

The corridor slopes downward and twists back on itself. After some time, we round a corner and come across a branch in the path: two tunnels lead in opposite directions. Damp air licks my face and moisture glimmers on the rounded stones, glittering as though from some other world. Our footsteps ring hollow—wooden planks beneath us stretch from one wall to the other.

Steel lets out a frustrated sound. "What kind of maze is this?"

"This is no maze," murmurs a quiet voice. "You are in the depths of the Palais Garnier. Or is House Leviathan no longer a patron of the arts?"

"You know him?" I ask the ghost, scanning the shadows. "How?"

"He forgets to mask his magic." The voice seems to come from over my shoulder. I turn, but no one is there.

"How long have you been following us?" Steel demands.

There's no one here, and no one could have passed us in the corridor. I look up. The ceiling soars upward into darkness, as though it was designed as a laundry chute, like the shaft above the sarcophagus. Stones jut out from the wall, tiny corners for the most part, but one is a large slab. A slab that sits under a shadowed alcove.

I narrow my eyes. An alcove, or an opening?

"Why bring us here?" Steel continues. "What do you want?"

"I do not believe I invited you."

"You invited *me*," I reply, trying to pierce the shadows. I can't let him get away. "You said you wanted to show me something."

"I wanted a conversation."

"You could have had that outside," Steel retorts. Thin rivulets of water drain from the walls and flow across the planks to his feet. "Not by luring her into your dungeon."

The ghost's deep laugh reverberates off the walls. "Please, monsieur. It is far from a dungeon."

"I didn't know Phantom demons had need of such tricks. Or such elaborate houses." I raise my eyebrows, waiting for his response.

It comes after a slight pause. "You know a great deal about our world, mademoiselle Locke."

"So, you *are* a Phantom," I reply. "Is that why you spoke to me, before? Because out of all of us, you didn't know who I was?"

"Out of all of you," the ghost replies, "I thought you would be the most reasonable."

"You gave up any chance of reasoning with us when you murdered Joseph Buquet."

"The man was an oaf and a cad. He should not have revealed me."

"And Sorelli?" I ask. "You can see why we'd find it difficult to believe the innocence of a ghost who admits he's murdered before."

"Yes, I can see your predicament." Amusement threads through the words. "I suppose I will have to find this killer myself."

I blink. "What?"

"I will not have the Sûreté traipsing through my opera. And if we lose any more dancers, there will be no opera to see."

"You will return with us," I command. "Help us find the killer, if that's what you want. We can rule out your involvement once we have answers."

"And have you string me up for the murder of one useless stagehand?" Another low, musical laugh. "That is not the crime that I will hang for, mademoiselle."

I raise my gun, levelling it at the shadows in the alcoves. "Then we will have to discover your other crimes, monsieur."

"Wait." Steel's whisper sends a shock through me.

"What?"

"It doesn't make sense," he says. "Why would he admit to killing Buquet without a qualm but balk from admitting to the murder of a woman?"

"He's still a *murderer*," I hiss. "We can't let him escape."

"Perhaps she doesn't trust you yet, Dragon," the ghost calls. "And she has good reason not to. How many humans has House Leviathan enslaved or slaughtered in the name of entertainment? Will mademoiselle Lyr be another in a long line of conquests?"

Steel flinches. "I never—"

"You are the heir, are you not? The sins of the father... Or in this case, the uncle."

I thrust my doubt aside. "Surrender," I demand. "Surrender, or I will fire."

"My dear girl. Do you really have the stomach to shoot me?"

My palm is clammy and the trigger feels slippery. But I can't let him get away. I can't let another murderer go free. I squeeze.

The report makes me stagger. Shards of rock break off the wall and thud to the ground. I missed.

"You have more spine than I credited you with." The ghost is smiling. Even though I can't see his face, I can hear it in his voice. Some prey instinct at the back of my brain shouts an alarm. "Enough games. If I am going to hunt down a murderer, I do not need either of you getting in my way. Nor do I need you revealing what you have seen to the Sûreté." A grinding sound, and the wall behind us closes. "A pleasant journey, mademoiselle."

The ground under our feet disappears and we plunge into freezing water.

CHAPTER FIFTEEN

The impact punches the breath out of me. Water closes over my head, so cold it feels like I've fallen into a bath of ice. I strike out, sweep water with my hands, claw at nothing. My skirt swamps my legs, clings, drags at me. I'm sinking. I can't see any light. I can't see *anything*.

Panic bursts through my chest and I reach up—*is* it up?—hoping to break through, find air, but my fingers meet more water. My lungs ache, shrinking with the need to breathe. Without thinking I open my mouth and choke on the taste of mud and silt. Is this how I die?

Someone grabs my arm and hauls me upward. I kick my feet uselessly, my boots leaden weights. Then the water breaks over my head and I can breathe. I cough, hacking up water until my throat burns. An arm around my waist keeps me above the water, just; it laps at my neck, my shoulders.

"Are you all right?"

"Steel?" I whisper, coughing again as the word snags in my lungs.

He swears, the word tinged with something that sounds like relief. "You can't swim?" he demands. "Why not?"

"I live in *London*," I snap back. "Where was I going to learn, the Thames? Have you *seen* the state of the Thames?"

"All right, all right." His breath puffs over my forehead. "I've never seen you panic before."

"I'm not *panicking*."

"Right," he says, with audible amusement, though tension lurks in the words like a banked fire. "Why didn't you say anything?"

"It's not exactly something that comes up in daily conversation," I manage, taking shallow breaths. I tilt my head towards the ceiling, if there even is a ceiling; everything is as black as night.

"You could have told me."

"Oh, sure." I push sopping hair out of my face with shaking hands. "By the way, just in case we get plunged into an underground lake in the future—I can't swim!"

"Remind me to teach you some day."

It shocks me into a stuttering laugh and I descend into another round of coughing. The arm tightens. "I'm a-all right," I whisper. My eyes adjust to the darkness and I make out the shape of his head, the darker shade of his hair on paler skin. He doesn't seem to be moving, just standing in the water with nothing beneath us but dark space. I sway my legs, boosting myself up until the water sits at my collarbones. "Are you?"

"Just about. I'm not strong enough to get us out, but I can keep us afloat."

"For how long?"

A pause and then he says, "Until I can't any more."

"Oh. We'll have to get out of here before then, in that case," I reply, seizing on the practicalities of the issue.

"I'm open to suggestions."

Right. Suggestions. I peer into the darkness, but the water could go on for miles and I wouldn't be able to tell. The ghost dropped us in here to leave us to die—perhaps there isn't a way out at all.

I cut that thought off. If a way out doesn't exist, we'll have to make one.

"The trap door," I say, gasping as a shiver wracks my body, "is it shut?"

"I can't tell. Can you reach it if I lift you?"

"I'll try."

He grips my waist with both hands, small spaces of warmth in the chill of the water. I lift my arms and raise them over my head, palms flat. Steel raises me out of the water. The surface seeps down to my chest, then my waist. The water touches my hips in the same moment that wood meets my fingers.

"Found it." I try to ignore the strange feeling of Steel holding me above the water and concentrate on the planks over my head. I can't feel any hinges. "It's closed. I can't tell how to open it."

"I will be having words with this ghost when we find him," Steel mutters.

"We'll have to find another way out." The cold of the water creeps up my hip. But I haven't moved. "It's filling up."

Steel lowers me with a loud exhale. "I was hoping you wouldn't notice."

"You *knew*?"

"More water's coming in from somewhere below. I expect it's being pumped in from the river."

"So, we have a mere four or five feet of space before we drown."

"That's about the state of things, yes."

I kick at the water, frustrated. "Wonderful."

"If it's coming in, then we can get out the same way," he says. "We just have to find out where."

"And how do you propose we do that?"

"I can look for an opening." He hesitates, then adds, "But I'd have to leave you while I search."

We can't hang around until I learn to swim. "Just be quick."

"Cup your hands like this." He grips my hand, pushes my fingers together. "Pull the water down, like you're climbing a ladder."

I follow his instructions. The water laps at my chin, but I'm afloat. "I'll manage. Go."

He hesitates another moment, then the shadow of his face nods and dips out of sight. A rush of water swamps me as he dives, and then I'm alone in the dark.

My breath rasps, loud against the whisper of water. I stare up at the dark ceiling, trying to map out the shape of the trap door in my head, keeping my mind off the feeling of empty space under my feet. If the doors opened outward, towards the water, then perhaps it has hinges that I missed. If we could unpick the screws, we could open the door that way.

At the rate the water is rising, we'd be making a serious gamble. If we can't undo the hinges in time, we'll be dead.

We're four floors below ground—at least—and underneath the foundations of the opera house. Paris has catacombs, doesn't it? We must be close to the tunnels. Could we break through the walls?

I don't move my hand quickly enough and I sink in the water, ducking under the surface. I surge up, spluttering, my heart thundering so loud it silences my breathing. For the first time in a long time, I feel helpless. I'm completely dependent on Steel to stay alive.

Is this how he felt in London?

With a gasp Steel breaks the surface, sloshing me with another wave. I shake it out of my face. He grips my waist again, pulling me out of the water.

"Any luck?" I gasp out.

"I found a grate. I might be able to break it open."

"That's great," I reply in relief and Steel snorts a laugh. "That was not a pun! This is not the time for puns!"

"Sorry. Hold on to me." He turns in the water and pulls my arms around his shoulders until I'm pressed against his back. "How long can you hold your breath?"

"Excuse me?"

"Joking."

"Not funny."

He strikes out across the water with smooth, even strokes that send out ripples I feel more than see. Moving as we are, I should be able to see the walls close in around us, but there's nothing.

"How big is this place?"

"Huge," Steel replies. "I can't tell where it ends."

Not a river, then. An underground lake? Had the ghost engineered this, too?

We swim—or, Steel swims and I cling—across the whatever it is. The cold seeps through my skin until my very bones ache with it. I'm conscious of the impenetrable stone over our heads, getting nearer with every second.

"Here it is." Steel stops and I slip off his back, treading water the way he taught me. Above is a faint golden glimmer, just enough to illuminate the intricate pattern of metal between us and freedom. "It might be a sewer entrance. Hopefully, we won't survive this just to die of dysentery," he adds and I grimace.

"I'll be glad just to be out of here."

Steel reaches up and grips the grate with both hands. He barely needs to lift himself out of the water to do so. "It's iron. And rusted over. I'll have to break the bars."

"Can you?"

"With enough time."

I refrain from mentioning the deadline that's creeping up over my ears. "Please feel free, Mr. Steel."

"By that I assume you mean, '*Get on with it*'."

"You're very astute." Something brushes against my leg. I jerk away from it. "Something's in the water."

"I was wondering where that rat went."

"Wonderful," I mutter, trying to peer into the darkness below my feet. The endless empty space could be filled with a hundred rats, all about to swarm up and feast on my legs. My breath quickens and my chest tightens with fear.

"You've faced mutilated corpses without flinching," Steel murmurs, "you're not going to faint on me now, are you, Miss Locke?"

"It's a distinct possibility," I reply, gritting my teeth. "Are there demons that live in water?" Is that why we were dropped in here? Not to be drowned, but to be eaten alive?

"Put your arms around my shoulders," Steel suggests. He doesn't look away from the grate, intent on his work. I hesitate. "It'll be easier for me to keep you afloat."

Not doing so seems foolish when the alternative gapes open underneath me. I kick out and fling my arms around his shoulders.

"And you're less likely to get eaten," he adds and I scowl.

"You *do* think there's something in the water."

"Let's hope it's merely a rat."

I tuck my legs against his side, knees tightly together and pressed against his ribs. He doesn't take his gaze off the metal grate, as if he doesn't notice my sticking to him like a very tall limpet. "Am I... I'm not too heavy, am I?"

"You're as light as a feather, Miss Locke," he replies, as sardonic as ever.

"And you're an ass."

"Now, now," he says, grinning. "Language."

I keep my gaze on the water and away from his ridiculous face. "Are you never serious in the face of certain death?"

"Only when it's absolutely certain." A series of snaps follows the words. Pieces of metal splash into the water. I look up and thin light streams down through the gap. "That's better."

More snaps, and the gap widens. I breathe out my relief. Steel notices.

"You didn't think I'd let you drown, did you? I'm not that poor a partner."

"I forgot to factor in your arrogance," I mutter.

His grin widens.

The cold makes me shudder, causing my voice to hitch. "W-where does this lead?"

"No idea. Somewhere better than here, I hope." He lets go of the grate, dropping us back into the water. But we're a lot closer to the grate than we had been. "After you."

He grips me around the waist again and lifts me up. I grasp the edges of the hole, lever myself over the rim onto cool stone. I reach back and help Steel pull himself up. He rolls onto the ground beside me. Through the hole, the water looks dark and fathomless. As I watch, it creeps nearer to the grate. Finally, just as it laps against the stone, it stops.

"It's s-stopped rising."

"Excellent," Steel mumbles from where he lies on his back, his eyes closed.

Another shiver wracks me. Without the warmth of Steel to cling to, the chill wicks through my muscles unchecked. I hug myself and look around. It's a stone passage, limned by the glow of a distant torch. The walls, though, are not the same blank stone that we traversed in the opera house. These are packed with skulls.

"We're in the c-catacombs." The torchlight flickers over bared teeth and shies away from the black spaces where eyes used to be. "M-must be under th-the city."

Steel opens his eyes to peer at the walls and grimaces. "This might be an appropriate time for an '*out of the frying pan*' joke."

"N-never."

He looks at me, frowning.

"A-are you alri-right?" I splutter, through my chattering teeth.

"Am *I*—?" He huffs. "I'm fine, Locke. *You're* the one shivering out of your dress."

"My d-dress is perfe-fectly fine."

"You're soaked." He holds his hands over my body, keeping his palms a few inches away from touching. Water seeps out of the fabric and drips onto the ground, leaving my clothes damp but not drenched.

"That's us-useful."

"The ghost isn't the only one with tricks." He does the same to himself and water streams off his suit, pooling on the mud.

The ghost. "I-if I hadn't sh-shot at him—" He said he thought I'd be reasonable. Perhaps I could have talked to him. Perhaps I could have stopped him.

"You did what you thought was necessary. Even if it *was* a foolish idea," Steel adds, under his breath.

Bitter regret snatches my breath away. Or is that the cold? "S-stupid idea." If I'd been smarter, aimed better—

"Stop." Steel grips my shoulder, his fingers warm through my icy dress. "This wasn't your fault."

It's all I can do to stare at the blurry white collar of his shirt. "I let-t another k-killer go free."

"We don't know how strong he is. Even if you *had* managed to hit him, you might not have killed him."

My teeth lock together, my jaw too tight to get any more words out. I try to tell myself he's right, but the dark thoughts linger. If the ghost kills again...

Steel touches the back of his hand to my forehead. "You're freezing. Shit." He wrenches off his jacket and throws it around me, yanking the lapels together. "Warm up," he orders.

I make a *tch* sound through my teeth. He doesn't seem to hear me. I try to flex my hands, but they feel like heavy blocks. A dull ache creeps into my knuckles, my knees. My back hits something hard and I realise I've slumped to the floor. Despite the water that's still draining out of my clothes, the cold seems to be spreading.

"You can't faint here, Locke. What if the rats come up through the grate?"

I hunch over my arms, the words little more than residual noise. A curse. I'm moved and then long legs slide alongside my own. Steel pulls my back into his chest, warm and solid. He rubs at my upper arms, quick, brusque movements. Heat seeps into my body, gradual at first, then quickly enough that my shivers worsen.

That's good. My brain clings to the thought. Shivering is better than stillness.

"That's it," Steel murmurs and wraps his arms around my chest, jacket and all. His breathing is rapid and uneven by my ear.

I concentrate on his warmth, on the solid strength of his body encircling my own. He holds me as I shake until the ice in my bones thaws. Prickling spreads through my fingers, then my toes. I make a pained noise.

"What? What is it?"

"Hurts," I manage, swallowing to warm my throat. "Fingers hurt."

He loosens his hold and pulls my arms out. Putting my hands together he rubs at them with his own. "Better?"

Not really. In fact the pain worsens, but that's only the blood rushing through my fingers.

"Yes," I whisper. His palms are calloused, rough and warm on the backs of my hands. "Thank you."

"I wasn't going to let you faint. Or worse." He huffs, warming the side of my neck. "You forget: we have a case to solve." He pulls my hands up to my shoulder and breathes over them. "How's that?"

I have to swallow. "Better."

"Are you all right to stand?"

We can't stay here forever, in a corridor lined with human skulls. Even if, for a brief moment, I want to. "Yes."

Steel peels away from me, standing upright. He holds out a hand. A lone butterfly takes wing in my stomach, braving the ice around my heart.

I seek a distraction as he helps me to my feet. "We can't be far from the Palais Garnier." My voice is hoarse, but I'm glad of it. It disguises my weakness.

"So, follow the light?" Steel suggests. "Can you walk?"

I glance at the skulls rammed into the walls and nod, trusting my legs better than my voice.

Steel takes the lead, looking ruffled in shirtsleeves and waistcoat, his dark hair a tangled mess. I pull his jacket closer around my shoulders. Any scent that might have clung to it has been washed out by the silt-infused lake water.

"Do you still have the gun?"

"No." It had been in my hand when I fell. "It'll be at the bottom of the lake by now."

"That bastard demon," mutters Steel. "He could have killed us."

"No doubt that was his intention." The ghost said he wanted to investigate, as if he was concerned about Sorelli's death. Unless that had been a lie, for our benefit. Regardless, we need to catch him before he takes it into his head to dispense justice.

A torch is set into the wall, burning steadily. The iron sconce has rusted in places. Up ahead is the light of a second and we move closer. Then I stop, catching Steel's elbow.

"Look." Footsteps mar the dirt path in front of us. A single pair, turning on itself.

"Someone maintaining the passages?"

"As a crypt? Why?"

"A good place to hide your dead," he replies, grim-faced.

We continue, tracing the footsteps. At first, I try to place my feet in their steps, but as the footprints grow it becomes impossible. More than one person has been down here, and recently. At one point, the dirt is marred by a long, wide streak that goes on for over fifty paces. The torches remain spaced far apart, leaving an air of unease to lurk between them.

It seems like hours before we turn a corner and come to a ladder flanked by two more torches, burning low. No sound apart from our breathing disturbs the musty air, but the ground at the base of the ladder has been trodden and retrodden and marked again with that wide swathe, as though something had been dragged down the corridor. I'll have to ask Dumont what kind of criminal activity might be attached to this area.

"Come on." Steel climbs the ladder and puts his shoulder to the iron cover at the top. He slides it off, revealing dark grey sky, and hauls himself out. I follow as fast as I can, flinching at the mental image of the cover sliding back into place, leaving me trapped.

Steel helps me out and covers the hole back up. We're in a small, unlit alley in the back streets of Paris. I pull together the sodden strands of my hair and twist them into a damp knot.

"We should go back," I whisper. "The others will be looking for us." I feel Steel's gaze on my face, but he says nothing and I lead the way back to the Palais Garnier.

Agent E. Wilson

Eve wakes when it's still black outside the window. She squeezes her eyes shut in the vain hope that sleep will swallow her again. Earlier—yesterday?—she'd drilled with a rapier until dinner, and her muscles haven't stopped complaining. It's been too long since she sparred; Khurana hasn't had much time for exercise lately.

Something, some imbalance in the air, jerks her from her half-asleep musing to full attention. Eve slips her hand under her pillow, disguising the motion as a stretch, and curls her fingers around the hilt of the dagger she keeps there. She scans the room through her lashes, looking for anything out of place.

Nothing seems to have moved.

She exhales and, in the pause before her next breath, listens intently. There.

Lurching upright, she flicks her wrist and the dagger becomes a flash of silver. It lands in midair with a soft, fleshy thud.

"You know," Cassius says, shimmering into view and wrenching the blade out of his arm, "your manners could use some work."

Eve stares at him. Distantly, she realises she's in her night-gown and bonnet, but the more pressing concern is that she only keeps *one* dagger under her pillow. "What the hell are you doing?"

"Thinking." He tosses her blade onto the dresser.

"You can do that in your own room. Get out." She looks past him to the adjoining door, which still holds the key in its lock. "How did you get in?"

"You have two doors," he explains, in his most condescending voice.

"Well, obviously I wasn't expecting you to break into my room in the middle of the night! What time is it, anyway?" she adds, flustered and annoyed about it.

"If you didn't want me here, you should have locked it."

"That's not how privacy works!"

He scoffs. "You're an *agent*. There's no such thing as privacy, anymore; I'm always going to be twenty feet away." He says it without glee, as if he's as irritated by the prospect as she is.

"That's at least ten feet further than you are right now," she says, "so, please feel free to leave."

"Is this all you have?" he asks, gesturing to the wardrobes.

"Did you go through my things?"

"Like I said, privacy is an entitlement we no longer receive. Why, we're practically married." This he adds with a salacious grin.

"I will stab you again," she promises, and he drops the act.

"Ask Maia to get you some better clothing."

"What? Why?"

"You can't enter society dressed like a servant."

"I'm not entering socie—Cassius—"

He stays visible as he goes to the door, letting her see him ignore her as he leaves. She listens for the faint click of his own door before she retrieves her dagger and flops back on the bed. To hell with Phantom demons and their schemes.

She doesn't get long to consider Cassius' odd behaviour; Monaghan calls them into his office after breakfast.

"How are you getting along?" the Professor asks, meeting her gaze in a way that makes her feel both respected and inadequate at the same time.

"Fine," she answers, "sir." No need to give him the details; a good agent can make any partnership work.

"Excellent. In that case, I have a job for you." He hands her a map of the East End. A small asterisk has been drawn over a house on Flower and Dean Street. "We have reason to believe that a powerful breed of demon has been living, undetected, in the Whitechapel district."

"The Ripper case?"

"It is unlikely that they're connected to those murders. The demon would have been discovered by now, if that were true."

"Then, what are your orders, sir?"

"I want you to bring it back to the Agency," he says. "With as little damage as possible, though you'll need to be prepared for resistance. This demon will be strong."

It's Reaper agents who bring down suspects. Hound and Phantom agents carry out the investigation—Hounds for tracking, Phantoms to verify culpability and deal with the local authorities. Reapers are physically stronger than either; they're the Agency's warriors. Jacob should be dealing with this. "Where's Agent Horner?"

"I sent him on a case with our two new agents. This particular demon—" He taps the map. "—requires a deft touch. With the recent murders in Whitechapel, the locals will be on edge. Be discreet."

"Yes, sir." She pauses, but he adds nothing else, so she gives him a crisp bow and retreats. Outside, she takes a minute to memorise the map and then folds it into her pocket.

"Is your sword blessed?" Cassius asks.

Her gaze darts to his arm. Fortunately (unfortunately?) her dagger isn't, so his wound had healed by morning. "No. Blessed weapons are kept under lock and key." Except for Khurana's cane-sword, which the woman had gotten secretly blessed by three different holy figures just to cover all eventualities.

He makes a dissatisfied noise.

"Besides, I can't carry a sword through London. We'll pick up something else." She's better with daggers, anyway. Perhaps she should follow Khurana's example and stop by a church later. "How long can you stay hidden for?" she asks, wondering if she needs to get him a blade, too.

"A few hours. Why?"

She outlines her plan, forgetting her dislike of the man in the wake of the goal Monaghan gave her.

"We should wait for Horner," says Cassius, afterwards, his mouth tight. "Going in alone is a stupid idea."

"We have our orders." This is her first case as an agent. She isn't going to let Monaghan think her a coward. "And you get a chance to prove you're worth keeping around."

He doesn't rise to her bait and they make their way to the East End in uncomfortable silence.

CHAPTER SIXTEEN

W alking into the front entrance of the opera house bedraggled and muddy and stinking of petrichor draws the attention of everyone in the building, and the French don't bother to keep their voices down as we pass. Ruefully, I glance at Steel. His expression is all disdain.

"There you are, thank God," Dumont calls from the huge marble staircase. He hurries down, followed by René and the two managers. "We came back to the first cellar and you were gone. What happened? Where have you been?"

I raise my hands, wait for him to stop. "I'm sorry we caused you alarm."

"Speak for yourself," Steel mutters.

"Are you hurt?" Dumont asks me, over him.

I shake my head. "Nothing a good night's rest won't cure. And you?"

"Fine. We searched for you, but… Where did you go? Why are you…?" He gestures at my dress, no longer saturated since Steel's little magic trick, but clearly the worse for wear.

"We found the ghost," I reply and the managers let out a startled exclamation.

"What do you mean, you *'found the ghost'*?" Moncharmin demands. He laughs, his gaze darting from side to side at the people nearby. "There is no ghost in the opera house, madame."

"Perhaps we should have this conversation in private," René suggests.

"I think that's a good idea," I agree. "Let's talk in your office, messieurs."

Moncharmin has to be shepherded upstairs by Dumont, while the people in the lobby regard us with narrowed, suspicious eyes. We make it to the office unchallenged and shut the door. I sink into the nearest chair without waiting for an invitation.

"A glass of cognac for the lady," Dumont orders.

"I'm fine," I reply, but Richard is already responding, "Of course, of course," and pouring out a glass. He thrusts the amber liquor at me. On instinct I want to refuse, but the alcohol will help steady me for this conversation. I down it, wincing at the sudden flare of heat, and set the glass on the desk with a crack.

"There are hidden passages under the cellars," I tell them. "That's how the ghost has been getting around. And how he gets into box five without anyone seeing him."

"Nonsense," Moncharmin replies. "You are hysterical, madame—"

"I am *not* hysterical." They all look at me in surprise. I scratch the back of my knuckles, take a deep breath. "Steel was with me when we found it."

The demon nods, supporting my story without interjecting.

"The ghost was in there. He triggered some sort of trap and dropped us into an underground lake."

"First tunnels, now an underground lake?" Moncharmin says. "You expect us to believe this, mademoiselle?"

"You investigated without us?" asks Dumont. "That was dangerous and irresponsible. You should have come back as soon as you found the corridor."

Steel shifts and irritation flickers at the back of my head.

"We couldn't." I wave my hand, hoping the gesture illuminates the hopelessness of the situation. "The door shut behind us and we couldn't find a way to open it."

"Then you should have called for us."

"We tried," Steel interrupts. "It's not as though we *wanted* to get dropped into a freezing cold lake."

"Regardless of how we got there," I say, "we confronted the ghost but couldn't subdue him. As you see."

"Where is this ghost now?" Dumont asks. "How did he get away?"

I wince and Steel replies for me, "As she said, he trapped us down there. We barely escaped with our lives."

The agent tucks his hands behind his back, his brows doing their best to fight each other over the bridge of his nose "We'll have to tear down the walls. Find where he's hiding."

Moncharmin jumps to his feet. "You will do nothing of the sort."

"Now, now," Richard murmurs, flapping his hands. "I'm sure we can come to some kind of arrangement."

"No." Moncharmin stares at Dumont, ignoring his partner. "You've come here with a private investigation team," he says, gesturing at Steel and me, "and without any sign of your superiors. What would happen if I walked down to the Sûreté now and reported you?"

Dumont's throat bobs.

"I thought as much," the manager continues, smug now. "I doubt Commander Auguste even knows you're here. You will leave this office, at once, and speak to no one of what happened."

"You cannot be serious," René cries. "You would deny the Sûreté? Deny the right to justice?"

"I deny nothing," he replies, levelling the demon with a cold look. "This is *our* opera house, and we have tickets sold through to the summer. I will not have police officers tearing down walls or frightening off our patrons."

"Sir," Dumont says, facing the man's stare without flinching, "your opera house is haunted by a murderer. How many more deaths do you think it will take before your patrons stop coming?"

"No one knows that the deaths are connected to the Palais. Even *you* cannot be sure."

"That is a gross underestimation of the situation."

Moncharmin flares his nostrils. "I have said all that I care to say on the matter. If you will." He gestures at the door.

Dumont's hands clench at his sides, but he strides out of the office. The manager turns a stony gaze on us, so I hurry out after him. The agent is halfway down the corridor already and I run to catch up.

"Well?" Steel demands, his long legs getting him there first. "Surely your Sûreté will back us now that we have proof."

The agent draws to a stop before we reach the stairs. His fists are still clenched and he watches the opera's finely dressed patrons trickle past.

René, having been close on our heels, puts a hand on the man's shoulder. "If we make too much noise, they'll put us behind a desk," he says. "It's only their respect for Dumont's mentor that is stopping them from doing that now."

Dumont exhales and relaxes his hands. "And your skill," he murmurs.

The demon shakes him gently. "What happened to being a no-good troublemaker?"

"So, what do we do?" I ask.

"We keep investigating." René shakes his head when Dumont moves as if to protest. "No, you told me that you became an agent because you wanted to protect the less privileged of this city. Was that a lie?"

Dumont twitches out of his grip. "Of course not."

"Then that is what we will do. This ghost is a murderer. It is our job to catch him."

"There's something else," I say. "The ghost told us that he had nothing to do with Sorelli's death. He claimed he wasn't the killer."

René makes a scornful sound. "Is that not what they all say?"

"What about the hanging of Joseph Buquet?" Dumont asks. "Did he deny that?"

"No. That's the odd part. He admitted to one, but not the other." I rub my hands together, chasing out the last few chills. "We were as good as dead, in his mind. He'd have no reason to lie."

Dumont shrugs. "Perhaps to cause you doubt, in case you survived. Only a fool reveals all of his truths, even when he thinks he's beyond consequence."

Of course, Dumont's right. But I was wrong before. Could I be mistaken again? "He also said that he would try to find the murderer himself," I add. "That he didn't want us getting in his way."

"Regardless of the woman's murder," Dumont says, "he still killed Joseph Buquet. He will be caught and tried and convicted, and we will hang him from the gallows before the week is out."

That's the fate of murderers and I should be glad of it. Somehow, I'm not. Because of his voice? Because I was charmed by a ghost?

No—because I have a doubt, and I cannot ignore it.

"We need to interrogate him," I say. "Before he is hanged, at least. We must be certain."

"We must catch him first. I will concern myself with the rest once that task has been accomplished."

"If the place is riddled with more of these lake traps," René mutters, "then that may prove difficult."

"Before we rush back down to face the monster," Steel says, some of his dry humour resurfacing, "Locke and I need some sleep. And we need a better plan than pulling down the walls."

"You have a point." Dumont straightens. "We will return here in the morning. Get some rest." He nods at us like we're his agents and heads down the stairs with René.

"And here I thought I wouldn't give your agency a second thought," Steel says. "At least it had a soft bed and a hot meal."

I think of Maia and her cooking. What did they tell her, when we left? Does she miss me? What has Monaghan told them?

"You're thinking too much." I glance at Steel and he offers me one of his crooked smirks. "Sleep, first. Then think."

"I'm better at thinking."

"I know. You're a restless sleeper," he says and I look at him in surprise. "Come on. Best we get out of here before the managers reemerge."

He seems content to take the route back to the hotel without speaking, which leaves me to comb through my memories of our encounter with the ghost and figure out how I might have succeeded.

CHAPTER SEVENTEEN

The shared hotel bathroom is small and, at this time of night, lit by a single sputtering oil lamp. I have to scrub to get the smell of lake water out of my hair and it's only the awareness that Steel is waiting for his own bath that forces me to stop and get dressed.

He slips out when I return and I stand by the window, unable to think about sleep yet. Unable to let go of that moment when I'd shot at the ghost. If I hadn't tried to follow him through the wall, we wouldn't have been separated from Dumont and René. If I hadn't acted so rashly, he'd be in custody right now.

If, if, if. So many options, so many ways I could have succeeded. I try to map out the optimum path: could I have acted differently in the cellar? Done something to draw the ghost's attention?

My dream flashes through my head; Monaghan's hand on my shoulder, Rayne bleeding out on the bed. Flinching, I hasten to the wash basin, plunge my hands into it and scour them clean.

"What are you thinking about?"

I jump. I hadn't noticed Steel returning. "The ghost," I reply, rubbing harder, ignoring the sting. "I shouldn't have shot at him."

Behind me, Steel makes a thoughtful noise. "What happened to '*we need absolute proof*'?"

"I couldn't let another murderer escape."

"Another?" asks Steel, suddenly sharp.

I stare at my hands as I scrub, at a tiny spiral of blood in the water where my skin has broken, but he sees what I'm trying to hide.

"You're not blaming yourself for what happened to Rayne," he says, and it doesn't sound like a question.

"*I* happened to Rayne," I reply. "I was the one that killed him."

Steel grasps my arms. "Stop."

I freeze. His body is a line of warmth at my side, his grip gentle on my forearms. He lifts my hands out of the water and steers me to sit on the bed. I can't summon the effort to challenge him, so I stay silent. Steel clasps my hands where I'm trying to fuse them together and untangles my fingers, smoothing the torn skin, avoiding the scratches. He turns over one of my hands, sets it palm up in my lap. My right hand. The hand that held the blade that killed Rayne.

"We need to talk about this," he says.

I almost twitch my hand out of his grasp. With an effort, I keep still. "Talk about what?" To my credit, my voice remains steady.

"Don't. It wasn't your fault."

"I don't know what you mean."

He brings a soft white towel from the basin and pats my hands dry, gentle where the skin is rubbed raw and bleeding. The smooth rasp of his movements is calming and he doesn't look up from his task. Ashamed, I glance away. I'm supposed to be a professional, a hunter of demons, and yet I can't even manage this.

"How do you do it?" I ask, not sure I want to hear the answer. "How do you...deal with it?"

"I keep it locked away." A bitter, self-deprecating smile slides over his mouth. "But despite my best efforts, it always finds me."

"Then, what do you do?"

"When I find out, I'll let you know." He releases my hands. My skin is cold without him. "I'm grateful, you know," he says.

"For what?"

"For freeing me."

"But I'm the one who trapped you," I protest. My hands curl instinctively. I flatten them again. "I'm the one that owes *you* gratitude."

His gaze stays on my hands. "You don't owe me anything."

I do. I owe him more than I can ever repay. "I'm not going to argue about it," I say, with the ghost of a smile.

It works; he chuckles and rubs his brow. "This is a ridiculous situation," he mutters, glancing at me from under his hand, his eyes shining silver.

This moment of stillness feels like a chance to voice the things that have been preying on my mind. But now that I have it, I don't know what to say.

"I appreciate your help," is what leaves my mouth, in the end.

"You say that like I'm not getting anything out of this partnership."

"Are you?"

"I am." He leans back on both hands. "More than I expected."

"Charming," I reply, finding comfort in the jest, and he barks out a laugh. It lifts the heaviness. I look at my palms. "How did you know?"

"Despite what it looks like, I do pay attention, sometimes."

I sigh. "Sometimes you seem to know me better than I do."

"Yes." Something in his voice makes me look up. He's frowning and the crease between his brows deepens as I watch it.

"What?"

"Nothing."

"Clearly it's not nothing," I say, tensing. "What's going on?"

He bites the corner of his lip. "Have you...noticed what I'm feeling?"

At first I think he's asking if I've been paying attention, and then I think he's asking if I've noticed some specific emotion that's been troubling him, and *that* thought stops my heart like a hurdle, making it skip a string of beats. "I don't understand what you mean."

"Sometimes I know when you're angry, or upset. Or I know where you are when I shouldn't."

Now I have no idea what he's asking. "What?"

He drops his head into his hand, sighing. "This is hard to explain. I think the spell we performed in London, to separate us—I think it had some side effects."

My stomach clenches. "What kind of side effects?"

"Nothing that would affect your mind," he hastens to reply. "Just a...a faint sense of each other. Like seeing something out of the corner of your eye. The odd...unusual dream."

I'm starting to grasp what he means, but it feels too alarming to think about closely. "And the something that I'm sensing is you."

"Yes, exactly."

I'd thought I'd sensed his emotions sometimes before, but I assumed I'd read it from his face. "Why didn't you mention this before?"

"Because I've never heard of anything like this before. But then, what I know about my heritage could fill a thimble." The muscle in his jaw flexes. "Maybe I made a mistake, when I recast the spell, screwed it up, somehow."

"It won't affect us? I mean, beyond telling me where you are and what you might be feeling? And the—the dreams." The dream of corpses and shattered glass—*his* dream?

"I don't think it will. That level of magic would need—well, a lot more blood, for a start. That I *do* know."

It hasn't caused me any discomfort and in a way, it could prove useful. "Would distance separate it?"

He looks at me quickly. "It might, yes."

So, when he leaves Paris after he solves his case, it won't be an issue. "What you did helped us escape London," I say. "We can deal with the consequences for now."

"Yes. All right."

Curling my hands inward, I let out a long breath. "I wish Turner were here," I say, impulsively. "She'd be better at this than I am."

"I don't know about that."

His kindness always takes me by surprise. It makes me forget what he is. "I wish you'd met her. She would have liked you."

"I would've liked her, I think. I admire the kind of person who can hide a cipher in a piece of embroidery. That reminds me." Steel leans down and slides something out from under the bed. He holds it out to me. "This is for you."

Bemused, I take it. A simple pen and a leather-bound book. I flip it open and find blank white pages inside. "You got this for me?"

Steel squints at something on the ceiling. "You had one in London, so. I thought you might need one. That you might find it useful. For codes, or notes, or—whatever you want."

Gratitude swells in my chest, so warm and full that my eyes sting. "Thank you," I manage. "It's perfect."

He shrugs, still examining whatever on the ceiling has snared his interest. I can't seem to get rid of the warm melting feeling in my chest. Dangerous. Kind or not, Steel is still a demon.

"When did you buy this?"

His eyes roll towards me in a sheepish, guilty look.

"You *stole* it?"

"It's the thought that counts, right?"

Exasperated, I do my best to hide my smile. "Honestly."

"Will you use a code, like Turner?" he asks, after a while.

"I don't know. That must have taken her weeks, if not months, to come up with." Spreading my hand over the first blank page, something occurs to me and I ask, "Could I use it as a kind of demon lexicon?"

"What, like an encyclopedia? Why are you asking me?"

"Because I'd need your help to fill it."

Steel glances at the blank pages, his brows ticking up. "You wouldn't...let anyone see it?" he asks and there's wariness in the words.

After Monaghan, I can't blame his caution. "No. It's just for me. To help me understand your world a little better. And for the case." And, perhaps, for a day when I can choose my own cases.

"All right." He lets his legs sprawl out over the floor between us. "Where do you want to start?"

The question sparks a brief debate about how to organise the compendium: Steel wants to start with his own family, but I want to order it like a reference book, the less powerful classes first. He capitulates eventually and we forget about sleep as Steel talks and I hurry to take notes, interjecting with questions every now and again.

Occasionally, my mind flits back to the ghost, but each time I go to blame myself, I hear Steel's voice at the back of my mind, telling me, *Don't*. Perhaps I should be worried that it's taken root there so easily.

AGENT E. WILSON

Flower and Dean Street is a twin row of brick cottages that frame a cobbled road. It's still early and the only people around are labourers hurrying to their factories or drunks huddled in shallow doorways. And a group of children playing a rhyming game, spinning in a circle with their hands clasped.

The house that Monaghan's map indicates sits further down the street, as nondescript as the cottages flanking it. Eve raps on the door. Any noise Cassius might be making is masked by the shout of a pedlar plying his wares and the sing-song chant of *'A tissue, a tissue, we all fall down!'* She only knows he's close by the absence of the spell tugging at her chest.

An older woman opens the door. She takes one look at Eve and snorts. "Bloody 'ell, am I gonna be visited by the Devil himself, next?"

Eve clenches her hand on the hilt of the dagger she'd chosen, tucked unobtrusively into her belt. "Been a busy day, has it?"

The woman's hair might be white and her skin aged, but the glint in her eye is as keen as the edge of Eve's blade. "A busy bloody month. You'd better come in, 'adn't you?" After ushering that gracious invitation, she turns her back and retreats into the house.

It might be a trap, but who would know to expect her? Eve ducks inside, waits until a brush of fabric tells her that Cassius has joined her—stamping down the bubble of relief that swells when he does—and shuts the door.

The door leads to a single room, so there must be others living above. A rocking chair is parked in the corner, which the woman heads straight for, and an old cooking pot sits on the stove, emitting a stench that makes Eve wrinkle her nose.

"Have the police been by?" she asks.

"Is 'at what you lot are calling yourselves, these days?" She speaks with a little difficulty, her face afflicted with what looks like a case of phossy jaw. Matchstick girls don't usually live long, not with a wound like that.

Eve tightens her grip on the knife. "Our lot?" she repeats. "An agent came to see you?"

The air splits and Cassius is there. He grabs the woman by the throat, bracing his other arm against the back of the rocking chair. "Blood Drinker," he spits and there's acid in the words.

She merely smiles. "Took you long enough," she says. Her hands rest on the chair's arms, her nails long and sharp. The dim light had softened their edges, blurred the danger.

Eve's heart beats strong and fast. "Wait."

Cassius stares at her. "We have orders, remember?"

"Orders to take her back," she snaps, "not murder her in cold blood."

"He wasn't that specific."

While they argue, the woman watches them.

"You were visited," Eve says to her, ignoring the growl Cassius emits. "By who?"

"It's by *whom*, actually," the demon says, exaggerating the *h*. She drops the accent in her next sentence and both come so smooth and easy Eve's not sure which is an affectation—if either. "And I don' remember if she gave 'er name."

"I think you remember everything." Eve finds herself conscious of her own accent, grown in slums by the river. She puts careful emphasis on her *T*s. "You're just choosing not to tell us."

Cassius flexes his hand on the woman's throat. His own claws are smaller than the Blood Drinker's, not as powerful or as sharp, but so close to her jugular they still pose a threat. "We should at least take the head," he says, dispassionate. "Monaghan will want the teeth."

Eve watches for a flex in the woman's expression. She can't tell if Cassius is playing up his aggression for the sake of the impromptu interrogation, or if he actually means it. A sinking feeling tells her it's the latter.

"Tell you what," the woman says, her eyes falling to half-mast, gleaming beneath her white lashes. "Let me go, an' I'll tell you wha' I know."

Khurana would have mentioned it if she'd come here, so the only *her* that this demon could be speaking of is Hazel. Finding out why she was here might give Eve some insight into why she fled.

But it would mean disobeying her orders. On her first case as an agent, too.

Her dagger's hilt is slippery in her palm. "Very well." She jerks her head at Cassius, signalling him away.

For a moment he doesn't move and Eve's blood heats at the thought of a fight. Then he releases the woman and steps back. The tight-eyed glare he throws at her promises they'll have words later.

The Blood Drinker tucks one foot behind the other, apparently unaffected by the bruises blossoming across her throat. "She said 'er name was Locke, but it was 'er demon that interested me."

"Oh?"

"You don' often see royalty in London. And I ain't talking 'bout she who wears the Crown. Though you don' see 'er round 'ere, neither."

"He's Leviathan's spawn," interrupts Cassius, "not Lucifer's."

It's Eve's turn to glare. "What do *you* know about it?"

He looks away.

"If I 'ad to guess," the Drinker continues, "I'd say the Leviathan was 'is dam. It's the *sire* you wanna look at. Cause no Leviathan 'as eyes like that."

Eve doesn't care about Steel or his past. "What about Hazel? Why did she come here?"

The woman's ever-present smile curls at the corner, as if Eve has said something amusing. "She was lookin' for a Wraith demon. Didn't find it, in the end. Or found it too late, maybe."

Lavender. Eve deflates. This must have been during those early days when they still thought there was a chance that Turner's demon would return. She's given up her first case for nothing.

"You have two days," she says, stepping backwards to the door. "If you're still in London by then, the deal expires."

The woman glowers at her, but Eve slips through the door into the street. In the daylight, the danger of the moment feels diminished. She has to sidestep the children, who've collapsed, puppy-like, into a pile.

"What was that?" she demands, when Cassius appears at her side. "Is that the kind of thing you did for Rayne? Slaughter demons without verifying their intent?"

"Of course," he replies, breezily. "How else could I have made him the best?"

She curls her lip. "Next time, don't act without my authorisation. And what was that about Steel?" she adds, in a tone that should make it clear that the words are not a question.

He starts to look shifty. "Diamond class demons don't take orders well. He would've torn down the Agency, if given the chance. We're better off without him."

She ignores the '*we*' part of the response. "Tell me what you know," she orders.

"It's not my responsibility to correct your ignorance. Besides," he says, as she prepares to argue, "he's not here anymore. What does it matter?"

Eve's annoyed to find that she doesn't have a suitable retort. "Come on," is all she says, in the end. "We should get back."

CHAPTER EIGHTEEN

"What the hell is going on?" Steel mutters out of the corner of his mouth, looking rather like a cat that's been presented with the suggestion of a bath.

"I have no idea." I jolt out of the way of a couple dressed in feathered masks and early seventeenth century clothing, too elaborate and vivid to be real. More masked people fill the lobby and perch on the wide staircase that leads up to the boxes. We'd come in hopes of speaking to Christine again, with the intention of questioning the ballet dancers about Sorelli's last known movements, but we've stumbled into some kind of celebration.

"Isn't the opera supposed to have finished for tonight?"

Music does come from somewhere, but it sounds as though the players are half-drunk and heading for full at some speed.

"There's Dumont," I say, spying the man looking harassed at the centre of a group of young women. "He must have had the same idea." I ease past a rambunctious gentleman in a raven's mask and slide between three young women attempting to waltz with each other at the same time.

René sees me and calls, "There you are," reaching past the group and pulling me to Dumont's side. He laughs at the women as he does it. "Our pardon, mademoiselles, but we are engaged tonight. Perhaps we can visit you later," he adds, with a wink.

The women pout but flit away, sharing a bout of merry laughter. Dumont's mouth stays open for a moment, then clicks shut. The demon chuckles.

"M-mademoiselle Locke," the agent stutters, ignoring his partner. He nods to Steel, who returns the gesture. "I was not confident that you would return, after what happened last night. Are you well?"

"Yes, thank you, agent. We were hoping to speak to mademoiselle Daaé and the other dancers about Sorelli."

He exhales. "We completed an initial interview upon the discovery of her body. Nothing conclusive, I am afraid, although we had hoped to follow up with them. Daaé, in particular. She and Sorelli were close. But..." He trails off, gesturing feebly at the chaos whirling around us.

"Is this the best time for a party?" asks Steel, waving away a servant with a tray of drinks.

"The managers are trying to drum up more interest in their opera," René answers. "All the costumes are from this evening's rendition, and it seems like all of Paris' elite have been invited."

I glance at a couple tucked into a shadowed corner. "It's easier to act on your impulses when no one can see your face."

"I do not like it," Dumont says, frowning. "The ghost is still at large, as dangerous as he ever was, and there is no way to know who's here and who's not with all these masks and costumes. I will find the managers."

"And here I was hoping for a dance," interjects René, with a lopsided smile that he directs at Dumont first, then the nearest revellers.

"We are *working*." Dumont's dark skin doesn't show it, but I suspect he's blushing.

"We'll look for Christine," I suggest. "Let's meet you at the statue, later." I indicate a stone woman holding aloft a cluster of candles.

Dumont and René head up the stairs towards the circle, and Steel and I head down, into the wide round chamber that leads backstage. We find a quieter group here, older guests and actors who've chosen conversation over carousal.

I stop beside one of the smooth red marble columns. None of the people here have Christine's long dark hair, nor are they wearing wigs that could hide it. "Perhaps she's still backstage."

"Isn't that the Comte?" asks Steel, nudging me.

The Comte de Chagny stands at the edge of the round chamber, his pointed shoes just touching the circular mural paved into the floor, as if he'd been caught before he could enter. Two women stand with him, both masked, one with greying brown hair and the other sleek black. A man in his mid-thirties stands beside them, without a mask. He regards the Comte with a charming smile.

I take another look at the two women. The elder holds a familiar black cigarillo. "That's madame Bellemeure. The lady with her must be Chang Mei." I walk the perimeter of the mural until I'm in hearing distance, and tuck myself behind a pillar, out of sight.

Steel follows, leaning on the red marble beside me. "Suspect?" he whispers.

The Comte had debts. Perhaps Sorelli was caught up in them. "Suspect," I confirm.

"I have to admit," says the stranger, "I was surprised to hear that you had become a patron of the Opera." The military tunic he wears is sky blue, adorned with golden epaulettes. He would be an inch or two shorter than me, if we stood aligned, and his brown hair is as neatly combed as his thin moustache. The man from the soirée, I realise, the hotel owner.

"Not me," the Comte replies. "It is my brother who has become a patron, monsieur."

"Ah, of course. It is your brother then, who is a devotee of the arts."

"I would say that my brother is more of an admirer of this opera's *prima donna*." The Comte's bitterness can't be hidden.

The woman taps her cigarette onto a little holder that she carries in her other hand. "Perhaps the Marquis von Tier could introduce some more worthy heiresses," she suggests. It *is* Bellemeure.

"Indeed," the Marquis says, taking the cue with grace. "My hotel is about to host a very pretty, very *wealthy* young lady from Spain. You were interested in investing—perhaps you and your brother might come and visit."

The Comte looks uncomfortable. "Yes, well. I have not yet fully considered the benefits of your proposition."

"Let's say I cater to a particularly...elite group. The entertainment I offer is unparalleled—at least in Paris. In Austria, we do things differently, but I aim to bring the best that my house has to offer and leave the worst behind."

"Your hotel has been running for less than a year," the Comte replies. "Perhaps, when a little more time has passed—"

"By then, it will be too late. I need an answer soon, Comte."

"And you will have it. For now, I must find my brother." De Chagny gives them a curt bow and marches across the chamber and through the doors that lead backstage. If Raoul is back there, Christine must be, too.

"Entertainment?" Bellemeure asks, in a voice so icy that it stops me from pushing off the column and following him. "I thought we had an agreement."

Von Tier eyes her, still with that charming smile. "Come now, Fraulein—No, it's madame, isn't it?—I must give them some reason to follow me."

"Not by drawing this kind of attention."

"My people are built for violence," he says, "not for pretty words and dresses, like yours. Besides, our deal is complete, is it not? Or is there something else that you want from me?"

They stare at each other for a moment, the Marquis wearing his smile, Bellemeure impenetrable behind her glittering mask.

"Good evening, Marquis," the woman says, the dismissal evident in her voice.

The man bows, clicking his heels together. "Madame. Mademoiselle." He turns and walks away, cutting across the mural's centre, not far from where I stand. Bellemeure tilts her head, as if she's listening to something. Then she turns and looks straight at me.

I pull back behind the column, wondering if she saw me, if I can weave a story that might explain our presence. Von Tier marches past, going straight to the stairs. This close I see that his eyes are black and over-large, as if he'd dilated the irises with drops.

Steel grips my arm so tightly I jump.

"What?" I whisper. "What is it?"

"That man is a Revenant," he says, hoarsely.

"Von Tier? Are you sure?"

"I couldn't smell him before—that woman's cigarette—but I'd recognise that scent anywhere."

I grip his elbow. For all the fierceness of his expression, he looks like he might slide to the floor at any moment. "What does that mean?"

"It means," he says, his jaw clicking, "that we've found our murderer."

"Wait, hold on." I have to pull him back to keep him at the pillar. Bellemeure and Chang Mei have both disappeared. "We don't know that, yet. We only know that he's a demon."

"You saw the burns on that woman's body," he returns, hotly. "Revenants are masters of fire. He's the one we're looking for."

"Even so, we can't start a fight here," I whisper. "We need more information. He's a Marquis, he won't be unprotected, and I doubt he'll be alone, either. Can he smell you?"

"No," Steel rasps. "Revenants can't scent well. They only smell the smoke of their own *flames*—" The guttural agony in his voice throttles the word. Grief and rage not my own surge through me, smashing through walls that weren't prepared for them. We'd been ready to face his mother's killer, not this connection to his father's.

On the other side of the chamber, the doors leading backstage fling open and Christine hurries through. She wears white and silver again, her mask a dainty, feathered thing. Behind her come Raoul and the Comte, arguing in low voices.

"Christine," I call, hoping to distract Steel a moment longer, give myself time to plan.

The woman pauses at my voice and makes her way over to us. The two brothers halt as Raoul tries to follow her and the Comte grabs his arm, hissing something at him.

"Good evening, mademoiselle." Christine's smile carves lines into her cheeks where it's drawn so tight.

"Is everything all right?"

"Everything is fine," she says. "How can I help you, mademoiselle?"

"Do you know anything about the Marquis von Tier?" Steel interjects.

"The Marquis?"

The Comte approaches us, frowning. "What do you want to know about von Tier?" he asks. Raoul takes the opportunity to go to Christine's side, tucking himself into her shadow.

"We have reason to believe that he might have something to do with Sorelli's death," I reply.

"Don't be foolish," the Comte replies. "He is a Marquis." The words aren't heated, just the knee jerk reaction of an aristocrat when his peers are threatened.

"Did he ever meet Sorelli?" I ask Christine.

She rubs a finger under her mask, smoothing a couple of wayward feathers. "Once or twice, yes. He wasn't a paramour, but everyone knew he was looking for people to work at his hotel. He refused the other dancers, though," she adds. "He only asked Sorelli."

Because she was a demon? I glance at Steel, who's gone tense under my hand.

"And he never came back," Christine says. She glances up the stairs towards the rest of the party. Von Tier is no longer in sight, absorbed by the other guests. "Do you really think he had something to do with her murder?"

"Yes," answers Steel, promptly.

"Perhaps," I amend. "It's too early to know for sure. He is, at least, a suspect."

"And if you proved that he did it," she muses, "then it would remove suspicion from the ghost."

It's not a question, but I answer anyway. "Yes."

"Von Tier's a demon," Steel says, making me glare at him, because *for God's sake*. "Just like the ghost."

"What is all this talk of demons?" the Comte demands. "Who are you people?"

I open my mouth to reply and the noise from the party drops. The sudden silence has all of us turning towards the stairs and I let go of Steel, bracing for whatever new attack might come.

It's not an attack. A figure draped in a scarlet cloak and wearing a mask shaped like a skull advances to the top of the stairs. Costumed figures part before him and the opera house fills with whispers. The man's posture is rigid, his arms straight and his hands balled. He keeps a wide space between him and the other guests, and each step looks as though it pains him. His gaze never leaves Christine.

The ghost. I think the words are in my head, but then I realise that people are murmuring them, the realisation spreading as the figure walks towards us. The ghost is here.

He descends the short flight of stairs that lead into the round chamber. It echoes with his footsteps, with the soft drag of his cloak on the marble. He reaches the bottom and pauses, his eyes little more than dim sparks at the centre of the mask's sockets. The entire building seems to hold its breath, waiting for him to speak.

But it's Raoul who breaks the silence.

"Demon!" He starts forward, reaching for a dainty costume sword at his hip. It makes a very real noise as it slides from its sheath. "I won't let you terrorise Christine any longer!"

The Comte grabs his arm. "Don't make a scene, Raoul!"

"Let go of me, Philippe!"

I bound up the stairs and find Dumont and René shouldering their way through the onlookers. "Time to end the party," I tell them.

Dumont spins and starts to shepherd everyone away from the stairs. "Sûreté business!" he calls, startling them. "Everyone outside, please! Now, madames! Messieurs!"

Raoul has wrenched free of his brother's hold, but Christine has his attention. "Is it true?" she asks the ghost, who merely looks at her. "You're a—a devil?"

"He's no one," the Comte says, trying to work his way between the ghost and Raoul. "He's just some deranged lunatic playing us for fools. Arrest him!"

"*Is* it?" Christine asks again, the words strained and high-pitched with desperation, and the ghost's chest deflates as he sighs.

"Devil is a word created by man," he says. "Another might call me angel just as easily. *You* did, after all."

"And you let me." She steps back, towards the stairs. "You let me believe what I wanted to believe."

"I made you great." The teeth of his mask march to the edge of his jaw in a monstrous grin. "Is that not what angels do? Grant prayers?"

"Did you kill my friend?" she asks, her voice low and level, the tendons in her wrists straining.

The ghost regards her for a long moment and even Raoul goes still. "No," he says, finally. "I would never hurt one you cared for." Repressed emotion rings in his voice, making the words tremble as though he and Christine are putting on their own opera.

She nods. "Thank you," she says and Raoul makes a furious sound.

"He is manipulating you," he calls, yanking his sword up into an *en-garde* position. "Do you have a weapon, monster? Or shall I cut you down where you stand?"

With a laugh, the ghost tosses his red cloak over one shoulder. "If you think you can, Vicomte," he mocks.

For God's sake. "Stop them, will you?"

Steel looks at me as though I asked him to step onto burning coals. "*Stop* them?"

"If we're going after von Tier, we don't have time for this nonsense." We've already wasted too much on the ghost's drama.

As I think it, Raoul lunges. His blade stabs through empty air. Another laugh echoes against the marble ceiling and the ghost reappears behind the man.

"Not quite," he taunts. The Comte makes a move as if to intercept and the ghost tuts. "I wouldn't, Comte. My promise does not extend to you."

"Demons do not keep promises," Raoul says, whipping around.

"An interesting gambit, monsieur," the ghost says, "given that I promised *not* to harm you. Or would you like me to?"

Half of me wants to put a bullet in one of them just to make them shut up. "Steel, please."

He makes an exasperated noise but moves to grasp the back of Raoul's coat, gripping the hilt of the sword in his other hand. "Enough," he says, roughly. "Or do you think this is going to endear you to your lover?"

Raoul blanches and twists to look over his shoulder. "Christine—"

But the stairs where she'd been standing are empty. Christine is gone.

CHAPTER NINETEEN

Raoul rushes up the stairs, shouting her name. I hurry after him, cursing the woman. The twin statues that flank the stairs to the upper circle loom over empty space. The guests are gone. There's no sign of Christine.

The ghost is right on my heels, visible now. "Where is she?" he demands, spinning in a circle, his scarlet cloak streaming behind him like a trail of blood. "What have you done with her?"

"I did nothing!" Raoul snaps. "*You* were the one threatening her! You terrified her!"

The ghost growls. "You have a poor affection for her if you think that."

Raoul slashes at him and, instead of disappearing, the ghost seizes the bare metal and tears it from his hold. The sword goes clattering across the floor. The demon advances on Raoul, his figure flickering in and out of view. The Vicomte brings up his fists, as valiant as he is naïve.

"This has nothing to do with Raoul," the Comte protests, though he avoids getting between the two of them.

"Where is she?" the ghost demands, ignoring him. "Where is Christine?"

Dumont appears in the doorway to the lobby and René bumps into him as he stops short. "What is going on?" the agent asks. "We could hear you outside!"

The ghost goes as still as a hunting cat, focused on Raoul. "I should have killed you when I had the chance, Vicomte."

I grab his arm. "Enough!"

Before I know it, his hands are around my throat. "*Do not touch me*," he breathes, his eyes burning in the holes of his mask. "*Hazel!*"

My thoughts click into place like puzzle pieces, revealing half a dozen different paths. Call for help: I'm dead, or the ghost is, if Steel is quick enough. Try to escape: I get hurt and Steel hesitates, meaning I'll probably end up dead. Fight back: I'm *definitely* dead, and then the ghost will be, and who knows how that ends for Steel.

So, I look him in the eye and make my voice very, very cold. "This will not help you find her." My pulse beats strong and fast against his fingers. I wonder if he can feel it through his gloves. "Release me. We have a better chance of finding her together, than alone."

His gaze flickers over my face, searching for something, some crack in my composure. "I have your word that you'll find her."

"You have it," I promise.

He snorts and his hands come away from my throat. It aches, but I suppress the urge to touch it. Steel's at my side in an instant, examining me, his mouth tight.

"I'm unhurt," I murmur. "Did you see mademoiselle Daaé in the foyer?" I ask Dumont.

"I did not notice her, no."

"The *prima donna*?" asks René. "She was with the Marquis." We stare at him.

"The Marquis?" Raoul repeats. "Are you certain?"

"Where?" the ghost asks. "Where did you see her?"

René turns to indicate an area of the foyer and the ghost rushes past him. "We sent all the guests home," adds the Sentinel demon. "I did not see where they went, or if she left with him."

"She knows he's a suspect, why would she—" I stop. She'd asked if proving his guilt would clear the ghost's name, and I'd foolishly said yes. She went to him *because* he's a suspect. I look at the Comte. "She told me the Marquis asked Sorelli to perform at his hotel. Do you know where it is?"

The man glances at his brother, then at the ghost flitting around the foyer. "Republic plaza," he answers. "It is still in the process of being remodelled."

The plaza lies to the north west of the cemetery, where we'd found Sorelli's body. But it's too far for people not to have noticed someone dragging a struggling young woman, or a corpse.

"We'll start there. Comte, you have a relationship with the Marquis, correct?"

The ghost chooses that moment to burst back into our conversation. His cloak and hat are gone, no doubt hurled across the foyer somewhere. "She is not here," he says, his voice pitched high and thin. "We must find her."

Taking heart from my composure, De Chagny ignores him, focusing on my question. "The Marquis is looking for investors, but I have already declined. He won't see me."

I narrow my eyes at him. The conversation I'd overheard hadn't given me that impression.

"Please, Philippe," Raoul begs, his face beseeching. "Please, I love her."

That earns a snarl from the ghost, but de Chagny sighs. "Very well," he says, heavily. "I can request an audience. Perhaps, to-morrow—"

"Now," I interrupt, before the ghost can do more than shriek in outrage. "We go now. Can we rely on the Sûreté's help, Dumont?"

He lets out a self-derogatory laugh. "Not at my request and not against a marquis. I might as well tell them that I want to arrest Sadi Carnot. We're on our own."

"All right," I say. "Then we'd better hurry."

CHAPTER TWENTY

The hotel sprawls alongside the plaza, its fresh cream façade garnished with black railings at each window. Empty planters line the pavement outside, the same grey stone as the road. Our carriage stops by the bronze statue of a woman holding aloft what could be either a torch or a sprig of leaves; it's too dark to tell. When neither man moves to get out, I hold in a sigh.

We'd been too many to take a single cab, so we'd split into two parties. The first, in the carriage behind us, comprises Dumont, René and the de Chagnys. The second, unlucky group consists of me, Steel and the ghost. The latter has his arms folded and stares at us through the holes of his skull-like mask. The embers of his eyes catch the light from the gas lamps on the street; twin specks glittering in the dark.

I'm too tired to bother with niceties. "Get out," I command. I don't need to look at Steel to feel his surprise and I wonder if that's a sign of the lingering ritual spell. I reinforce my order by opening the door and jumping out, wincing as I land in a puddle and icy water drenches my stockings.

The second carriage has stopped just behind us and Raoul is already outside. Only the cab that trots past him without a care keeps him from barrelling across the square towards the hotel. By the time I've paid the driver, Steel and the ghost have disembarked and are glaring at each other.

Irritation makes my skin itch, but I can't blame it on either of them. If I hadn't wasted so much time on the ghost's trail, on this ridiculous operatic drama, we might have found von Tier before now. We might have already solved the case.

The bronze woman makes a decent gathering point—other groups linger under her gaze and one man slumps against her plinth, steaming with the scent of alcohol.

"Is that the place?" Raoul glowers at the building as though he could burn it down with the fire of his glare.

"Don't be foolish," I tell him. He blinks, darting a look at me, but the words seem to derail his train of thought. "If we're going in, we need a plan," I add.

"*If*, mademoiselle?" the ghost asks, silkily dangerous, but Steel relaxes, as though he's stepped onto familiar terrain.

"You know the Marquis, Comte," he says. "You can handle the introductions."

"We'll come with you," I add—unnecessarily, perhaps, for Steel isn't much better than Raoul for how he scowls at the building.

"I'm not staying here," interjects Raoul. His face twists in anger and grief. My heart aches for him, even though I scold it for the deficiency. "You can't make me."

"Stay close, then," I reply, hoping I don't regret it.

"And do you have an order for me, mademoiselle?" The ghost's voice dares me to give him one.

I refrain from touching my throat. "How long can you stay out of sight?"

He bristles. "As long as necessary."

"Good. Then don't wander off."

Dumont examines the hotel, his gaze lingering on the two guards in blue and gold livery that flank the hotel's tall metal gates. "They may be prepared for a Sûreté agent," he says and adds, with a wry smile, "I *am* fairly distinctive."

"Try to find a back entrance," I suggest. "We might have better luck with the servants, anyway. I can't imagine they'll have Revenants cooking meals or cleaning suites, but there might be others."

"Such as copper class demons," he muses. "I see."

I realise no one has voiced their disagreement or challenged me, but there's no time to wonder why. Brushing my hands together, more of a nervous gesture than to shed the nonexistent dust from my hands, I nod and say, "After you, Comte."

The man's mouth quivers, but he glances once at Raoul and then marches towards the hotel. Dumont touches his forehead at me and he and René lope away. The ghost shimmers out of view and the rest of us follow de Chagny across the square.

Instead of slinking past the guards as though he has something to hide, the Comte pauses in front of them. "Is the Marquis inside?" he asks, cool and confident. "I have an answer for his proposal. The name is de Chagny."

They glance at each other—human, by their eyes and the way they move—and reply, "Yes, monsieur. The Marquis is at dinner."

The Comte sweeps past them before they can finish speaking, his chin cocked arrogantly high, his shoulders slanted as though no weight has ever touched them. We move into a large square courtyard and he murmurs, almost to himself, "I may not be able to trade on coin, anymore, but I still have my name. *Our* name," he adds, with a bite, and Raoul looks away.

The entrance lies on the far side of the courtyard, adding another few minutes to our approach, as if we're petitioning a king. No more guards bar the way, however, and we slip through the black double doors without being challenged.

Inside, the hotel is a picture of grand elegance. Crimson fabric, gold stucco and plush carpeting, all reminiscent of a kind of imperial irreverence that grants the hotel a grand air. Guests wear smart dressclothes and silk gowns. An open set of doors lead to a room from which comes the clink of glasses and loud conversation. Even the Halloween party we attended in London hadn't matched this level of luxury.

De Chagny pauses, looking floored. "I..."

"The concierge," I suggest, eyeing the desk that lies across the lobby, manned by a handsome young man with polished gold buttons marching down his uniform.

As the Comte nods and makes his way over, I take a moment to examine the guests. There are less than I'd thought initially, the lush brocaded curtains and gleaming wooden tables filling more space than the people that flit between them. And the women outnumber the men by at least three to one.

I turn to Steel, hoping to ask him about their humanity, but his gaze roams over the lobby and his fingers tap against his thighs. "Is there anything we should know about Revenants?" I ask, instead.

"Don't let them touch you," he responds immediately, as if he'd already been thinking it. "Their fire dies soon after it leaves their skin, so the further away you are, the safer you'll be."

I should have asked Dumont for a second revolver. "Anything else?"

"They're bad trackers; they won't smell us coming."

He'd said as much at the opera house. "Well, I suppose that's something."

"Mademoiselle Lyr?" The voice startles me and I spin around. The young woman who'd acted as Bellemeure's companion stands in front of me. Her voice is smooth and throaty, with a light accent. "Are you here to see madame Bellemeure?"

"No," I reply, shaking my confusion away. "We're here to see Marquis von Tier. Do you know where he is?"

She pauses. Her gaze moves across each of us, then to the Comte at reception. "He and madame Bellemeure are engaged to dine together. Perhaps you would care to join them." It's not phrased as a question, but she bows and opens her hand to indicate a side room. "I will engage the Comte," she adds, as I glance over to him.

"Thank you." I incline my head and follow her directions, checking to make sure Steel and Raoul are with me. I don't dare to ask if the ghost is close—if there *are* Revenant demons nearby, they might hear me.

The room we enter is a modest parlour, set up for an informal meal. The rest of the room is decorated with the same care as the lobby: golden bookcases grow out of the walls and chairs sit tucked into the corners, cushioned in red velvet. Bellemeure lounges in one by an open window, her ever-present cigarette dangling from one hand.

Something flashes over her face as Steel enters and her eyelids drop down quickly, veiling the emotion. "It is a delight to see you again, mademoiselle, messieurs. Mei, will you bring us something to drink?"

Mei, who had just entered alongside the Comte, bows and retreats.

"Forgive me the habit." Bellemeure taps ash into a small dish on the windowsill. A wintry breeze blows the smoke back inside and I repress a shiver. "It is becoming quite trendy, you see, and I am not one to fall behind the latest fashions." This is said with a smirk that I think is aimed at self-deprecating. I eye her gown, at least ten years out of style. But then my sense of fashion is, at best, minimal.

"Not at all," I return. "Mademoiselle Chang told us that you were dining with the Marquis."

"Where is he?" Raoul cuts in, quivering.

"The Marquis? I believe he should be here in a moment." The woman smiles at Raoul, not unkindly. "Why don't you sit down? I'm certain I can help with whatever it is that brought you here. What *does* bring you here, if I may enquire?"

Raoul opens his mouth, clearly about to tell her everything, and I interject, "The Comte is interested in discussing a potential investment. Although it does not seem as though the Marquis requires it. The hotel is beautifully decorated."

Her eyes go vacant. "Von Tier can always use money."

"Why?" I ask—too bold—but she smiles again.

Mei sweeps into the room holding a tray of glasses. She offers one to the Comte first, who takes it with a stiff nod, sweat beading at his brow, then to Raoul, who downs half the glass in a single gulp, red staining the corner of his mouth.

"Ah," says Bellemeure, delicately. "Perhaps I should have called for something stronger. But French wine is the best in the world. Or, so I am told."

Steel and I take a glass each when offered, and Bellemeure has the last, taking a small sip. Her long nails are painted a dark colour that looks almost black against the ruby red wine. Steel and the Comte, who seemed to have been waiting for her to drink, mirror her. I cup the glass with my other hand, swirling the crimson liquid. I don't want anything to cloud my mind.

"How do you know the Marquis, madame?" I ask.

She stabs her cigarette out on the dish, crushing the paper into a twisted stump. "He helped me with a task, some months ago. Although it seems our collaboration will be short-lived."

"Oh? Why is that?"

"Because Mei is going to kill him."

The words ring in my ears. "I beg your pardon?"

Bellemeure smiles. "Von Tier is a member of House Asmodeus. Well, he was. It is his greatest desire to create a new Revenant House, here in Paris."

"What?" Steel grits out.

On my other side, the Comte stumbles, clutching at a bookcase to keep him from falling. Raoul slumps in his chair. His glass rolls onto the floor, spilling wine onto the carpet.

No, no, no.

"That is what you came for, is it not?" Bellemeure says. Mei circles around to her side, watching us, and Bellemeure hands the woman her glass, still full. "You and the Leviathan."

The air seems to freeze in my lungs. "You knew?"

"Of course I did, my dear," she says, as if pitying me. "They may call themselves diamond, but my kind have been around for far longer."

A cool wind swims through the room, clearing the last lingering scent of smoke. Steel makes a tight, distressed noise. The glass falls from his hand, thunks onto the floor.

"What are you?" he whispers.

"Your ignorance is far from impressive," she replies, her thin brows two perfect arches.

He staggers and I lunge to hold him, but his weight drags me to my knees. The Comte slides to the floor, boneless. Raoul's head is already tipped back, his eyes closed.

The ghost. The ghost might—

The door opens and von Tier strides into the room. Steel lets out a low growl and struggles to stand.

"Well," the man says, "this is a surprise. Are they gifts? Bellemeure, you shouldn't have."

"Thankfully, I did not." Bellemeure stands and Mei closes the window behind her. "They know what you are. In fact, I believe they came to kill you.

"Ha! How interesting. And you stopped them for me?"

Mei hands her a pair of dove grey gloves and Bellemeure pulls them on, running the silk up to her elbows. "I have other plans," she says. "But this one may interest you." She gestures to Steel, who is leaning fully on me, his breathing ragged.

"Stay away," I spit.

"A child of Leviathan?" von Tier says, with no small degree of wonder. "Did you *miss* one, madame?"

Miss one?

"Take a closer look."

Von Tier bends at the waist, considering us. I draw away, tugging Steel to me protectively, but the Marquis grips my arm and flings me aside. My head bounces against the wall. Pain dazzles me and I slump, trying to blink away the black spots dancing over my vision.

The demon grasps Steel's hair, examining his face. He whistles. "My demons will pay highly to fight one of Lucifer's brats."

"Don't touch him." My voice comes out little more than a whisper.

Von Tier releases Steel and the demon collapses like spilled water. "First a *prima donna*, then this." The Revenant chuckles. "What a profitable day."

"What do you have to do with the *prima donna*?" Bellemeure asks.

"She came to evidence her suspicions. I thought I'd keep her."

"That is not what we agreed."

"Would you rather I throw her into the ring, too?" His voice is soft with delight, as if he wants Bellemeure to say yes.

"I would rather you stop altogether."

He tuts. "If I am to build my own House, I must provide a reason for my fellow Revenants to join me. My brother would never countenance something like this."

"For good reason," replies Bellemeure, her voice hard. But she turns away from him and gestures to Mei. "Have the guards dispose of them," she tells her and then asks von Tier, "You have somewhere you use for this purpose, I assume?"

"Of course, madame," the Marquis replies, with a smirk. "I am a most proficient host."

I shift to Steel's side, trying not to be noticed. "Steel," I whisper. "*Steel.*"

He doesn't twitch.

The click of footsteps makes me look up. Mei meets my gaze, her face implacable. She draws back her arm.

"Don't—"

I see a flash of her fist and then nothing.

AGENT E. WILSON

Eve is so busy trying to predict Monaghan's reaction that she stumbles straight into the painter. He mutters something in a language she doesn't recognise and crouches to mop up the droplets of paint she'd made him spill. She splutters out an excuse, halted by the whirlwind of activity in the lobby. Half the walls are already a crisp, clean white, lightening the entire room. Another labourer perches on a ladder in the centre, halfway through installing an ornate chandelier. A stuffed adult tiger is being lugged up the stairs by three more men, generating an outcry when its tail scrapes against the freshly painted wall.

"He's moving faster than I expected."

She glances at Cassius. "What does that mean?"

"It means," he says, heavily, "that we should have killed that demon when we had the chance."

Ignoring his odd attitude, Eve skirts around the ladder and heads for the kitchen. "Maia, are they restocking the taxid—"

She stops short. The man standing at the range is not Maia.

"*Vite, vite!*" he shouts, to someone in the scullery. "And knead 'arder," he says to a young cook at the worktable bullying a ball of dough. "Put your shoulders into it."

"Who the hell are you?" Eve asks, forgetting to be polite. Maia doesn't let anyone cook from her range, and she doesn't even tolerate Hazel helping in the scullery. "Where's Maia?"

"The Agency's 'ousekeeping is under new management," he replies, his French accent thickening the words almost to incomprehension. The man's cheeks are rosy from the heat of the fire, his curly brown hair tucked under a puffed white hat. "Out, please. I won't have maids in my kitchen."

Eve contemplates throwing her dagger into his hat. His head can't be big enough to fill it. "My name's Agent Wilson," she says. "And this is *Maia's* kitchen."

He regards her with derision and replies, "No longer. Now, out! Out, I say!" He advances as if he's prepared to throw her out with his own hands, and he's such a broad bear of a man that she's not sure he wouldn't succeed.

"I'm speaking to Monaghan," she threatens, but his reply is a contemptuous *bof*.

"Out with the old," Cassius says, as they escape.

Eve takes the stairs two at a time, dodging the tiger, who's gotten stuck in the balustrade. "Maia!" she shouts.

Khurana meets her on the first floor, her posture slumping when she sees Eve. "You have returned," she says, the words rushing out on a sigh of relief. "Are you hurt?"

"No, I'm fine. What's wrong?"

The agent casts a look at the workers struggling to extract the animal's tail and motions her along the corridor. She and Isis both wear heavy coats and gloves, and a bonnet dangles from Isis' hand.

"Were you on your way out?"

"We were coming to find you," she says, walking so fast that Eve has to work to keep pace. "You had a case, yes?"

"Yes. A Blood Drinker in the East End." Isis makes a hissing sound and Eve throws her an astonished look. "If you think I can't handle myself—"

"I believe *I* was the one handling things."

"It is not that," Khurana replies, speaking over Cassius. "You are skilled, but you are inexperienced. A demon of that calibre should not be confronted alone. Monaghan should not have sent you." Khurana rarely lets her emotions seep into her face, so the clear worry in her drawn expression makes Eve tense.

"What's going on downstairs?" she asks. "Where's Maia?"

"Gone."

Eve feels as if a thread inside her has been cut without warning and flaps, untethered. "*Gone?*"

"He has dispatched her to a colonial office in Calcutta. She left an hour ago."

Eve halts in the middle of the corridor. "He sent her back to India?" Without even giving her time to say goodbye?

"Fear not," Khurana says, her grey eyes softening. "I have put her up at a hotel. We have a few weeks before the Indian office reports her absence."

"This is starting to sound like a plot against the Commissioner," drawls Cassius, leaning against the wall and propping his foot on it. "Another man might call that treason."

"It is lucky, then, that you are not a man," Khurana counters. Both she and Isis hold themselves with restrained energy, and it's seeping into Eve's limbs, making her want to bounce on her feet—or run.

"I don't understand what's going on."

The noise on the stairs drops. Eve turns and stiffens as Monaghan strides down the corridor, his demon at his shoulder.

"Wilson, you're back sooner than I expected." His head tilts and his green-eyed gaze flits between them. "Where is the demon?"

Eve pauses and then says, "It wasn't there. I was just asking Agent Khurana for her assistance in tracking it down."

In the stillness as they regard each other, the entire corridor seems to shrink, closing in on her like a cage.

"That will not be necessary," Monaghan says. "I have a more urgent case for you. You will pursue miss Locke."

The words take a full minute to register. "You want me to go after Hazel?"

"The police agree that she took the ferry to Boulogne. You will follow her from there. Cassius is familiar with her methods from the Ripper case," he continues, indicating the Phantom demon, who regards him with a fixed expression. "He can help you."

Khurana shifts at her side. "Professor," she says, "as a Hound agent, I can better support—"

"No. You and Horner will go to Ireland. I have received reports of dissent that must be investigated." He folds his hands behind his back. "Agent Wilson is to leave straight away."

Eve jolts. "But—"

"We can delay no longer. We must bring back miss Locke and her demon to face justice."

Khurana's hand clamps down on her arm. "Thank you, Professor," the woman says. "This is a great honour."

Eve bows at the waist, unable to muster the grace for a curtsy. She takes a moment to glare at the floor. *This* is what the strings were leading to. *This* is the payment that she's going to have to make to keep her position, prove her loyalty.

Stay calm, her mind says, in Hazel's voice. She straightens, her expression under control. "Thank you, sir."

"I don't need to remind you, Agent," he says, "that a great deal depends on the reputation of this Agency. Without the support of the government and Her Majesty the Queen, we will not have the means to protect the lives of those who work here. I hope I make myself clear." His gaze is steady, his expression impassive, so he can't mean it the way it sounds—as a threat.

"What about the Blood Drinker?"

"Tiberius will take care of it." The Reaper demon regards them inscrutably. "You have one hour, Agent." He waits for them to acknowledge the order and then leaves, ignoring the workers on the stairs who all stop to tug their forelocks.

"Come," the agent commands. "We will help you pack." She and Isis lead the way in silence and even Cassius offers no barbs to pierce it.

They enter Eve's room and Khurana goes to the small trunk each member of the Agency owns, swinging it onto the bed. The thin mattress bounces.

"Be easy," murmurs Isis, taking it from her. "I will do it."

Khurana takes a step back, breathing out and clutching her cane in a grip that makes the leather of her glove creak.

"If he wanted to send someone after Hazel," Eve says, still trying to piece together whatever this puzzle is, "then he should send you and Jacob. It's a retrieval mission, not a case." And, as Khurana said, she's inexperienced.

"But he is not," the agent says. "He is sending you."

Cassius gives a crow of laughter, making them jump. "You really are naïve," he tells Eve.

"I'm in no mood for cryptic comments," she snaps. "If you have something to say, say it."

"The Agency has gone from an under-funded embarrassment of an institution to a powerful branch of the government, headed up by someone second in authority only to the Prime Minister. All on the back of *one case*." He bites off each word. "Isn't that convenient?"

Isis, partway through folding one of Eve's dresses, pauses. "The Ripper case was a series of murders," she says, in her quiet voice. "Most likely committed by Agent Rayne."

Cassius flicks his hand in a dismissive gesture. "Rayne wasn't smart enough to build this kind of web, and your tall freckled friend doesn't have the heart for it. I should have seen it earlier," he adds, with another dark chuckle.

"Get to the point."

"It's your Professor," he says. "Puppeteer, I should call him, given the strings that he's pulling. And now he's sending you off to prove your loyalty or die a traitor. I wonder if he knew how old the Blood Drinker was," he muses, "or if he meant for her to kill us. Rather a neat ending, if she had."

"You're grasping at straws," Eve replies, just as Khurana says, "That is unfounded speculation. Where is your proof?"

Eve frowns at her. "You can't think he's telling the truth?"

She and Isis exchange looks. "I will not discount any possibility," Khurana responds, after a moment. "The fact that he is sending you and not me... It is odd, is it not?"

"I'm closer to Hazel. I know her habits." Eve shifts, uncomfortable with how defensive the words sound.

"And what of you?" Khurana asks Cassius. "If you go with Eve, will you protect her?"

"How long do you think I'll live without her?" he counters. "He's already started purging England of its rogue demons. Without the Agency, I'm dead. The only way I survive is if *she* survives."

"I suppose that must do."

Eve raises her hands. "Wait. Are you saying that I *should* go after Hazel?"

"Perhaps this is why she ran," suggests Isis. "She discovered Monaghan's betrayal."

"If true, then we are *all* betrayed," Khurana says, casting us back into silence.

If it's true, then they have much, much bigger problems than an elderly Blood Drinker lurking in the East End.

"I'll find Hazel and bring her back," Eve decides. "She can help figure out what to do next. Will you both be all right in the meantime?"

"We will manage," is Khurana's response, which does little to set her mind at ease.

Someone knocks on the door. Cassius, the closest, pulls it open and dons a charming smile. "Yes?" he asks.

A servant Eve's never seen before drops a shallow curtsy. "There is a carriage waiting for miss Wilson."

"Agent Wilson," she and Khurana correct, at the same time.

The servant looks thrown and Cassius shuts the door on her. "Our time is up," he announces. "I hope you're ready."

She bares her teeth at him. "I hope *you* are."

"Do not tarry," Khurana orders, helping Isis snap the trunk closed. "We may not yet know what Monaghan's plans are, but separated, we are weaker."

Eve nods and takes the trunk. There should be words to mark this moment, to soften the pain of parting that she feels like a blow, but none come. She was never that good with words, anyway.

"Be safe," she says and follows Cassius out the door.

CHAPTER TWENTY-ONE

Wide green fields stretch out before me and I inhale the scent of lilies and fresh grass. From somewhere not that distant comes the friendly babble of a brook. It's still early. I can walk to town and back before mother prepares dinner. Or I could head into the woods, hunt the stag I saw yesterday.

(I don't know how to hunt)

A light strain of music reaches me. Town, then, if father's already playing; he'll have forgotten to visit the market. My fingers itch for a bow, though, for the lilt of Schubert or the soft aching notes of Chopin.

(I can't play)

In answer, the brook behind me gurgles. I inhale, exhale, calm the water again. Control. I must remember control. Flexing my hands, I examine the callouses on my fingers, the new ones the violin's strings have left. Cheap catgut, but it's not like we can afford better.

(Not my hands)

I jerk awake, a blinding pain in my head that throbs in time with my heartbeat. My fingers and toes are almost numb with cold.

The Marquis. Steel.

I open my eyes a sliver. At first all is dark, until faint grey light picks out furrows in the surface in front of me. Old stone. I keep still, moving only my eyes. A plinth, topped by a crumbling steeple: a tomb.

"Beeilung," someone mutters, close by, and someone else responds, "Ya, ya."

The vibration of heavy footsteps reverberates through my limbs as they approach. I hold my breath, peering through my lashes.

A tall, broad man enters my field of vision, dressed in a long coat and leather gloves. He leans down, partially eclipsed by the tomb. He lifts something, using both hands. Then there's a sharp crack. He hefts the thing over his shoulder and it's then that I see the golden hair, the moustache. The Comte.

With a grunt, the stranger dumps the body. It disappears with a delayed thump. A grave, the same as Sorelli. We're in the cemetery.

Planting my hands on the ground, I shove myself upright and run. One of the strangers shouts something—German speakers; von Tier's men—and their heavy footsteps come thumping after me.

My brain informs me that Mei knocked me unconscious with a blow to the temple and that running might not be the best decision. I ignore it, skirting a divot in the uneven cobbles and then swinging left to dart between a line of mausoleums. The man grabs my arm and yanks me to a halt, making me stumble backwards. Steel's warning about letting them touch me flashes through my mind. I go limp. Surprised, the stranger drops me, releasing my arm.

I kick out at him, relishing the yelp when my boot connects with the side of his knee. Cursing follows and he reaches for me again. I twist away from his grip. A second man lopes into view behind him.

"Fang sie!" he calls, his voice hard but low, as if he's afraid of being overheard.

My attacker regards me. His eyes are black, the irises so wide there's little white to be seen. A Revenant demon.

Someone yelps. Both of us turn, startled, towards the man who'd shouted. He claws at his chest, where the tip of a black rail protrudes. It's sucked back through his body with a hideous squelch and then it stabs through his throat, spurting blood over the cobblestones.

The demon next to me lets out a wordless shout and rushes forward as his companion falls. The air ripples, a figure flickering in and out of sight. So, the ghost didn't abandon us.

I grab onto the Revenant's coat and haul backwards with all my strength. It only makes him stumble, but it's enough. The ghost appears before him and slams his makeshift weapon through the demon's heart. The meaty sound of the rail entering his torso makes me gag and I drop my hold. The ghost ignores me, dealing a second precise blow to the throat.

Only when the Revenant has fallen does he speak. "Running was idiotic," he says. "You made things difficult for me."

"Oh, *forgive* me," I snap, gingerly touching the wound on my head. "If you'd done that earlier, I wouldn't have needed to run."

"I had to look for a weapon." He flings the rail into a tuft of grass on a nearby tomb. It looks like one of the prongs from the fences that line the larger mausoleums.

"Is it blessed?"

"No. It is much easier to kill demons than most would have you believe."

"And that's why you couldn't save the Comte?" I ask.

The pause before his response is too long.

"You *let* him die?"

"It is the Vicomte whom I promised to protect. You should be grateful that I deigned to assist you at all."

It annoys me that I *am* grateful. Whatever skills I might have, I'm human. I wouldn't have survived against the two demons for much longer. "If you care that little, why didn't you stay at the hotel to find Christine?"

"Mademoiselle," he replies, "I am a genius. I am not suicidal."

"Right," I mutter. Both corpses seep blood, coating the cobblestones in thick tacky liquid that shines even in the darkness. More deaths to add to my tally.

I flex my hands. These were different. These were necessary.

"Hide the bodies," I say. "We don't want the police on our tail."

He makes an outraged sound, but I march back to the place where I'd woken. The Vicomte is there, curled on his side, still unconscious. I take a breath, brace myself, and shake him awake.

"Vicomte—Raoul. Wake up."

His eyes flutter open. "Christine...?" he murmurs. When he sees me, his face falls. "What—what happened? Where in God's name are we?"

"A cemetery. Raoul, there's something—"

"Where is Christine? Where is my brother?"

He must see something in my face. He pushes me aside and scrabbles to his feet. Upright, he wavers a moment, then stumbles towards a rectangle of dark open earth.

I crouch on the cobbles, my mind numb, watching as he freezes at the edge. Without a sound, he sinks to his knees, his hands falling limply between them.

"Revenant demons," I say, after a long moment, reluctant to press him but conscious of the time draining away as we wait. "The same ones that have Christine." He twitches at her name and I hate myself for using it. But the guilt doesn't stop me from adding, "If we hurry, we might still be able to find her."

"And how do you propose to do that?" The ghost is still wearing his death's mask, although a small crack runs from the socket to the temple. "If you had not noticed, mademoiselle, you are human."

"I am well aware, monsieur." Standing, I brush mud off my skirt, using the moment to think. Bellemeure is planning to have von Tier killed—if she'd been telling the truth, that is—so she and Mei will be focused on him. They won't be happy to see Raoul and I return, alive.

And then there's Steel.

I turn in a circle. Jagged tombstones and crypts sit silent and dark, a deserted city of the dead. I look again at the grave where the Comte's body lies—the headstone has a chunk missing where Steel tore off the rose marker. The same grave that Sorelli had lain in a week ago. Dumont can't have had time to get it filled in.

How had they brought us here?

The ghost shifts. "Mademoiselle—"

"Quiet, please," I say, absently. "I'm thinking."

"The fact that you must work at the task does not inspire me to confidence."

A carriage could have conveyed us, but in the crowded streets surrounding Republic plaza, the risk of being noticed is high. If it was me, I'd want a better chance of security, a way of moving bodies that wouldn't be seen by anyone, not even the guests—

An image flashes through my mind: the dirt floor in the catacombs, marked by footsteps.

"Is there an entrance to the catacombs near here?"

The ghost gestures to his left. "There are entrances everywhere."

I take a few steps in the direction he indicated. There is a narrow set of steps beside the high wall that encloses the cemetery, leading to a bolted metal door.

"Meet us there, will you? And if you can get the door open, I'd appreciate it."

He mutters something uncomplimentary but goes, deciding to give up on arguing for the moment.

I drop down by Raoul's side. "I know this is difficult," I begin, my voice as gentle as I can make it, "and if you'd prefer to wait here, I'll go on alone." I don't bother counting the ghost. "But if you want to find Christine, then we need to leave *now*."

He lets out a grunt of acknowledgement. I think for a moment that he's going to stay, but then he lurches to his feet. "Where is she?" he asks, his voice thick.

"I assume they're using the catacombs as tunnels. We can follow them back to the hotel."

Raoul runs both hands through his hair, dishevelling the golden locks. "Very well. After you, mademoiselle." He follows me without a glance at the grave, his walk lurching, unsteady. I'm not sure if that's because of grief or a lasting side effect of whatever Bellemeure used to drug us.

The metal door stands open on an unlit tunnel. "Well, mademoiselle?" the ghost asks, from his position lounging in the shadows.

I step inside, looking for—ah. A lantern sits against the wall, along with a box of matches. When lit, it illuminates dry cracked ground and mud walls. The skulls must be deeper underground.

"Shall we?" I ask and march forward without waiting for a response.

⁓⁓⁓

It's not long before the tunnel turns into stairs heading down. I have to place my feet sideways to fit the steps. We spiral deeper, spinning around a thick stone column. Sooner than I expect, the stairs straighten and we emerge into another tunnel, the ceiling so low I have to duck my head. As I do, I notice the prints. Boots, and more than one set.

"Someone was here." They blur in my vision, muddled by the pain throbbing in my temple.

"Likely they belong to some aristocratic buffoon, come to see the corpses," the ghost mocks. "These tombs are a pleasant day out for rich families with nothing to do."

The walls continue for some time, then my hand slips into empty air. As I move the lantern, the light illuminates an alcove stacked with leering skulls. Their black eye sockets seem to laugh at me.

"Are these tunnels underneath the entire city?" Something—whether it's the skulls or the risk of discovery—makes me whisper.

"The cemeteries were diseased." It's Raoul that responds, pulled out of his despair. "My father brought me down here as a child," he continues. "I had nightmares for months afterwards. Philippe would—" He cuts himself off, lapsing into silence.

"There is nothing to fear from the dead," murmurs the ghost, though even he keeps his voice down. "The living, on the other hand, are another matter."

"No *real* ghosts haunting the opera, then?" I ask, a poor attempt at alleviating the gloom.

"Not yet, although I can make the effort to provide some, if you wish."

"I'd rather you didn't."

The prints continue and we follow them. Our footsteps sound muffled, and even the rhythm of our breathing is swallowed by the tunnel.

"Wait." Raoul has stopped and leans against the wall, his head low. "I need—I need a moment."

I'd been walking fast, keen to find Steel. "Of course," I reply, biting down on my impatience. "Are you all right?"

"My head is swimming." He puts one hand to his forehead. "I don't know what she put in that wine, but it's stronger than anything I ever had when I was on leave."

"I would have thought a sailor would have a harder head," the ghost mutters.

"I'm not a sailor anymore." Raoul looks at the demon with a shadow of a smile. "I came back to help Philippe with the estate and then I met Christine."

They assess each other. I refrain from tapping my foot and ask, "Can you walk?"

"Yes. Yes, I'm sorry. Let's go." He pushes himself off the wall and we continue.

There are more skulls than wall, now. The light picks up the curve of bone, the holes between teeth. I tuck my hand under my elbow to keep the lantern aloft, ignoring the ache in my head as best I can. Ahead, the tunnel bends and I can't see around its corner.

Are those voices? I stop before the curve, tilting my head to hear better. Whoever they are, they're a way off, but they'll see the light coming well before we reach them.

I gesture at the ghost and he comes close enough to hear my whisper.

"Can you hear what they're saying?"

A pause, then he replies, "Not well. They speak German."

"You don't understand it?"

He scoffs under his breath. "There are indeed some languages that I cannot speak, mademoiselle."

"Can you at least tell me how many of them are there?"

Even through his mask, I recognise his look of annoyance.

"Fine. I hope you're prepared for a fight."

"Are *you*?" the ghost replies, as predictable as ever.

Shielding the lantern, I swing around the curve. The tunnel stretches onwards, dark save for a single light a few dozen feet away. A light that reveals two cloaked figures carrying a woman in a white dress.

"*Christine*," moans Raoul, as if the sight hurts him, and before I can react he lets out a ringing shout and races past me down the tunnel.

The two figures drop her. I'm already running to catch up, sending my lantern's light jerking over empty eyes and soulless grins. If I only had a *weapon*—

Raoul punches the first man in the jaw, the full force of his not inconsiderable weight behind it. The demon stumbles back. But the second reaches for him, flames flickering around his fingers like silk caught in a strong wind.

"Don't let them touch you!" I shriek and Raoul jerks back. Not quickly enough. The demon grasps his shoulder, wringing a cry from Raoul. The scent of sizzling flesh fills the tunnel, making my stomach turn.

"Raoul!" It takes me a moment to recognise the voice. Christine darts behind the demon and aims a kick at his legs. Shadows surge over the wall as though we're trapped in some kind of terrible play.

"*Move*," spits the ghost and I hasten to get out of his way. He launches himself at the Revenant holding Raoul, seizes its head and twists.

The second demon turns on the ghost. I heft the heavy lantern and slam it into the back of his head. Glass shatters and oil spills over his body and onto the floor. It catches fire instantly and the flames lick at my hands. I throw myself out of the way, my hand clenched on the lantern's metal frame. The hit was enough to drive the demon to his knees and I swing it a second time. The metal connects with a soft crunch. Dark liquid blots the dirt.

The other demon writhes in the ghost's grip, raking at his face, but his flames sputter ineffectually against the mask. A splintering sound cuts off his struggles and the demon falls limp.

The last demon uses the skulls in the walls to haul himself to his feet. I go to swing the lantern again, but the frame is twisted and broken. I throw it to the ground and use my weight to pry off one of the metal prongs. I grab it and hold it out, putting my other hand behind it to absorb the impact.

The Revenant runs straight into it. It sinks into his torso with a sickening sound that has me back in London, staring Rayne in the face. I blink it away.

This man is not human, though, and he stumbles away, jerks the metal out of him. It hasn't killed him.

The ghost locks arms around him, one hand on his chin, the other on his shoulder. In a quick movement, he snaps the demon's neck. The body collapses on its front and I'm grateful I don't have to look at its face any longer.

Breathing hard, I push hair out of my eyes and bend down for the torch. "Wounds?" I ask, lifting it.

The ghost shakes out his hands. The palms of his gloves have burnt right off, leaving scraps of leather dangling from his blistering fingers. "Nothing that will not heal," he says.

But Raoul is slumped on the floor. My heart shudders. If I've got him killed, him *and* his brother—

"It's a burn," Christine says, peeling back the collar of his shirt. He whimpers and she hurriedly lets go. "I think he'll be all right, but he needs treatment, a compress or something." She looks at me, desperation in her eyes. "I need to get him out of here."

"Go back the way we came," I direct. "It leads up to the cemetery. Can you take him home from there?"

She bites her lip and tries to get him to stand, but he drags her back down, a dead weight. "I need help." She looks not at me, but at the ghost.

"Leave him here," the demon responds. "It is not as though he will be missed."

"Please," she says, ignoring his snide comment. "I'm not leaving without him."

The ghost heaves a sigh. He bends and hefts Raoul to his feet, supporting him with an arm around his side. "Hurry, then. The sooner I am back at the opera, the better." He starts off.

Christine rubs her arms. "Will you be all right?" she asks me.

"Don't worry about me." I watch the ghost leave with trepidation, but I can't keep them here, not with Raoul injured. "There are Sûreté agents inside. I'll find them."

She nods. "The entrance to the hotel is up that ladder. They were going to get rid of me—I wasn't *accommodating* enough," she adds, with a grimace.

"Thank you. Be safe," I say and she's gone, along with Raoul and the ghost, the sound of their retreat eaten by the darkness.

I turn to the ladder. A small rose has been carved into the wall beside it. Taking a deep breath, I begin to climb.

CHAPTER TWENTY-TWO

I crawl into a room no larger than a closet, the earthen walls of the tunnels yielding to whitewashed plaster and smooth stone flooring. There's a door leading out and I press my ear to it. The murmur from the other side is distant. I risk cracking it open.

The three-inch gap reveals a corridor, papered in cream and gold, more doors sprouting along it. At the far end, one stands open, and through it comes the sound of shouting and jeers. I creep towards it.

Men in top hats and tailcoats roam a balcony, yelling encouragement or taunts at the flat square pit beneath them. Two figures grapple on the sand—neither are Steel, thank God. Their expressions are tense and desperate, and I'm reminded of the dog fights held in Whitechapel's back alleys. Someone is even calling out bets. This must be what von Tier meant by 'entertainment'.

They'd have to keep the competitors nearby, under lock and key. Steel must be here, somewhere.

I move back along the corridor, checking the doors nearest the ring first. Each one is marked with the same rose symbol as the grave and they lead to more empty corridors. One opens on a carpeted staircase with a red rope strung across the entrance.

A bone-shattering crack comes from the fighting ring, spurring a fresh flurry of bets. I need to hurry.

The next door opens onto a dim passage. Light glimmers at the far end and from it comes the regular clinking of metal. I'm about to move on when a distant corner of my mind flares with emotion; anger and despair, smothered in an odd kind of haze. Steel?

Quickly, I stride down the passage, trying to look as though I belong. At the end, the walls turn into rows of cells. Seated on a single chair outside is a guard. He taps his boot on the nearest cell door, slumped against the wall. A pistol dangles from his belt.

As I pass the cells, I glance through the bars. Half are empty. The other half are filled with lone inhabitants, all prostrate and silent. In the shadows in one, propped up against the wall, is Steel.

"Lazing around?" I ask and the guard jumps, sitting up straight and glancing around wildly. "I should report you to the Marquis for sleeping on the job."

"I—I wasn't sleeping." He looks me up and down, a frown growing as he takes in my dress and muddy boots. His eyes are a faded blue; human. "Who're—"

I override him. "Von Tier wants the Dragon for the next fight. Open his cell, then go check on the two who were dealing with that *prima donna*. They haven't returned."

He blinks. "But—"

"I don't have all day," I snap, letting very real frustration bleed into my voice. "Or do I need to call the Marquis to make you obey? Or perhaps mademoiselle Chang?" I add, gambling.

"No, no." He springs to his feet, fumbling for the keys, though he still eyes me with doubt.

I go to stand by Steel's door and cross my arms, the picture of impatience.

He fits an old key into the cage door and shoves it open. "What did you say your name was?"

"I thought he was fit for the ring," I say, ignoring the question.

"He is."

Putting my hands on my hips, I nod at Steel's slumped figure. "Then why isn't he awake?"

"He's awake." The guard stomps over to him and aims a kick at his ribs. "Oi. Get up, you lowlife."

I lunge for the pistol. The man shouts in surprise, twisting to grab me. I tug the gun free just as he grabs my arm.

"What the hell are you—"

I can't shoot, the noise will be too loud. Instead, I use the pistol as a club, putting all of my strength into the blow. His head hits the wall with a crack and blood splatters the stone. The guard's gaze goes foggy as he drops. I wait a moment to see if he'll recover, but he doesn't move.

Panting, my hands shaking, I drop the pistol and kneel at Steel's side, put my hand on his shoulder. "Steel."

His dark lashes flutter and a gleam of silver appears between them. "Hazel?"

The word is slurred, but relief floods me with warmth. He's talking. If I can get him out, he'll be all right.

He squints at me. "You—you came for me," he whispers.

"Of course I came," I reply. "I'll always come for you." It's a promise I make without thinking, without even hesitating. I can't bring myself to regret it.

"Can't." He takes a deep breath, curls his fingers into his palm. "Can't feel."

"Can't feel what?"

"Magic." His expression is lost, confused, as if being cut off from his magic is like losing a limb.

I curse Bellemeure. This must have been how she'd overcome his family—cut off the connection to their magic, leave them insensate like this, then send in her assassins.

But the ritual had blocked him from his magic, too, until we'd changed the spell. There must be a way to fix it.

"Come on." I get his arm over my shoulders and heave. He's heavier than his lanky frame would make him seem and I struggle to get him upright. "Come *on*, Steel, stand up."

He manages to get his legs underneath him, rickety as a newborn colt, and I haul him through the cage door.

Somehow, I have to get him past the crowd and out of the hotel without anyone noticing. I'm so caught up in the problem that when I look up, I don't at first recognise the figure in front of me. When I do, my blood runs cold.

Chang Mei regards me with narrowed eyes, her lips parted over white teeth. She's changed from her dress into a baggy coat and breeches, the kind of thing any labourer in the city might wear. Her black hair is pulled up under a cap.

"You should be dead," she says. Her gaze doesn't leave my face, but it's impossible for her not to recognise Steel.

"And you should be with Bellemeure," I reply, trying to scrape together a plan.

She stares me down, not responding. Did she come here to fetch the ring's next victim?

"You can't be part of this," I burst out. "You're a demon, aren't you? It could have been you, in one of these cages." Something passes through her expression and I chase it. "You *are* a demon, aren't you?"

Mei snorts. "You English know nothing of my people."

"Then why are you here?" I ask. "Bellemeure's having you murder other demons, making you complicit in her crimes. Why stay?"

"Because it was those demons that destroyed my clan," she replies. "And it is those demons that drug us and pit us against each other for their own amusement. Are you truly defending them?"

"Not *them*," I reply, clutching Steel close. "What possible harm could one Leviathan demon do to you? To Bellemeure? I certainly won't stop you from taking revenge on von Tier."

She looks amused. "Let me guess: you want me to let you go. To let *him* go, so he can hatch some foolish plan for vengeance. That *is* why you came to Paris, is it not?"

I parry her question with another. "What about von Tier? Bellemeure told you to kill him, didn't she? Can you?" If I can goad her, perhaps I can figure out a way past her.

"If we have our way, every House will fall. Asmodeus is merely our next target."

Asmodeus is one of the Revenant Houses. "And them?" I jerk my head at the other cells. "What are you going to do with them?"

"Where are the keys?" she counters.

"Why?" I hit back.

The woman exhales and goes to tug on her cap, then seems to recollect herself and looks at her hand with a hint of surprise in her widened eyes. "If you believe that I am going to leave them here," she says, "then you deserve your fate."

"You tried to kill us," I point out. "And because of you, the Comte is dead."

"Oh?" Her brows arch up, interested. "I was partly successful, then."

A chorus of shouts go up from the ring, making both of us twitch. At the sound, Steel stirs against my side, putting more of his weight on his own feet. I need to play for time.

"That wine was drugged," I say, theorising aloud. "It was the same drug you used on House Leviathan, to suppress their magic. That's how you killed them. What *is* it?"

"His kind are so arrogant they disdain any art that is not born from their blood."

"What is that supposed to mean?" I examine her blank expression. "You don't know what's in it, do you? She hasn't told you."

"She doesn't need to," Mei snaps. "I do not create the drug. There is no honour in that."

"But there's honour in dispensing it? In murdering those who can't defend themselves?"

She makes a cutting gesture. "You have barely stepped into our world. You have no idea what is at stake."

"If you—"

Von Tier appears at the other end of the corridor and I click my teeth together to swallow my words. He is trailed by two guards, both demons. A frown flickers over the Marquis' face, but it vanishes as he approaches.

"Fraulein," he greets Chang Mei. "I thought you would be on your way to Vienna, by now. Is there something that bothers you?"

Mei turns sideways, keeping us all in view. Then she seems to make a decision and turns to face von Tier, putting her back to me and Steel.

Not that doing so helps—she's still standing between us and the door. As are von Tier and his men.

The movement catches Steel's attention. "It was you," he mutters, pushing off me, fixated on Mei. "It was *you*."

I try to pull him back. We can't fight all four of them.

"Perfect," von Tier purrs. "I'd thought to save the Dragon until later, but the ring is empty and my demons are starved for a fight. Bring him."

I shove Steel into the cell and swipe the guard's pistol from the floor, levelling it at von Tier. "Stay where you are," I command.

"Please, Fraulein." The demon chuckles. "You are human, and even with this Eastern savage to help you, you stand no chance against me."

Mei goes very still. "I would not have regretted killing you," she says, and pulls a long thin knife from inside her coat, "but now I will regret it even less."

I lean left, changing my target to the nearest guard, and pull the trigger. The demon falls back with a shout, clutching his wounded soldier. Mei lunges at von Tier and strikes at his stomach. He pivots. The blade scrapes through his jacket and gold buttons ping off onto the ground.

Again I pull the trigger, but this time the pistol is silent. Empty. Swearing, I flip it over in my hand so I'm holding the barrel and club the guard's outstretched hand as he leaps for me. Fire flickers over his fingers and sparks drip from his coat. I back away, but he follows.

"Aren't you going to help your master?" I gasp out against the sound of fighting.

"After I deal with you." Fire bursts out of his palms. I dodge and my nose stings with the scent of scorched fabric. I slap a smouldering ember out of my dress.

There's nowhere to go except a cell. I rush into the one that holds Steel, grabbing at the door to close it. The demon slams his shoulder against it, shoves it open. He clutches onto a handful of my skirt and pain shoots through my hip as the cloth blazes.

Steel lurches between us. He seizes the demon by the throat, ignoring the flames that simmer against his hand. They grapple for a moment, grunting, then Steel sweeps the demon's legs from under him and topples them both. The guard groans in pain. Without hesitation, Steel grabs his head and slams it into the stone floor. Once. Twice. Three times. Only when the flames sputter out does he stop. The demon's face is unrecognisable.

I tear my gaze away. The second guard has fallen, his neck almost severed, but von Tier fights on. I can barely see Mei, just a blur of black hair and the flash of her knife. Her cap has fallen off, a detail I notice as if from far away.

With a smothered groan, Steel staggers through the cell door. He clutches at the wall to steady himself, glaring through strands of dishevelled hair. Rage flickers at the back of my head, rage I don't feel.

"Wait," I call, reaching for him. "You can't fight them both, you're not strong enough."

Letting out a growl that reverberates in my chest, he launches himself at von Tier. The Revenant isn't expecting it; he pitches forwards, struggling to throw Steel off his back. Flames erupt over his body. Steel clamps on tighter, pinning von Tier's arms to his sides.

Mei stills, her coat fluttering in the wake of her movement. She levels her knife and plunges it into von Tier's chest. Steel lets out a sound. His hold loosens and he staggers back. I catch him, sickened at the burns on his arms and the blood on his shirt. The tip of the knife protrudes from the Marquis' back.

"Foolish girl," von Tier whispers. "You choose to make me an en—"

Mei puts a foot on his ribs, uses it to yank her knife free, and buries the blade in his throat, ending his last words in a wet gurgle. Then she jerks her arm to the side, spraying blood over the walls and over her coat.

The Marquis paws at his throat as the flames on his body turn to smoke. Then Mei stabs him a third time, right through his heart. She keeps the weapon in him as he crumples, bearing him down to the ground. When he hits it, she leans on the knife, pushing it as deep as it will go. Only when half the hilt has disappeared into his chest does she let go.

Silence pools in the corridor until Steel lets out a weak growl. Mei looks over at us.

Fear climbs up my throat. "You've done what you came to do," I say. "Leave. I'll make sure the demons here are freed."

"I haven't finished," she replies, eyeing Steel.

"You're wounded." Part of her clothing has burnt away, revealing flesh that's black and red and blistered.

"So is he."

"He heals faster." It's true; already Steel's wounded skin is growing pale and smooth. "Do you want to risk your life to fight one demon?"

She pauses, deathly still, a cat before it pounces. Then a shout comes from far away, and a low rumbling, like hundreds of footsteps. Then I realise it *is* footsteps.

The shouting becomes clearer: "Put down your arms! You are under arrest!"

Scowling, Mei turns and vanishes, blurring out of view. A few minutes later, a group of uniformed officers burst into the passage, led by Dumont and René.

CHAPTER TWENTY-THREE

The agents take us to a private room while the rest of the Sûreté sweep through the hotel. I help Steel to a chair and he falls into it, his burnt and blood-drenched hands dangling over the arms.

"Some of our missing demons are here," René tells Dumont. "I suspect the others did not survive the ring."

"At least we can save these."

"Do you have a handkerchief?" I ask him.

He blinks at me, but René fishes in his pocket and hands me a lacy blue one.

Steel's palms and forearms are healing steadily, and as I wipe off the blood he stirs and mutters, "Where is she?"

"Gone."

He hisses and tries to pull away from me.

"You can't fight her like this." His health is more important than revenge.

"What happened to the Marquis?" Dumont asks. "That was his body, among the rest, was it not?"

"Bellemeure's companion, Chang Mei. I've never seen a demon move as fast as she does." I offer the handkerchief back to René—now more red than blue—and he takes it between two fingers, wrinkling his nose.

"A specific Asian genealogy?" he guesses.

"We're wasting time," Steel mutters. He claws his way out of the chair, taking an unsteady step to the door. Then his legs give out and he flops to the ground.

I grab him before he topples over. "You can't go after her, the drug is still in your blood."

"It will pass," he grits out.

Dumont steps between him and the door. "I think it is beyond time that you tell us the truth." His gaze is stony and René moves to stand behind him, shoulders back, alert.

"What do you mean?" I ask, cautiously.

"If you were investigating for a client, you would not be this invested. You are hiding something."

I swallow. Dumont's expression does not change. Telling the truth now would be admitting that we were lying all along. As much as I've grown to trust them, they're still agents.

Steel makes the decision for me. "They murdered my family," he growls. "And I want them dead."

Dumont's face softens in sympathy, but he says, "Revenge is never the answer."

"What would you know about it?"

The sound of crashing wood breaks through the quiet of the room, then the booming call of "*Arretez!*"

René twitches. "That's Auguste," he says. "They must be having trouble with the surviving Revenants."

"We can't stay here," I add, holding Steel upright. He shivers as if he's freezing, but heat resonates through my hands where I touch him. "I need to get Steel somewhere safe."

"You haven't told us everything, yet," Dumont says. "How did—"

"Not now." It comes out in English and with too much of a snap. "Please," I add in French, forcing myself to modify my tone.

The agent exhales. "The Sûreté," he says. "Everyone is here; it will be empty."

"Auguste will want to interrogate us," René warns.

"Then we had better get out of here before he *finds* us, yes?" Dumont counters.

I blanch. An interrogation will mean dealing with other agents, and if they've heard anything about us from Monaghan... We've already taken too many risks as it is. "Help me get him into a carriage."

"*No*," Steel protests, trying to clamber to his feet. "We need to go after her—"

"You can't even walk straight," I retort. "What good will you do, dead on your feet?"

He flinches, but he stops trying to free himself.

"René, take his other arm."

The demon glances at Dumont, who nods his permission. "I'll find a cab," the agent volunteers. "Bring him through the kitchen. Auguste won't think about questioning the servants yet."

René loops Steel's arm around his shoulder and takes some of his weight. Steel scowls, but his legs shudder, not strong enough to keep him up.

"Come on," I murmur. "The sooner we get you healed, the sooner your magic's back."

That seems to bolster him; he takes a faltering step, then another, and soon we're out of the room, staggering through the servant's corridors.

From somewhere nearby comes a crackle and a shout, and as we pass an open door something flashes orange-red.

"Damn Dragon," René says. "You couldn't have waited to get drugged until *after* the fighting was done?"

Steel lets out a huff of breath and says nothing, doesn't even attempt a witty rejoinder. My stomach tightens.

We pull him through the kitchen—abandoned, pots still simmering—to a double door that leads onto a refuse-laden alley. Dumont, a little ahead of us, beckons us into the street.

"I've hailed a carriage," he murmurs. He offers to take Steel from me but I can't release him, so he settles for putting a hand on my back, directing me forward.

The cab's waiting, the driver yawning on his perch. He sees us and says something to Dumont. The agent replies with a strained laugh, something about too much good wine and too little French spirit.

I hustle Steel inside. René piles in behind me and Dumont swings up beside the driver, apologising to the man for the inconvenience. The driver takes it in his stride, retorting with a jest about weak English blood, and then we're moving.

I don't pay attention to Paris as it flits by. My whole body is trained to the sound of Steel's laboured breathing, to the muscle clenched in his jaw.

"We're nearly there," I murmur, though I have no idea if it's true. "Just a little longer."

He snorts halfheartedly.

When we stop, René jumps out and helps me pull Steel onto the street. Dumont pays the cab and it trots away, revealing the looming grey agency building, as forbidding now as it had been in daylight.

"It is a rear entrance," Dumont explains, hurrying to let us in. "It's best if no one sees you for now. Then we can figure out what to do."

It's silent in the halls of the Sûreté, but enough lamps are lit to lead us to a foyer.

"Where do we put him?" René asks and Dumont replies, "The second room, behind the little study. No one uses it unless there's an emergency—"

"Sebastien!" We stop, Dumont in front of me, partly blocking my view. Jacques appears, wringing his hands.

"What is it? Are you well?"

"There is an English woman who wants to see you."

"What, another one?" mutters René, on Steel's other side. "Are we being invaded?"

"A woman and a demon," Jacques says. "They've been waiting for hours. They wouldn't leave."

Then comes a familiar voice that makes me startle and lean past Dumont to see better. "My name is Eve Wilson," the voice says. "And I am here for Hazel Locke."

Dumont steps aside. It *is* Eve, thinner than the last time I saw her and with blue streaks cupping her eyes, but still *Eve*.

"Eve," I choke out, before all the reasons why she would be here come rushing back. And that's when I see the lanky red-headed demon at her side. "*Cassius?*"

He lunges towards me and the foyer erupts. René drops Steel and slams the Phantom back, halting his attack.

Cassius snarls at him. "Out of my way!"

"Stop!" Eve yanks him to her side. "What did I say about acting without my authorisation?"

"You have orders, remember?" Cassius demands, shifting under her grip but not fighting back. "We should take her now."

"I'm not going to drag her back to London against her will," Eve replies. "Besides, how far do you think we'd get before the police arrest us for kidnapping? If you'd stop being a fool and *listen* to me—"

He bares his teeth, part grimace, part grin, and I look again at Eve's face, horrified. They're *bonded*.

Steel makes a winded noise beside me.

"I'll do whatever you want," I say, which is a bald-faced lie, "but right now I need to take care of Steel. Dumont, could you take us to a room, please?" The woman stares at me. I drag Steel forward and Dumont ducks under his arm to take René's position.

"It's through here," he says and then adds, "Jacques, settle them somewhere and fetch us some water."

Cassius says something, too low and muttered for me to catch. *Cassius.* The last time I saw him he was fleeing the Agency after Rayne's—after I killed Rayne. What is he doing here, partnered with Eve? What is Monaghan thinking?

René leads the three of us to a small room tucked between a parlour and a dining hall, little more than an alcove. The walls are white-washed stone, undecorated and marred by chips and scratches. The single pallet has a sheet, at least, and the mattress looks thin but clean. I press Steel onto it. He folds without comment, tucking his long limbs over the edge.

"Is there any chance we could get some hot tea?" I ask. "With sugar, if possible."

René arches an eyebrow. Dumont draws him away and a surge of gratitude warms me. "We'll see what we can do," he says. Then they're gone, and it's just me and Steel in the cold dark room.

I sit on the bed next to him, leaving some distance between us. "How are you feeling?"

He curls his hands into fists on his knees. "I need to find her," he mutters.

"Steel..."

"She can't escape." His pupils fluctuate, serpent-thin one moment, fat and round the next. "I can't let her escape."

"You're not well enough," I say, reaching for his shoulder and then drawing back, unsure if this would be permitted. "You need to rest."

"I can't *rest*," he snaps. "You don't understand, it was *her*—" He tenses as if he's about to claw his way out of the room and hunt down Chang Mei and Bellemeure by sheer force of will.

I do press on his shoulder, then, urging him to stay seated. "I know."

"You *don't* know. You *can't* know." He knocks my hand away and stands, and I stand to match him.

"Please, Steel, you're still drugged—"

"It was her fault!" He takes a step and stumbles. When I catch him, he struggles. "It was *her fault*—" One moment he's fighting me and the next he's collapsing in my arms, his words swallowed by harsh, choked sobs.

CHAPTER TWENTY-FOUR

I t feels like a long time before Steel sleeps. I don't think he would have, if not for the drug. It saps his strength and blurs his mind, to the point that he mutters incomprehensibly as I help him into bed. But when his head hits the mattress his whole body deflates, as if all he had to do to find peace was to let go.

His mother was killed not long before I summoned him, and his father not long before that. He hasn't had nearly long enough to grieve.

The door behind me creaks open. "I brought you tea, mademoiselle."

"Thank you, Jacques." He lays it on the floor next to the bed. "Is he well?" the boy asks, his gaze skipping towards Steel.

"He will be." I crush the doubt that says otherwise.

"Agent Dumont is grateful for his help. He does not say it often," adds Jacques, with a twinkle in his blue eyes that makes him appear older than he is. "He and René don't have partners."

Is that what we are? What we could be, perhaps, in another world. "I'm glad we could help."

Jacques says, "The English mademoiselle is waiting."

A sigh seeps out of me. I'll need to face them sooner or later.

"I can stay with him, if you like," the boy offers, nodding at Steel.

"That's very kind, Jacques. Thank you." I try to ignore the odd wrench in my chest that comes when I step away from the bed. "I won't be long," I hasten to add, reassuring myself more than the apprentice.

The corridor is deserted, but I hear voices from somewhere nearby. I follow the sound until I turn a corner and find Dumont and his demon.

"You will give yourself wrinkles, at this rate," René is saying, folding up the sleeves of his shirt. Both men have discarded their jackets and something about the two of them reminds me of the easy camaraderie Jacob had found with Max. Homesickness wells in my heart.

The deep furrows between Dumont's brows do not fade. "We should have arrested the ghost when we had him. Commander Auguste—"

"What Auguste doesn't know, won't hurt us," his partner replies. "Von Tier is dead and the fighting ring is done with. We can pursue the ghost in our own time."

Dumont still frowns. "What?" he asks, at René's smirk.

"Nothing. Nothing at all."

"That is not what your expression says."

"Oh, so *now* you know when I'm lying. I will remember that, the next time you try to throw me to Auguste. And stop that. You'll give yourself wrinkles."

"If I have wrinkles, it is because *you* give them to me—" Dumont breaks off, catching sight of me. He coughs and straightens. "Mademoiselle. You are well? Your demon?"

"Sleeping," I reply, nodding at René. "Jacques is with him."

"Your companions are in there," the demon says, gesturing at the closed door behind him. "Although I would not be inclined to go in, myself. That demon looks as though he'd be delighted to skewer you if given the chance."

I take a deep breath. They've earned the truth. Part of it, at least. "I owe you an explanation."

"Indeed you do," Dumont says, folding his arms.

"We discovered a corruption at the root of our agency," I explain, saying only as much as I can afford to. "No one would believe us and we...we were in danger, staying there."

"And you decided to take up another case?"

"Something like that. I wanted to help Steel find justice."

Dumont glances away—down the corridor and back, checking for listeners—and bites his lip. "An agency should protect its citizens," he muses. "*All* of them, whether they are human or demon."

It was the copper class demons that had suffered the most at the hands of von Tier, the lower class demons that Dumont had been searching for. "Whatever their class?"

"Perhaps corruption is inevitable," he mutters, rubbing a hand over his closely cropped hair. "With that kind of power and wealth, what can you do against it?"

I think of Monaghan and any reply withers on my lips.

René eyes us, then sighs explosively. "Does that mean we should not try?" he points out and rolls his eyes towards the ceiling.

It pulls a smile from Dumont. "I do not know what plans you have, mademoiselle Locke," he says, "but you have proved your capability. I would be honoured if you would consider joining the Sûreté in some capacity."

A position in an agency, hunting evil and protecting the vulnerable—it's everything I could ever want.

And yet, I can't say yes. Eve is in the next room, all of Monaghan's will behind her, and Steel lies unconscious and recovering from the drug.

"I will consider it," I say, unable to reject the offer outright, "if you can give me some time."

He nods, satisfied.

"There's a favour I would ask of you," I add.

"Oh?"

"Transport to Vienna, for Steel."

A glance from René—his eyes are too keen—but it's Dumont who replies, "The Express d'Orient leaves for Vienna from the Gare de l'Est. I can arrange for a ticket, when he is ready."

"Thank you." I hesitate, torn between Steel's command to keep his secret and returning the respect and trust these two men have shown me. Even if Steel is right that revealing it might put us at risk, I can't imagine that they would betray us. "If there was a way to alter the binding ritual," I begin, "a way to remove the distance limitation, would you want to know it?"

I'm ashamed I did not ask sooner, by the longing that leaps into René's eyes. "Yes," he says, hungrily. "Do you know of one?"

"René," says Dumont, alarm in his voice. I tense, wondering if I was mistaken, if Dumont cares for the rank and power that his demon grants him, and not for René himself. "If I have kept you here against your will—" he continues and my unease evaporates.

"Do not be a fool," the demon replies, fond affection in his voice. "Of course, I know that you'd leave the second I asked it of you. I will not abandon you. But think of how much more we could do without being tied at the hip."

Dumont's relief is tangible.

"And there may be others, who we could share it with," René adds. "Perhaps even some of those demons we rescued would be interested, if it were a choice and not a compulsion. Assuming that such a possibility exists." Their gazes latch onto me, too desperate to ignore.

Such a cause could remake an agency, make it worthy of devotion. "I'll speak to Steel when he's awake and we'll help." Just those two words, *we'll help*, ease the heavy weight in my chest.

"Thank you, mademoiselle."

I can't delay any longer. "I had better go in."

Dumont opens the door for me with a small bow and closes it after I've entered the room. It's Spartan, and only one of the half dozen gas lamps is lit, giving the room a dark, haunted look. Four wooden chairs surround a low table and on two of them sit Eve and Cassius.

The former stands as I enter, straight-backed and clear-eyed, despite her obvious weariness. The latter slumps in his chair, eyeing me with a familiar smirk. I suppress the urge to curve my shoulders inward, to hide.

"How did you find me?" I ask.

"The sailor at St. Katherine's Way remembered you," she replies. "And you made an impression at Boulogne. It wasn't hard to eliminate the possibilities from there."

"Well?" Cassius interjects. "Are we going to take her, or not?"

I look at Eve. "'We'?"

She shifts one shoulder back and forth, her mouth a line. "The Professor didn't want to waste a Phantom demon if he could avoid it."

"A Phantom agent." The first woman in England to become one, as far as our records went. "Congratulations."

She lifts her chin, but there's a shadow behind her eyes. "Thank you," she says, stiff and distant, as through we're strangers.

I open my mouth to ask the question that burns in my chest, but no words escape. Swallowing, I push past the blockade with an effort. "What about—what about Rayne?" I expect Cassius to jump in with a sneering comment, lauding over the fact that he was the first to reveal the truth, but he merely watches me.

"Monaghan told us." Eve hesitates, then says, "Apparently, Rayne was trying to stop you."

"Stop me?"

"From killing again."

It doesn't make sense, at first, but as I stare at her, the meaning registers. "He's saying that I'm the Ripper."

"Under your demon's influence."

I put my face in my hands and swear under my breath. Even if I wanted to go back to England, I can't. Monaghan's destroyed that possibility better than if he'd set fire to every ship in the Channel.

Eve starts pacing, as if she can no longer bare to be still. "He ordered us to bring you to London to face justice."

"It's not justice while *he* leads the Agency," I spit out. "*He* was the one—he and Tiberius—We had nothing to do with it."

"He," says Eve, stopping in her path. "You mean Monaghan. Monaghan was the Ripper."

"Yes." But she's not looking at me, she's staring at Cassius.

"You see?" he murmurs. "As I said."

Of all the things I was expecting to come out of his mouth, that was not one of them. "As *you* said?"

Eve shakes her head and goes back to pacing, slower this time. "It was a theory."

My gaze goes to Cassius, who grins at me. "Your Professor is taking over England," he says. "It's Shadow Commissioner now, but I don't doubt that he'll be Prime Minister within a year. Woe to any demons left roaming free. He'll make quick work of them."

I drop into one of the chairs, propping my arm on the table to stay upright. "So, it's true, then? He's Shadow Commissioner?"

"On the back of his success in the Ripper case," Eve says, with unconcealed disgust. "We weren't certain that he was the culprit, though. When you ran..." She trails off and the weight of blame makes the pause swell.

"I'm sorry." My head throbs with dull pain, demanding attention now that the immediate danger has passed, and I press my palm to my temple. "He would have killed us to protect his secret. I didn't know what else to do."

"You should have waited for us. We could have helped."

"I'm sorry," I say, again, the words inadequate. At the same time, I don't regret running. "What now?" Eve doesn't answer at first and dread blooms in my stomach. "Eve?"

She sighs and says, "We have to go back."

"We can't," I reply, astounded that she'd even suggest such a thing. "They'd commit me, and God knows what they'd do to Steel. You can't be serious."

"What else do you expect me to do?" Eve asks. "He has my family."

Stung, I reply, "They're my family, too."

She casts a look at the wallpaper dotted with tiny golden primroses, at the heavy velvet drapes. "Yes, I can see how badly you miss them."

"That's uncharitable," I say, as guilt mauls my chest.

She puts her hands on her hips, gnawing at her lip. "Perhaps it is," she announces, "but if you'd stayed, we might have been able to stop him taking the others hostage."

"Is that what he's doing?"

"What do you think?" she counters.

It's exactly the kind of thing he would do, manipulating Eve with veiled threats towards the people she cares about.

"He tried to send Maia away," she adds. "There are new servants, new stuffed animals in the taxidermy room—" She breaks off.

"This isn't just one man," I protest, "this is an *Empire*. How do you plan on stopping him?"

"I don't know!" Eve's voice rings through the room, making the silence that comes after sound hollow. She collapses into her chair, hunching over her knees. "I don't know," she says again, quieter. We sit for a moment and then Eve huffs and asks, "Why are you even here? Why Paris, of all places?"

Grateful for the opportunity to change the subject, I tell her about Steel's quest—as much as I think he'd want her to know—and about Bellemeure. Eve listens in thoughtful silence, her attention caught by the details of the case despite herself, and when I'm done she says, "This woman must have a network of contacts to create this drug. She can't be working alone."

The gravity of how much I've missed her presses down on me. I give a small laugh. "You'll make a good Phantom agent." I surprise a hesitant smile out of her.

"Mademoiselle." Jacques hovers in the entrance, the door open just enough for him to stick his head through. "Your companion has woken."

I'm standing before he finishes the sentence. "I have to go."

"Not a chance." Eve's up, facing me with a look that I've only ever seen her use on suspects. "We're not done."

My exhaled breath fills the space between us. "Are you going to stop me?" I ask.

She returns my gaze and for a moment I think she might.

"Spare me," Cassius groans. "If we're not going to take her, then we should get out of Europe while we have the chance."

Eve makes an indignant noise. "We're not *leaving*!"

"Why not? Your little friend is right." I glower at the description, but Cassius continues, "The Professor has an Empire at his fingertips. If we don't return, he'll send others. And you are two women. What do you think you're going to do?"

"Listen, demon—"

"We'll think of something," I interrupt, cutting short what promises to be a long tirade, "but right now, I have to see Steel. I'll come straight back." Eve gives me a reluctant nod and I duck outside, heading towards the little room.

Although I hate to admit it, Cassius is right. I can't go back, but I can't stay in Paris either, within Monaghan's reach. My heart aches; the sting of an infant dream so quickly snatched away.

I find Steel lying on his back, his eyes open. I move to the end of the bed. "How are you feeling?"

"Like I've been beaten up by a few Revenants." He makes a face at the ceiling. "Otherwise, not too bad."

"And your magic?"

The wry expression fades. "I can almost feel it," he whispers. "It's different from the ritual, it feels...muted, somehow. I don't know how to explain it."

"It'll come back." When he doesn't respond, I say, "I may have promised Dumont and René a way to alter their binding spell."

He glances at me, one corner of his mouth quirking. "I should have known you'd try to help them. Very well. We do owe them, I suppose." He returns his gaze to the ceiling and says, in a flat voice, "I have to go after her."

"Von Tier mentioned Vienna," I say.

"House Asmodeus is in Vienna."

The rest of von Tier's House. "There's a train from the Gare de l'Est. Dumont has agreed to purchase a ticket for you, when you're ready."

His eyes sparkle. "Thank you." He pushes himself up to his elbows, dark brows dipping towards his nose. "Wait. Aren't you coming with me?"

"I came to help you find out who murdered your family." I lift my shoulders in something too vulnerable to be a shrug. "And in that at least, we've been successful." He has no more need of me. My stomach clenches at the thought.

Steel runs one hand through his hair. "You've paid any debt that you owe me," he says, staring at the unmarked flagstones under his feet. "You could leave, if you want. Go back to England, or stay here."

Neither of those options are open to me any longer, but I bite the inside of my cheek. I don't want his pity.

"And..." he adds, "you'd be risking life and limb if you came with me. Bellemeure is courting war with the Houses."

If he goes alone, he could die and I'd never know it. "You'd be taking that risk."

"I'm prepared." He inhales and faces me, something resolute in his expression. "I have no right to ask this," he says, determinedly, "I know I don't, and you should know that too. I mean, I don't ask this because I feel like I have a *right* to it, or that you should be obliged—"

"Steel," I interrupt, a smile pulling at my mouth, "what exactly are you asking?"

His throat bobs. "Come with me," he says, more of an order than a request. "No debt, no obligations."

"Work together, you mean?"

Relief makes his mouth soft. "Yes. Be partners. Officially."

Partners. I want that. I want to go to Vienna with him, on a case worth solving, doing work that needs doing. But... "Eve is here."

"Eve?" He tenses. "Monaghan—?"

"Just Eve. Well, Eve and Cassius."

"*Cassius*? What the hell is he doing here?"

"It seems to be a long story," I reply, "but they've been ordered to take me back. To take *us* back."

"No. He'll kill you if you go back. And me, too."

"He'll send others." Jacob, Max. Maybe even new agents, now that he has the power. His ambition might have no end.

"So, we'll fight them." He looks grimly satisfied at the thought.

"What about Eve?"

"She can come with us." I glance at him, surprised. "To Vienna."

"And Cassius?"

"Him, too," he adds, with reckless abandon.

I sigh. "I suppose it's better to have him tied to Eve than free to work whatever mischief he has planned. At least we'll be able to keep an eye on him." Vienna won't save us from Monaghan, but it might buy us some time. Time to come up with a plan.

"So?" Steel stands and holds out his hand. "Partners?" His expression is cautious, as if he can't read the emotions surging through me.

I take his hand, ignoring the way my heart skitters and stumbles. "Partners," I whisper and realise the danger too late; the ice around my heart has long since shattered.

Keep reading for more in the Locke & Steel series

EXTRACTS FROM HAZEL'S JOURNAL

~~Hazel's Journal~~

Call it something more impressive if it's going to be about me

It's not about you.

A Compendium of Demons

Better?

It'll do

Stalker

Class: Copper

Known: Whitechapel demon

Summon component: Tarantula carcass

Abilities:

Low level mimicry (voice)

Hide in shadows

Strong eyesight

Transmutation – giant spider

Components? Planning on replacing me Locke?

I'm capturing it for posterity.

Well, if you're looking at posteriors, may I suggest—

Posterity, not posterior. And no.

Scout

Class: Copper   Known: None

Summon component: Bat claw

Abilities:

Influence dreams

Hide in shadows

Strong eyesight

Transmutation - giant bat

A bat?

Well. I've never seen it happen. but these lower ranked demons are bestial first and human second. That's why they can transform so easily

How many more are there? What else can they change into? How big do they

Time for a break

Strike

Class: Copper   Known: None

Summon component: Scorpion tail

Abilities:

Strong sense of smell (inferior to Hounds)

Low level of ivnisibility

Strong eyesight

Can they transform?

Not a clue. When we
meet one. I'll ask

Hound / Sentinel

Class: Copper

Summon component: Wolf fang

Abilities:

Enhanced senses (especially smell)

Superior strength

Ability to detect magic

Known: Isis & René

I don't know why your agency calls them something different, they're basically the same demon

Phantom

Class: Silver

Summon component: Eagle or
Owl talon

Known: ~~Cassius~~
Opera Ghost
Cassius

Abilities:

Invisibility

Superior strength *(only to humans)*

Blood Drinker

Class: Silver

Summon component: Snake
fang

Known: Flower &
Dean St. demon

Abilities:

Superior strength

Sap blood

Teeth

Are teeth an ability?

They are when you have
more than a shark's

Reaper

Class: Silver

Summon component: Tiger claw

Abilities:

Exceptional strength

Good sense of hearing

Emits fragrance off-putting to other demons

~~sound~~ *pressure*

Known: Maximus

& Tiberius

Wraith

Class: Diamond

Known: ~~Raven~~

Summon component: Unknown

Abilities:

Superior strength

Superior senses

Invisibility

Ability to detect and cast magic

Houses:

Beelzebub / ~~House of Flies~~ (2nd ~~House~~)

Beleth / ~~House of the Cat~~ (destroyed - was 4th)

Houses pool magic and protect against malicious spells

Like the ritual spell?

Exactly

Revenant

Class: Diamond   Known: Von Tier

Summon component: Unknown

Abilities:

Superior strength

Ability to manipulate fire

Terrible sense of smell

Useless at magic

Houses:

Asmodeus / House of the Beast (3rd House)

Mammon / House of Wolves (4th House)

Dragon

Class: Diamond

Summon component: Unknown

Abilities:

Superior strength

Superior senses

Ability to manipulate water

Ability to detect and cast magic

Houses:

Lucifer / House of the Morningstar (1st House)

Leviathan / House of the Serpent (destroyed - was 2nd)

You can draw me if you like — No, thank you.

Known: Steel

We don't have to include this.

For posterior. right?

POSTERITY

ALSO BY

Thank you for reading *The Rose and the Ghost*, book two in the *Locke & Steel* series. If you enjoyed it, I'd be incredibly grateful if you could leave a short review or rating. Your feedback will help other readers to decide whether to read the book, too.

To read the short story prequel, *House of the Serpent*, and get notifications of new releases, join my email list by visiting my website, www.lemedlock.com.

House of the Serpent

A once great house, fallen. A perilous quest for revenge.

Follow this vengeful journey of a demon as he seeks justice for his slain family.

A companion short story to the Locke & Steel series.

ACKNOWLEDGEMENTS

Thank you first and foremost to my Family, who are so big I think of you all with a capital *F*. For your warm-hearted generosity and support, I am forever grateful. A huge thank you to my earliest readers, my aunties Diane and Rita, and to my godmother and aunt, Theresa. Thank you to uncle Kevin, head of our own wild ragtag House, and to all of my uncles, aunts and cousins for your kindness.

Thanks also go to my editor, Nicola, and my fantastic beta and sensitivity readers, Stephanie, Yssa and particularly to Tessy, who beta read this novel without reading book one, and immediately went out to buy *The Agent's Demon*. You gave me confidence in this story when I needed it the most.

Thank you to mum, for supporting me all this time and constantly giving me encouragement, and to Dad and Kevin and Liam for your support and for being part of my life.

To my bestie Elaina, the words you gave me after reading book one still make me cry (in a good way!). I'm so grateful that you took the time to read it and so incredibly happy that you loved it.

To my sister Becky, I cannot put into words how delighted I am that you enjoyed book one. Thank you for giving it a shot. Fingers crossed you like this one too!

To my friends and family, I don't say it enough, but know that I adore you and I'm so glad to know you.

ABOUT THE AUTHOR

L. E. Medlock has been writing stories since her first school writing assignment, and reading books long before that. She initially decided it wouldn't make a great career choice and went to University to study Egyptology and Classical Civilisation, but the writing never stopped. At the end of her master's degree, she decided to try and turn professional. Some fourteen years and six novels later, she published her debut, The Agent's Demon (the "light-hearted" one). She enjoys stories about flawed gods and monsters who look like us. She's much too addicted to video games and dreams of one day being a cat owner.